WICKED
BEAST

Also by Tawny Taylor

Dark Master

Real Vamps Don't Drink O-Neg

Sex and the Single Ghost

Published by Kensington Publishing Corp.

WICKED BEAST

TAWNY TAYLOR

APHRODISIA

KENSINGTON BOOKS

http://www.kensingtonbooks.com

APHRODISIA BOOKS are published by

Kensington Publishing Corp.
850 Third Avenue
New York, NY 10022

All Kensington Titles, Imprints, and Distributed Lines are available at special quantity discounts for bulk purchases for sales promotions, premiums, fund-raising, and educational or institutional use.

Special book excerpts or customized printings can also be created to fit specific needs. For details, write or phone the office of the Kensington special sales manager: Kensington Publishing Corp., 850 Third Avenue, New York, NY 10022, attn: Special Sales Department, Phone: 1-800-221-2647.

Aphrodisia and the A logo Reg. U.S. Pat & TM Off.

ISBN-13: 978-0-7582-2678-5
ISBN-10: 0-7582-2678-0

First Kensington Trade Paperback Printing: February 2009

10 9 8 7 6 5 4 3 2 1

Printed in the United States of America

WICKED
BEAST

1

To full-time waitress and part-time wannabe author, Cailey Holm, writing was a thrilling adventure. Her stories whisked her away from the blah rut her life had sunken into: miserable job. Pathetic social life. Depressing finances.

For a few hours a week she could be someone else, cover-model perfect with a thrilling job, loads of loyal friends, and a great wardrobe. She could be pursued by a sexy alpha guy, both a masterful, dominant lover and patient, caring partner.

The world's perfect man.

But most importantly, she could lose herself in her characters' problems. Knotty predicaments that were always untangled by The End.

Writing was fun. Relaxing. But that was before last week's Big Experiment.

It was Cailey's critique partner, Mia Spelman, who'd come up with the oh-so-brilliant idea. Everyone in their group had to sit in a circle and confess their worst fear. Brought to mind that perennial preteen sleepover game "Truth or Dare." Same girlie giggling and embarrassing confessions. The only thing missing were the Barbie footie pajamas and prank phone calls.

The sad part—three grown women playing a kiddie game—wasn't lame enough. Oh no. It got worse. After they each admitted their fear (something that would've been totally humiliating if the other two hadn't been so much more embarrassing) they had to promise to write a story in which their heroine would have to conquer that same fear. By doing so, Mia claimed, they would—in some way Cailey had yet to comprehend—cure themselves.

Big, huge sigh.

Cailey'd said it time and again: Mia read too many pop psychology books. Miss Freud Wannabe defended her choice of reading material by claiming the books helped her with her writing. The girl boasted she could cure the world.

Funny, since the same woman who could recite Jung's personality theory from memory took a bath wearing a life preserver.

Despite the fact that Cailey figured the whole thing was futile, she was desperate enough to get over her crippling phobia of cats to give the exercise a half-hearted attempt. Besides, shape-shifter stories were hot with erotica publishers. Could be good timing. Who knew? Maybe she'd accomplish two things at once: finally produce a saleable manuscript and get over her irrational fear.

Then again, maybe she'd write three hundred pages of dreck and remain phobic for life? There were worse things that could happen to an ailurophobic waitress in metro Detroit.

Like she could be forced to attend a Lions game . . . with a stadium full of *real* fanged felines.

"You must have them doing *it* while he's in cat form." Mia twisted the knob on the faux mission-style stained-glass table lamp, parked next to her on the cherry veneer side table (this waitress couldn't buy solid cherry).

Snap, snap. The light blinked on. That made five lights. In a room the size of a large closet. How was it she hadn't noticed Mia's abuse of wattage before now? Was Mia afraid of the dark as well?

Cailey took a break from ruminating over Mia's issue with darkness long enough to comprehend her critique partner's suggestion about her story. Had Mia just suggested . . . ? No way! Cailey's stomach twisted. She lurched forward, perched on the edge of the faux-leather chair cushion. "What did you say?"

"Interesting. I think Mia's onto something here." Insane Critique Partner number two, Lisa Goddard, flopped one knee over the other and tapped her fingertips on the couch's over-stuffed arm. "Everyone knows it's not technically bestiality if the character still possesses his human mind."

"No. Way!" Cailey repeated, too horrified to say anything else. A sour taste filled her mouth, making her cheeks implode and her lips pucker.

"But it makes sense," Mia continued, obviously not realizing how disgusting—how utterly revolting!—her idea was.

A woman doing *it* with a huge animal? Can you say ewwww? Mia nodded. "Think about it—"

"That's just it," Cailey interrupted. "I don't want to think about that. I can't think about it or I'll—"

"My point exactly!" Mia dropped her flattened hands on her thighs so hard and fast they made a loud slap when they struck her faded denims. "I realize you don't want to think about cats having sex—"

"Heh. Yeah!" *No shit, Sherlock.*

"—but if the scene's hot enough, you'll forget all about the guy being a lion," Mia continued. "You can't be afraid of something that arouses you. Get it?"

Huh?

Cailey shuddered so hard her teeth chattered. "I'm not following. What part of *that* is going to arouse me? A woman being screwed by an enormous, fanged, clawed cat? Nope. Not working for me. No happy tingles here. Nuh uh." Maybe this had been a worse idea than she'd thought.

"Hang on. I think it's too soon." Lisa studied Cailey with sharp eyes. "We're pushing her too hard."

The voice of reason.

Lisa continued, "Cailey's phobia is pretty bad. She needs to ease into this slowly. Maybe write a safe scene to start, where the heroine just sees a cat. Then, she can write another one where the heroine touches a cat. That kind of thing. We need to take this one tiny step at a time."

"Yes. One teeny, tiny step," Cailey agreed, holding up her hand and pinching her index finger and thumb together to illustrate. Before Mia could make another totally insane suggestion, Cailey shifted the conversation from her project to Mia's. "So what's your story about? Is your heroine going to fall into some deep water or something?"

"Not exactly." Mia lifted her chin and plucked up the manila envelope sitting on her lap. She flipped up the flap and pulled out a stack of pages. "I'm writing a paranormal. About an Egyptian god. It's humming right along. I already have seventy pages—hey!"

"Wait a minute!" Cailey swiped the pages from Mia and stared at them in disbelief. Her crap-meter gonged in her head like a metal soup pot being beaten by a toddler. "What's this? *Dark Surrender*? That's not fair. You've been plotting this Egyptian god story for weeks. We're supposed to be pushing ourselves, trying new things. Plus, you're supposed to be writing about your fear of water, you big chicken."

"That's true." Lisa nodded, now turning her squinty-eyed gaze to Mia. "Although calling names is so not cool."

"But neither is breaking the rules of your own friggin' game." Cailey skimmed the first page of the synopsis and handed it to

Lisa. "Just as I thought, there's no mention of the heroine being afraid of water. This is your typical Mia Spelman alpha-hero story."

Mia snapped the rest of the pages out of Cailey's hand. "Yeah, well, my character's fear is in the story. Take my word for it."

Lisa handed the first page back to Mia. "If it's not in the synopsis, it can't be a major part of the conflict."

"Well, it is." Mia crammed the stack into the envelope. "My character's phobia is a secondary plot. And this is a short synopsis. You know we don't always include secondary plots in short synopses. There's no room for them. Not when there's so much else going on. The romance and suspense—"

"This is too funny." Cailey couldn't help it. She laughed as she set the bowl of corn chips on top of her own printed pages. "It's your game. Your rules. But hey, if you don't want to follow them, then I'm good." Had she found an out from this insanity? Did she want an out? "I could dump the were-lion thing and write the vampire story I've been dying to start."

"Aw, come on! Don't go getting all I-quitish on me." Mia scooped up a handful of chips, eyeballing the pages under the bowl. "I swear I'm playing fair. What do you have there? Aren't you going to let us see it?"

Cailey resisted the temptation to ball her pages up and toss them in the trash. Thanks to the difficult subject matter, this story wasn't coming as easily as they usually did. She'd struggled for days to produce twenty pages she didn't hate. But difficulties aside, she had a pretty good feeling about what she'd started. She was reaching, growing.

Desperate for some moral support, Cailey looked at Lisa. "Tell me you're following the rules and I'll stick with this thing to the end."

Lisa smiled brightly. "I am. I'm writing a romantic suspense."

Romantic suspense?

Cailey let loose with a sigh-of-the-betrayed and tossed them both a dose of mean eyes. "No way! Come on you two! You're *both* cheating? Lisa, you always write romantic suspense."

"I know. But in my story, the heroine's fear of guns is a major part of the conflict." Lisa pulled a stack of pages from the red canvas tote sitting at her feet and dropped them on the coffee table's glossy top. "See? It's in the synopsis."

"Well, at least you have that." Cailey skimmed the pages. "Wow. This sounds good! Can't wait to read it." She handed the stack to Mia. "Fine. I'll keep going with the lion thing. But I have to tell you guys, it's really hard to write this stuff. I mean, really hard."

"Yeah." Mia said, reading Lisa's pages. "I know what you mean. Say, is it safe to have your hero—cool, she does it with two men?—like, use his gun in some erotic way? He could maybe stroke her with it. Intimately."

Cailey swallowed a guffaw. "Guns? Where? Not that I know anything about this stuff, but I don't think it's safe to have them down . . . *there*."

Lisa frowned. "You have got to be kidding me."

Mia looked up. "What? No, I'm not joking. It should be okay as long as they're not loaded."

"You have got to be kidding me," Lisa repeated.

Mia shook her head. "It's kind of an adaptation of counter-conditioning. You're replacing a fearful response with a differ-ent kind of—"

"Yeah, yeah. We got that part. But we both want to know how you're going to eroticize water," Cailey challenged.

"Oh, I know!" Lisa said, her expression brightening. "She can have her heroine doing it tied up . . . in a lake."

Mia stared at Cailey, aghast. "I will not!"

"Yes! That's perfect!" Cailey gave Mia a smug grin. "If you're going to make my heroine screw a cat, and Lisa's do insane things with a gun, yours can do the nasty in water."

"No, I can't."

"Why not?" Lisa asked.

"Because . . . uh . . . it's not safe to be tied up while in water."

"Puhleez." Cailey snatched up some chips and dunked one in the bowl of salsa. "The hero is not going to let the love of his life drown. Okay, how about this: you could go with a blindfold. That would work, too." She stuffed the tomato- and pepper-loaded chip into her mouth. Yum. Tangy, with a hint of lime and a little spicy kick. Just enough zing to make the taste buds stand up and take notice.

She loved critique group night. Not only because the two girls sitting there in her living room really did help her with her writing, but also because it was the one night she allowed herself to eat anything she wanted. She followed up the first chip with a second. And a third, while enjoying the lively discussion her idea had sparked between the levelheaded Lisa and the not-so-levelheaded Mia.

She'd definitely touched a raw nerve in Mia. But it served Miss Counter-conditioning right. If she was going to push them so hard, she should have known Cailey and Lisa were going to give her a shove right back. Seriously, why wouldn't they? This had been her idea.

Mia was in the middle of a totally illogical argument against blindfolding her heroine when an eardrum-splitting crack of thunder blasted outside Cailey's window. Cailey's head spun around, her eyes focusing on the scene outside. She half expected to see a blaze in the courtyard behind her apartment building, maybe one of the towering oak trees on fire.

The lights flickered.

"Wow, that was loud," Lisa said.

"Sure was." Mia shifted nervously in her seat, her eyes wide as saucers. "I hope the power doesn't—"

The lights cut off, leaving them sitting in the middle of Cailey's dinky living room in near pitch black.

"Shit," Mia whispered.

"Sorry," Cailey said, blinking to try to adjust her eyes to the darkness.

One of the shadowy figures she could make out was moving around quite a bit. Mia, maybe. Poor thing. She'd looked terrified. Cailey was beginning to believe that water wasn't the only thing Mia was seriously phobic about.

Cailey jumped to her feet, smacking her shins on the coffee table. Biting back a few choice curse words about her apartment building's volatile electrical system, she groped her way across the living room Helen Keller style. "Mia, are you okay?"

Another blade of lightning lit the sky outside for a split second, casting the room in a weird blue light.

"Sure. I'm ffffffine," Mia squeaked. "Ohmygod! What's that?"

"What?" Cailey lurched to the right and nailed her head on the corner of a wall. A few more four-letter words sprang to the tip of her tongue. In the interest of avoiding further panic, she bit them back.

"It's okay, Mia. It's only me," Lisa said. "I'm right beside you."

"Th-thanks. Hurry up, Cailey." Mia's teeth were audibly chattering as she stuttered the words.

"I'm going as fast as I can." Risking another whack on the head or a face-first collision with a large appliance, Cailey moved quickly on all fours, tracing the line of kitchen cabinets with one hand. She counted out, "One, two, three," stopped at the third one, stood up, opened the upper cabinet, and reached blindly inside. A shower of empty Tupperware containers struck the countertop, the hollow sound of plastic bouncing off laminate adding to the bedlam.

Her shaking hands knocked over a bud vase, sent at least one of her crystal candle holders sailing to the floor, and thinned her collection of salt and pepper shakers, all before she'd finally found the candles in the back.

"Ohhhh," Mia moaned. "I'm not feeling very well."

"Sorry! I'm trying. Can't see, damn it. The noise you hear is me, knocking things—"

Something huge smashed into her apartment's only entry, and Cailey dropped the candle she'd finally gotten a firm grip on.

What the heck was that? A tree? An elephant? A friggin' tank?

"Uh, that *wasn't* me," Cailey said, scrambling for the dropped candle and cussing herself out for having forgotten to buy batteries for her flashlight. It wasn't like this losing-power thing was a rare occasion.

A second enormous crash.

On her hands and knees, Cailey dropped her head and covered it with her hands. Then the crack of splitting wood ripped through her tiny apartment. Lisa and Mia shrieked. Cailey yelped and ducked lower, until her forehead whacked the cool linoleum floor.

"Ouch!" she shouted, fingering the sore spot. "Dammit, I'm going to look like I had a date with Max, The Boxing Chimp, if I knock into anything else." She fell back on her rump, sending a Tupperware container sliding across the linoleum floor.

"Cailey," a man's deep voice roared from the general direction of the door.

What the heck?

The lights started blinking on and off, strobelike.

"Cailey Holm," the man said, still standing out of the line of her sight.

Cailey wasn't sure if she should be scared to death or grateful. Did she know that deep, powerful voice? She couldn't be sure. Didn't sound familiar. Perhaps it was the building's maintenance guy, checking to see if she was okay?

The lights cut off again, and Mia whimpered.

As a concession to her five-foot-nothing, overgrown-chicken status, while making an attempt at being a reasonable adult (really, how likely was it for an ax murderer to come stomping into her apartment and shouting her name during a thunderstorm?) she crawled on hands and knees around the short wall cutting off the kitchen from the living room.

She saw a massive shadow, backlit by the vivid sapphire flashes in the window. The lights flickered on again, this time settling into a wavering yellowish glow. The dim light was just enough for her to get a semidecent view of the guy with the gruff voice. Longish hair. Square jaw. High cheekbones. Lips that were neither too full nor too thin. Big, solid frame. Muscular.

Wow.

She was staring, but she couldn't seem to stop. There was something about him. The way he moved. The way he looked. Savage. Feral. Dangerous. Sexy.

Familiar yet not . . .

His gaze slowly lowered, until he was staring at her.

Instantly, she felt small and helpless, like a mouse trapped in a corner by a huge cat. Her heartbeat launched into top speed as she battled the temptation to turn ass and run like a fool.

But her inner voice—the one that was reasonable—told her an attempt at breaking land-speed records wasn't necessary . . . yet. This scary-slash-fascinating feast for the eyes could be a maintenance guy. She didn't know them all. How stupid would she look if she ran for no reason?

"There you are," he said. One side of his mouth lifted into a lopsided smile that simultaneously put her fears at ease and amplified them. Weird.

"Er, yeah," she said, trying to gather up a smidge of dignity. On her hands and knees, like a dork. How silly was that? She ran her sweaty palms down her jean-clad thighs after hiking herself to her feet. "Are you . . . uh, with maintenance? What happened? Did a tree fall on the building?"

"Maintenance?" He visibly puzzled over her question for a split second. "No. Not exactly." He closed the distance between them before she'd taken her next breath.

Whew, that man moved fast. Practically super-hero, faster-than-a-speeding-bullet quick. What was up with that? She did a little backward hop then lifted her gaze to his eyes, prepared to lecture him about the dangers of invading a girl's personal-space bubble. But the second her eyes met his, she forgot what she was about to say.

His eyes were gold. Not your typical brown with flecks of hazel like Mia's, but solid yellow-gold. Like Lisa's Persian cat's.

Lisa's vicious Persian cat.

Cailey's stomach twisted, tying itself into a painful knot. She staggered backward.

His brows dropped. His naughty smile faded. Before she realized what was happening, he scooped her off her feet and flopped her over one shoulder, like a caveman hauling away a deer carcass.

She was the carcass. Not the most dignified way to travel.

"Hey!" she said. "I can walk, you know."

Evidently deaf, the caveman with yellow eyes turned toward the door and crossed her tiny living room in three long strides.

"Hey?" she shouted, getting woozy from the world bouncing around her. She planted her hands on his back and pushed up, lifting her upper body. "What are you doing, Conan?" When he didn't respond, she smacked his back. "This isn't funny. Put me down!" When that didn't produce the results she was looking for, she started kicking and punching, while simultaneously shouting, "Let me go!" at top volume.

The barbarian would set her down. Now.

Or else.

"Lisa? How about some help?"

Her friends were huddled gape-mouthed on the couch, clearly as stunned by her current situation as she was. Not a good sign.

"Lisa!"

Lisa started peeling Mia's fingers off one of her arms, but she didn't pry herself free of Mia's clutch before Conan had hauled Cailey out into the hallway.

Oh God! Was this a joke? What was going on? She broke into a fit of frantic motion, hoping he'd accidentally drop her before he made it to the end of the corridor.

No such luck.

"Lisa!" she screamed again. "Somebody, help me!"

As he stomped through the main exit at the building's front, she caught the edge of the door frame with her fingers and held on for life.

Why was he taking her outside? Couldn't be to show her the pretty stars.

Half inside the building and half outside, she shrieked "Heeelp!" to her friends, neighbors, enemies, anyone who might be within earshot. The barbarian pried her fingers from the wood trim one by one.

As he carted her outside, she threw her weight forward, figuring a concussion from a dive to the ground beat being dragged out of her home by some nut job. But he held her too tightly. She didn't budge.

Before anyone could stop him, they were across the parking lot and headed for the alley.

The rain had stopped, but suddenly the wind picked up, blasting against her face so hard she had to shut her eyes. A tingly sensation passed over her arms and legs, like millions of little scampering spider feet. The air popped and crackled like they were walking through a pocket of static electricity. She opened her eyes, her vision strobelike, thanks to the howling gusts continually making her blink. Bizarre colors swirled around them, iridescent, semitranslucent.

An instant later, it stopped. The wind. The colors. The funny creepy-crawly sensation. It was very dark. No streetlights. No buildings. No moon. They were standing in . . . a forest?

Strange. There were no woods around her apartment, not

within miles. How could the brute have taken her so far in such a short time? On foot? He couldn't have.

But he had.

She mentally shook away her confusion and resumed her battle to break free. "Let me go, dammit. What do you think you're doing?"

Not missing a beat, he answered, "That's simple enough to figure out, isn't it? I'm kidnapping you."

2

Lander Cornelius smiled to himself as he walked, despite the abuse he was taking from the woman draped over his shoulder—or perhaps in a small way because of it. He put up a silent thank-you to the witch who'd sent him into his captive's strange world as he carried his prize back to his lair.

When the witch had first appeared to him, he hadn't known how powerful his quarry's magic would be, how wonderful. How could he have? Who missed what they'd never known?

Thanks to Cailey, he could now smell. Taste. Feel. The world was no longer cloaked in shades of gray. Empty and odorless. Two dimensional. Oh, the joy.

Yet, the witch had given him an even greater gift. Once the woman on his shoulder had fully submitted to him, he could possess the power to change the past, the present, and the future. He could alter the events that had occurred years ago, and those yet to come.

Just think of the possibilities, the disasters he could prevent. Tragedies. Deaths. Yes, this was the ultimate gift to a king.

Cailey. She was the key to this power, for she possessed a

magic greater than even the witch. He could control it, once he had her complete submission. At least, that was what the witch had told him.

Oddly, he sensed a strange connection with his prey, an invisible tether ferrying thoughts and emotions back and forth. He only had to open his mind to hear her gentle voice in his head. To share sensations, emotions, and the occasional thought.

It was distracting, disturbing.

He shifted her weight back a bit, allowing her to breathe easier. "Not much farther."

"Fuck you."

He swallowed a growl.

Cailey was nothing like the lionesses he admired most. Sure, she was intelligent. And, of course, there was no denying she was beautiful. Stunning golden waves cascaded down her back and over her shoulders. Expressive eyes lent what some men might consider an ordinary face unrivaled radiance. Her body was soft in the right places, but also strong and well-proportioned. He couldn't wait to see her completely undressed. That would be soon, but definitely not soon enough.

But she was also outspoken, independent, headstrong.

His gaze momentarily dropped to the erection tenting the front of his black pants. Because of his nature, he was never too keen on wearing clothing; he'd never had a choice in the matter. But at the moment, the garments were bunching in the wrong places. He needed to make an adjustment—quickly—or to get rid of them entirely.

As he stepped up his pace, Cailey continued to beat his back with her fists, kick, and squirm. The pain didn't bother him. In fact, he was grateful to feel her blows. But he feared her wild thrashing might cause an injury. To her. His treasure.

He didn't want to think about the consequences.

Thankfully, his home was not far from the portal between their worlds. By the time he had her safely inside, she was breathless from her exertion and, gauging from the slowing pace of her punches, just about worn out.

Good. Her exhaustion would work to his advantage.

He took her straight to his bedroom and set her down on her feet. As expected, she immediately broke into a run, headed straight for the door.

It didn't take her long to figure out it was locked.

When she turned around, she drilled him with a furious glare. "How dare you! Let me out. Now!"

Clearly, she had no idea how to address a king. He realized, painfully, how difficult it would be to train this goddess to submit. No gift came without its price.

Control. She must always realize who is in control.

He leaned to the left, resting a shoulder against one of the eight-foot pillars at the corners of his bed. "But don't you want to know why I brought you here?"

"No."

She was lying. He sensed it in her voice.

"Or who I am?" he prodded, intensifying his gaze. "Aren't you the least bit curious to know who I am?"

"No! I don't give a damn who you are."

Another lie.

It was hard, but he forced himself to maintain an emotionless mien, even though the vixen had fought him since he'd snatched her from her home. His every nerve was stretched thin.

Adding to the tension was Cailey herself. Her beauty. The scent of her skin filling his nostrils. The sound of her voice humming through his body.

There was a lot to do. Sobering business. If he was going to train Cailey to use her magic for his purpose, she needed to learn to speak the truth. She needed to learn to respect him. And she needed to learn to admire both him as an individual and the strength and majesty of his kind.

He was King of the Werekin: shape-shifters of all species. He merely had to guide her to these truths—with an adequately firm hand.

She stood mute, her back to the door, her arms crossed over her chest. Her anger hadn't eased yet. He could smell it. Spicy and sweet. Delightful. Nearly as intoxicating as the sight of her lush lips and the ivory swell of her breasts, rising and falling with each breath.

Did she know how much he wanted her? How quickly his desire was building? Could she sense it the same way he could feel the longing and fear warring within her? He hoped not. If she did, she might use his desire against him.

He had to maintain control. Always.

He took a single step forward, but she tried to fend him off by lifting her hands and glaring.

"Don't come any closer or I'll scream," she warned.

He had no doubt she would shriek. She'd tested the limits of her vocal chords once or twice—or ten times—already. His eardrums had worn thin, thanks to the high-pitched screeching.

But there was no one to hear her now. At least no one who would do anything about it.

He studied the tension in her body, the stiffness in her limbs as he took a second step toward her. The tang of terror filled his nostrils. The aroma stirred his instincts to chase. Capture. Take. "You don't know our kind," he said.

"What 'kind'? What are you talking about?" She flattened herself against the door.

He stopped directly in front of her, using his size to his advantage. "I'm Lander Cornelius, King of the Werekin."

Recognition slowly touched her features, one by one. Her eyes widened. Her lips parted. The lower one trembled. "Oh. My. God," she muttered in a breathy voice.

"You will learn to respect me." He lifted a hand to her face but before his fingers made contact with her skin, she jerked her head to the side.

"Don't."

"Yes, I will touch you," he said, "whenever and however I wish. You are mine. My possession."

"No, no, no!" She shook her head. "It's impossible. I just started that story. It isn't published. I haven't posted it on the Internet. . . . How? Did you hack into my computer and steal it?"

Her question confused him. What was a computer? And then he realized she was suggesting he had stolen something from her. He took several slow, deep breaths and cleared the rage from his face and voice. "I don't have to steal anything. Computer? Internet? I don't know what you're talking about."

Her confusion and fear hummed along that invisible line between them and vibrated through his body. The sensation intensified the need swirling within him. Regardless of the anger, frustration, and rage, he ached to touch her, to get closer. Why did he react to this . . . infuriating . . . woman this way? He reached again, this time for her arm.

To his surprise, she didn't jerk away. Her gaze was down, fixed to the floor. She drew her eyebrows together and pulled the corners of her mouth into a frown. But she didn't run. Didn't flinch. Didn't move.

When his fingertips finally made contact with her warm skin, a blade of wanting ripped through his body.

Her gaze shot to his face.

Did she sense something? The bond between them? The hunger charging through his system? The desperate need she stirred in him? Her lips parted again. Her tongue darted out, tracing a slick path along her lower lip before slipping back into the sweet depth of her mouth. Damn, he wanted to taste her.

She would let him.

He tipped his head and met her gaze. "I do not have to steal anything. As king, it's my right to take what I want." The little gasp of surprise he heard roused the predator within him.

Seize. Dominate.

"You're not really a king. You're some kind of obsessive fan . . ."

"Fan of whom?" He lowered his head, until little puffs of warm, sweet breath cyclically caressed his lips. Soft like the stroke of a feather.

". . . who stole my story and wants to act it out . . . or something like that," she muttered, her voice shaky, her words disjointed.

"Act out a story? Why would I do that?"

"I . . . I don't know." She sighed.

A sign of submission. Progress.

It wouldn't be much longer. He would have complete submission. She would give it to him freely. And then he would possess the ultimate power, and free his people of all tragedy.

Cailey stood on legs softer than molten Cheez Whiz, staring at the back of her eyelids while simultaneously giving herself a mental kick in the ass. What the hell was she doing even contemplating kissing this guy? He was nutso. An obsessive fan who'd somehow hacked into her computer, stolen her latest work in progress, and memorized it.

Okay, so it was sort of flattering (in a very small way) that someone would find her work so riveting he actually wanted to live it for real. But still, she'd never gone for the newly sprung-from-the-psych-ward type. Especially crazy, pushy, overbearing guys.

That being the case, why was this guy looking sooooo good? And why did her body react sooooo strongly when he came near? It made absolutely no sense. The man was a stranger. Not to mention he'd kidnapped her! She should be shitting her pants . . . not creaming her panties.

Granted, he had yet to do anything truly threatening. Even though he put out this I'm-a-tough-guy vibe, he hadn't hurt her. If she was honest with herself (something she usually preferred to avoid) she'd have to admit she'd treated him worse than he had treated her. She'd punched him, kicked him, called him names.

And how had he responded? He'd done nothing but haul her like a sack of potatoes and give her this hot, I'm-going-to-eat-you-up stare. With those weird yellow eyes of his.

A look she was kind of appreciating.

Ohhhh. She was so in trouble! *Get your act together, girl!*

She heard herself sigh again. That was hardly the proper action for fending off the unwanted advances of a kidnapping, pushy, psychotic fan. She lifted arms that felt like they'd been enclosed in liquid concrete, heavy and awkward and unruly, and pressed her flattened palms against his chest.

That was one broad chest. Oooh. Nice set of pecs. She could feel the outline of developed muscles under his snug black shirt. Her index finger traced a line around one side then up toward the center. Was that a nipple? Her index finger skimmed over the stiff pebble under the thin fabric. Most definitely. Mmmm . . .

A funny sound rumbled within his rib cage. She felt it, like a vibration, in her hands. Her stomach. Her pussy.

Again, not what she wanted to happen. Or rather, not what she *should* have wanted to happen. Things were a little bit jumbled up at the moment—shoulds warring with coulds and maybes. She imagined a battlefield inside her head, little armored knights with big S's on their cloaks charging at other knights with intertwined C's and M's.

Yeah, she'd been to the Renaissance Festival once too often. Imagining a joust inside her head. Duh. She shook her head, knocking the little imaginary knights—who all bore a striking resemblance to the man standing in front of her—from her mind.

That was better. At least her head was clear again. For the time being. Sort of.

Distance. She needed some space.

Despite the fact that she secretly yearned for him to close that smidgen of a distance between their mouths—more than she wanted to take her next breath—she pushed on his chest. Hard.

He didn't budge. Instead, he laid his hands on top of hers, flattening them against his body. "I can see your desire. Your pupils dilating," he whispered. "Your heartbeat racing out of control."

She dropped her head back and scrunched up her face. Oh yes, she could feel every thump-wump of her heartbeat. Funny, though, she could feel his heartbeat, too. It was pitter-pattering almost as fast as her own. But that didn't mean she was ready to break out the toys.

This girl had some scruples. And some pride.

She did not dally with kidnappers.

She did not kiss kidnappers.

She did not lust after kidnappers . . . much. She could allow herself that small liberty. She just wouldn't admit it to him.

"Back off," she murmured in a phone-sex voice.

Heh. Hardly convincing. She might as well have pleaded with him to rip her clothes off and fuck her all night long.

"You don't really want me to do that," he murmured.

She made an attempt at sounding a little more convincing. "Sure, I do."

"Then why are you getting wet?"

Wet? As in . . . ? Ohhhh. He couldn't know that! Could he?

She sniffed the air but all she smelled was him. The sweet scent of his breath. His skin. The lingering aroma of coconut in his hair. And a touch of leather.

Oooh. Leather.

Time for a little believable denial. She lifted her chin. "I'm doing no such thing, you sicko."

He closed his fists around her wrists and, pressing his full length against her, wrapped his arms around her sides, pinning her hands behind her back. He gathered both wrists into one of his fists. "Shall I prove it to you?"

She could think of only one way to definitively prove that. He'd have to touch her *there*.

He'd better not.

Maybe it wouldn't be so bad. . . .

"No." She wiggled, but her squirming made her breasts brush seductively against his chest and her pussy grind against his leg. Oy. That had to say something very different from what she'd intended. Like, "Take me now."

She closed her eyes. Time to regroup. Time to do . . . something. While she scrambled to do *something*, the little voice in her head—the one that had formerly been so reasonable—echoed her body's unspoken plea: *take me now*.

No, no, no! She opened her eyes.

He tipped his head farther to one side and, instead of kissing her mouth, went for her ear.

Did he know how sensitive her ears were? How crazy-in-lust it would make her if he used his . . . tongue . . . ? *Oh yes. Just like that.*

His delightfully agile tongue teased her earlobe and she felt the fine hairs on the back of her neck stiffen. A little stream of breath tickled her ear canal, making her shiver. Her shoulder tightened and lifted. Goose bumps popped up all over her upper body.

"I see this drives you wild," he whispered as he tangled his fingers in her hair and gently pulled, forcing her head farther to one side. "Tell me everything about you. All your secret desires."

"I don't have any secret desires," she whispered, knowing full well she was in total denial. But seriously, how could she admit the truth, while she was standing there feeling so small and trapped and helpless?

What did he want from her? Was she supposed to just serve

herself up to this man on the proverbial silver platter? Let him do anything he wanted?

Granted, that notion did have its appeal.

No! She couldn't. She wouldn't. She was a levelheaded girl who never let her hormones override common sense. Never.

Except for that one time when she was PMS-y. But that was entirely different. She was pissed. For a damn good reason. Her jerk of an ex-boyfriend had deserved everything he got. All her friends had said so.

But when it came to love—or lust—she was entirely able to keep a handle on things. At least she had always been able to before.

She pulled on her arms, trying to break free of Lander, King of the Werekin, and his constrictorlike grip. No luck.

He chuckled, which doused the smoldering lust in her blood a smidge.

She tugged again. "When I get out of here, my first stop will be the closest police department so I can report you. You're going to be so sorry you did this."

"No, I don't believe I'll be sorry. Not at all." He nipped her neck, which sent a flash of heat blazing through her body. As if it would change her mind, he yanked on her wrists until the entire front side of her five-foot-nothing frame was smooshed even harder against his six-foot-plus one.

If he thought that was going to make her beg for *it*, he was so wrong. She was not into those kinds of games.

But she could be.

Shoving aside the temptation to grind her pelvis against his leg again, she rotated her wrists, hoping he'd let her go.

"What you really want . . . what you really need," he murmured against her neck, "is a man who will take control in the bedroom."

"What I really need," she snapped, "is some circulation in my hands. Like . . . blood? They're numb."

"We'll take care of that, then."

Finally, he gets the message! Yay!

Expecting to be freed from the man's tight embrace, she prepared to do a sidestep to avoid getting dragged back into another bear hug. Her legs tensed.

He didn't let her go.

Instead, he walked backward, pulling her with him until they were standing next to the bed.

"Uh. This isn't exactly what I had in mind," she protested.

"Sure it is." Still holding her wrists, he shuffled around in a circle, until he stood behind her and the bed stretched out in front. A very obvious invitation.

"I didn't say I was tired."

"I'm not expecting you to sleep." He pushed gently on her back, forcing her to bend over at the waist until her stomach and chest were flat on the bed. Naturally, being partial to breathing, she turned her head to the side. But the position didn't exactly allow for the widest range of vision.

He stood, his body pinning her hips and legs to the side of the enormous bed. He took both wrists, one in each hand now, and slowly pulled them out to the sides until her arms were straight and stretched perpendicular to her upper body. He massaged one hand until the pinpricks were gone, then did the same with the other.

"Don't move." The pressure on the backs of her legs lifted.

He was leaving? Finally! He really didn't expect her to stay put. Did he?

The way she saw it, she had two options. Number One: to lie there like an idiot. Or Number Two: to do whatever she could to get the hell outta there.

Decisions, decisions.

If he moved far enough away, she figured it would be a decent risk to test him. Really, why would she just lie there, like some mindless twit, waiting for him to do whatever the hell he thought he was going to do? Did he think she was a total idiot?

His weight shifted back and she dragged her arms inward, toward her center, simultaneously lifting her upper body off the bed.

"I said don't move!" he roared.

In a totally unconscious, knee-jerk reaction, she dropped back into position, chest and stomach down, arms out.

And then she got steamed. Both at him and herself.

Since when did she blindly obey the commands of some kidnapping putz? She didn't blindly obey anyone, sexy barbarian or otherwise!

It was clear from the sounds she heard clear across the room that Lander had moved well beyond striking distance. So, unless he was rummaging in the closet for ammo for his assault rifle, she figured it was pretty safe to move. Once again, although slower this time, she pulled her arms in and stood up.

He had obviously anticipated her actions. He stood about ten feet away, a leather whip in one hand and some black straps with little silver buckles in the other.

His expression spoke volumes—like a whole friggin' library. He wasn't happy with her? Aw, wasn't that too bad.

He had no right to tell her what to do. She stood defiant, daring him to do something about it. He wasn't going to hit her with that thing. Who did he think he was?

A deep burgundy color swept up his neck and washed over his face.

Uh . . . he was the big, angry guy with the whip and restraints, that was who.

When his wrist snapped, making the end of that lash whap against the floor, she eyed the locked door.

No go.

Spinning, she searched the room for an alternate escape

route. Surely the room had a window? Right? Wasn't that . . . like some kind of building code? That all bedrooms had to have a window or alternate egress, just in case there was a fire? Or was that just wishful thinking on her part?

"Time for some discipline," the barbarian with the whip said in a low, serious-as-death rumble.

Cailey shuddered and backed herself into a corner. He raised his hand a few inches and flicked his wrist again. This time, the tip of the leather thong cracked about twelve measly inches from her right shoulder.

Trapped!

Was it too late to go for Option Number One?

3

Cailey didn't like pain. Not in any form. Which was why she'd never been able to summon the guts to get that sweet butterfly tattoo she'd always wanted, or even a cute little belly-button piercing.

Nor had she ever thought to subject herself to a whipping by an enormous, blond-haired barbarian. As if he'd read her mind, he raised his arm higher, winding up to crack that whip again. She had the sickening feeling he wouldn't miss his target this time.

Time to swallow the pride and do some serious begging.

"Oh God!" she shouted, squeezing her eyes closed and crossing her arms to shield her head and face. "Please don't hurt me. I promise I'll listen. I'm just scared." When nothing happened after a hundred racing heartbeats, she opened her left eye.

Lander's arms were both resting at his sides. All but a few feet of the whip lay coiled on the ground in front of him, like a snake preparing to strike.

His expression was firm, threatening, his mouth drawn into

a taut line, his eyes narrow slits. "You will do as I say, or you will be punished."

"Uh . . ."

It had been a long, long, long time since anyone talked to her like that. So cruel and insulting. Like her hard-edged disciplinarian of a father.

The adult in her rankled at the tone The Barbarian's voice had taken. The child in her cowered from it.

Her gaze fixed on the man's angry glower, Cailey slowly lowered her arms. "I'm . . ." The word she knew he expected to hear snagged in her throat. She couldn't apologize. Her pride wouldn't allow it. She'd done nothing wrong. Any sane woman would be scared in this situation. Any sane woman would try to escape. "Why are you doing this?" she muttered. "What do you want from me?"

One end of the whip still clutched in his fist, he took a single step toward her.

Yikes! Why was he coming closer? Her insides bounced around in her chest like Super Balls ricocheting off her rib cage and breastbone. What would he do when he reached her? Would he strike her?

Or kiss her?

Which one scared her more?

Escape. Now.

Her gaze hopped around the room, springing from the closet, to the locked door, to the gigantic bed.

"I'm not going to hurt you," she heard him say, "if you do as I ask."

But she was too terrified to believe him. Of course he was going to hurt her! He had a whip. He'd already tried to hit her with it twice.

Just her luck, she'd found herself a sadistic fan who tortured women for kicks. She scrabbled through her memory, desperate to recall what she'd learned in the self-defense class she'd taken at the Y.

Make lots of noise. That'll scare off an attacker.

But wasn't that what you did *before* they'd hauled you into their torture chamber?

Fight. Kick them in the balls. Poke their eyes out. Crush their windpipes. Do whatever you must to get away.

But didn't that work better *before* they'd locked you in a room with them and their twenty-foot whip? Wouldn't her fighting back just feed his anger and make him lash out? Literally?

Play along, let him think you're going with the flow. Talk about yourself so that you'll become a human in his eyes, rather than a target.

Her gut told her that was her best choice, given her circumstances.

This wasn't going to be easy. The last thing she wanted to do at the moment was carry on a friendly little chat. Trembling inside, she dropped her arms to her sides. "Tell me what you want."

"To tell the truth."

"About what?"

"Everything." He took another step closer. Then another and another until he was once again crowding her personal space. "You will learn to submit to me. To do as I ask, without question."

"Submit? For what? Why?" she asked, staring into those weird eyes of his in a vain attempt to read the truth. The irises were the color of molten gold. So strange yet so . . .

"Because you must."

. . . beautiful. His eyes were gorgeous. And God help her, so was the rest of him. How was this possible? How could she be both terrified of someone and insanely attracted to him at the same time?

He reached slowly and took one of her hands in his. "You must trust me."

Her entire body was reacting to the gentle way he held her hand like it was a fragile, priceless work of art. Her face warmed. Her lungs collapsed, forcing her to gulp much-needed air in shallow, panting hiccups. Her insides simmered. "Trust? Now that's a funny one. You kidnapped me. Threatened me—"

"I did take you captive. I don't deny that fact." One of his hands skimmed up her arm. His gaze followed its ascent to her shoulder, halting at roughly chest level before lifting to her face. "But I didn't hurt you."

"You could have. If that whip had come a few inches closer—"

"I had complete control." His wandering hand was on the move again, this time gliding over her shoulder to her neck. One of his fingertips traced a tickly line up to her ear. "I knew precisely where the lash would land," he whispered.

"Uh . . ." She was having one heck of a hard time following this discussion, which really annoyed her. It wasn't like they were nattering about the weather here. No, this was much more crucial.

But the way he was looking at her, touching her . . . ohmygod. He palmed her cheek. His thumb teased the corner of her mouth.

Her eyelids felt like enormous anchors were weighing them down. Her mind was foggy, her thoughts fading in and out. The insane impulse to suckle his finger, swirl her tongue round and round the tip, popped into her head. She knocked that ridiculous notion aside.

What had he just said? *Oh yes. Something about the whip.* "But you didn't know if I'd move into its path."

"I most definitely did."

Strange. She believed him.

"I can read your body. It speaks to me."

She could almost believe that, too, considering the gentle

way he was touching her face. The soothing timbre of his voice. Darn it, he was being patient. Kind. And oh so seductive.

"Do you know what it's telling me now?"

"No." But she could guess. She wanted this. She wanted more touches. More sexy promises murmured in that husky voice. More moments like the last couple.

Why this guy? Had she been that starved for attention all these years?

"I'll show you." With a gentle pull to her hand, he led her back toward the bed.

She followed his lead, willingly.

Taking the whole kidnapping thing out of the picture, was there anything wrong with her going with this? Seeing where it was leading? Was there any doubt where it was leading?

She looked down at the enormous bed. Sure looked . . . comfy.

Guilt and desire clashed inside her, both fighting to control her mind. Guilt claimed a swift victory. Even though she was feeling warm and toasty inside, she couldn't let some things go. Not yet.

She firmed up her resolve, shrugged away from his touch, and met that sultry, gold-eyed gaze.

"Really. I'm being serious here. Tell me how you expect me to trust you? I've never met you before. You stormed into my house uninvited, hauled me away to . . . wherever we are, dumped me in your bedroom, then got all 'don't move or I'll punish you' and brought out the bondage gear. Plus, you're claiming to be the character from my unpublished book. Come on! Get real, pal."

He looked thoughtful as he rested a hip against the bed and crossed his arms over his chest. "When you put it that way, I can understand your ambivalence, but I cannot—"

"Ambivalence? I'm not ambivalent." *I'm horny.* "I know what that word means. It implies I have mixed feelings about the situation. There's no doubt what I'm feeling. . . ." *Lust.* She forced her gaze from his face to those broad shoulders. Strong. Muscular. Yummy. "I'm feeling rage," she said, her voice a little wobbly.

He shook his head. She caught the motion in the corner of her eye.

"And anger. Yes, extreme hostility . . ."

Why was he looking at her like she'd just said the clouds were made of marshmallows and the sea of blue raspberry Jell-O?

He couldn't read her mind. What she said was reasonable. Believable.

"What?" she snapped.

"As I said before, you must never lie to me." He straightened to his full six-foot-something height.

"I'm not lying," she said to his cotton-covered nipple, the part of his body that happened to be at eye level.

He gave her a little shove and she plopped onto the bed, landing on her butt.

Oooh! He was getting pushy. And shock of all shocks, she was liking it.

What's wrong with you?

She knew she should be getting totally pissed off. She should be shoving him back, demanding some respect. "Hands off, pal," she mumbled.

"What?" He planted both hands on the mattress, one on either side of her rump. His nose was so close she had to cross her eyes to see the tip.

She held her breath, partly because she felt so helpless. And partly because her face was flaming, and the heat was trickling lower . . . down her chest . . . to her stomach . . . "This tough-guy, push-the-girl-around act is so medieval." She raised her gaze from the center of his chest to his face.

Damn those eyes of his. She seemed to lose her scruples when she stared at them too long. She looked at his mouth instead. Wasn't much better.

"You like it."

Especially when he said things like that.

She closed her eyes and stared at the colors whirling around in the blackness. Ahh. Much better. Safer. "Why don't you do both of us a favor and unlock the door?"

"Why bother? You cannot leave, even if I did."

Of course she could. Couldn't she?

"Wanna bet?"

Big talk coming from a girl who was sitting nose to nose with six-foot-something of pure temptation, her eyes closed because she was lusting for him so badly the lyrics from "Gimme All Your Lovin'" was playing through her head at regular intervals. She wasn't even a ZZ Top fan.

"You can't afford to lose this wager," he taunted.

"Ha! You mean *you* can't afford to lose." She opened her eyes and poked his chest. Her finger, being a digit that enjoyed the terrain it had just been introduced to, refused to budge once it made contact. She felt herself scowling. Since when did her body parts have minds of their own?

Lander grinned. "You see? You're attracted to me. Admit it."

No way she was going to admit that! Because it was so not true. . . . Okay, it was a little-bit-of-a-lot true but he didn't need to know that.

"Are you ready to hear the terms of our wager?" He lifted a hand and curled his fingers around her index finger. Then he brought it to his mouth and—his gaze hotter than a nuclear reactor's core, his eyes making all kinds of shocking suggestions—he placed a kiss on the tip before releasing it.

"Yeah. Sure." She snatched her hand back and tucked it, along with its pair, under her butt. *There. Let's see him do that again.*

He chuckled as he stood. The sound of his low, rumbling laughter bubbled around in her tummy. "If I win, you will service me."

"And if I win, I'll go home," she said, trying hard not to acknowledge how pleasant that bubbly sensation had felt. He'd given her some breathing room. Her head was clearing a little. Troubling thoughts swept through her mind.

Only moments ago, she'd been scared to death, certain Lander was going to beat her or do something equally horrific. But now . . . she didn't want to explore her thoughts too deeply.

It was time for a reality check.

He'd done nothing substantial to ease her fears—besides setting that whip aside, kissing her finger, and murmuring some pretty cheesy lines. He hadn't unlocked the door. He hadn't clarified where he'd gotten her story. He hadn't explained why he'd kidnapped her. All he'd done was stand there, staring at her with those bizarre eyes, and been his charming, seductive self.

"You may return to your world." He scooped up the whip from the floor and looped it around his arm. "But not yet."

More lines from her book.

"I still don't get this. Why do you keep quoting my story?"

"I don't understand," he said, toying with the tip of the thong. "What story?"

"*Her Master*. It's mine. I wrote it. You've been reciting lines from the first two chapters." She shifted to one side, allowing one of her hands to slide out from under her rump. She tapped her chin. "So either you've lost touch with reality, or . . . something. Doesn't matter. Kidnapping is against the law. You've got to let me go."

"I can't. The witch said so."

"How about we try anyway?"

"Very well. But as I said, if you leave, you lose the wager." He stared into her eyes for a moment then went to the bedroom door. He produced a key from his pocket, and pushed it into the lock. His gaze fixed on her face, he pulled the door open and stepped to one side.

She didn't hesitate . . . much. She sprang to her feet and, starting in a slow jog, made a beeline for freedom. When she passed him, standing sentry at the doorway, she turned a grateful smile his way. "Bye. And . . . thanks for doing the right thing."

Oy vey, she felt terrible leaving like this, even though logic told her she had nothing to be sorry for.

He nodded. "You say that now."

She passed through the opening and stepped into an empty, glaringly white room. It was huge. Enormous. Like a movie set or gigantic factory. Lander's door slammed shut, closing her out. She looked around for another exit but saw none. The white surrounding her seemed to go on forever.

She inhaled. Cinnamon?

"Welcome to my world," a cloaked figure said, appearing out of thin air about twenty feet away. It pulled its white hood down, revealing an all-too-familiar face. "Hello, Cailey."

"What the hell?"

It was her, the woman who'd interviewed with their critique group a couple days ago. At the moment, Cailey couldn't re-member the woman's name. But she did recall how bizarre the lady was, and the creepy-crawly feeling she'd gotten around her. Mia and Lisa had felt it, too. They'd unanimously decided to turn down her request to join their group.

"The story hasn't reached the point where you can leave the room yet. When it does, you'll see what's out here." The woman's voice echoed, like they were standing inside a cave.

"This is so crazy. How do I get out of here?" Cailey shuffled forward, turned to the right, ran that way for several yards, then did a one-eighty and headed back to Lander's closed door.

"Like I said, you don't. Not yet."

"I don't get it." Cailey did a three-sixty where she stood. The only thing she saw was the deeply knotted surface of the door. Otherwise, it seemed that miles and miles of white noth-ingness stretched to eternity. "Where are we?"

"We're in your book."

"Impossible."

"Are you sure?" Bizarre Woman left Cailey to mentally masticate on that puzzling statement before continuing, "You must play out the story to its conclusion. Only then will you be able to return to your world."

"What the hell are you talking about?" she asked, scrutinizing the door frame. As she looked closer, she realized there wasn't a wall attached to it.

This was just too freaking strange. A doorway sitting in the middle of an empty room? How could that be?

Now on the verge of panic, Cailey fingered the door frame, following the edge up as high as she could reach. It had to be an illusion. Right?

"We'll call it the ultimate writing challenge."

"I'm totally not following you." Cailey looked down at her feet and realized there was no floor beneath them. She was sort of . . . floating? "How are you doing this? Am I standing on a glass floor?" She tapped her toe, expecting to hear something, to feel a hard surface. Nothing.

"It's magic."

"Heh. Riiiight. Magic." She wasn't about to admit Bizarre Woman's explanations were making more sense by the millisecond. There was way too much weirdness about all this to buy a completely logical explanation; however, that didn't stop her from desperately searching for one. "Everyone knows magic doesn't exist. It's all illusion. Disappearing 747s, Empire State Buildings, all that. Tricks. Illusions. Fake."

There's no such thing as floating or doors in invisible walls either.

"Do you have any other explanation for what you see?" the woman challenged.

I'm working on it. She took in her strange surroundings again. "I'm dead?"

"If you were dead, would you feel this?" Bizarre Woman poked her upper arm.

"Ow! Suppose not. Ummm . . ." She was really reaching now, desperate to find some kind of explanation that made sense. "I'm on a reality show?"

"Where are the cameras?"

Cailey looked up. Just more white. "Hidden? Oh! I've been hypnotized. That's it."

The woman shook her head. "How could I hypnotize you? I've met you once. In a public place."

"You were swinging your key ring."

"Now who's reaching?"

God, Bizarre Woman was right. She was reaching. Hypnotism. How sad was that? She didn't believe people could really be hypnotized, and yet she was more willing to accept that possibility as a plausible explanation for the bizarreness she was now entrenched in, rather than accept the alternative: that magic was real. Her stomach caved in. Her head started spinning. A chill swept through her body. "I don't feel so good."

"Come. This way. You're fading." Bizarre Woman steered her toward Lander's bedroom door with gentle hands on her shoulders. Cailey suddenly didn't have the energy to fight her; she just dragged her uber-heavy feet along, her gaze focused on the rough-hewn surface. Bizarre Woman pushed the door open, shoved a stack of paper and a pencil at her, and pushed her inside. "Write the story, and the magic will bring you home."

Drained, dizzy, and overwhelmed, Cailey stumbled through the doorway and staggered across the room. She plopped onto Lander's very real, very solid bed, dropping the paper stack beside her.

Lander waited several seconds before restating, "I am Lander Cornelius, King of the Werekin. And because you lost our wager, you must now serve me."

"I, uh . . . okay. You win." She looked at Lander's face, mentally ticking off the list of features she'd imagined when she'd written his description, right down to those spectacular eyes.

Her gaze wandered around the room, slower this time. She hadn't written a sex scene yet, but she had described this room in the first chapter. The polished, dark wood, four-poster bed, lush bedding, warm mocha-hued walls, and rustic, sort of medievalish décor.

She'd been too distracted to notice before. But there was no denying it. She was sitting in an exact replica of Lander's bedroom, as she'd described it in her book.

There was no way anyone could have found all these furnishings and recreated the setting, down to the minute details in the handwoven rug, in such a short time. She'd only begun the manuscript six days ago. And the description of this room had been written Thursday. It was Saturday. Two days?

She ran her hand over the gorgeous bedcovering, the intricate woven design masculine but not cold. She met his gaze again. This time she found comfort and a sense of familiarity in his eyes. She knew him.

A part of her wanted to believe it all—the explanation about her book, the bizarre connection with Lander, the overwhelming, inexplicable attraction to him. But there were still so many puzzling questions keeping her from fully accepting it. Like why? Maybe the answers lay with the woman who'd sent her to this place? What connection did she share with both of them?

"Can I ask you some questions, though?"

"Perhaps."

She took that as a yes. "You mentioned a witch earlier. Is she a friend?"

"No, she is not. I'd never seen her before. The witch does not live within my pride, nor is she a Werekin."

"Did she tell you her name?" she asked, pulling the thick coverlet around her shoulders. Were they even talking about the same woman?

"No." He helped lift a corner of the bedding up over her

shoulder. It was a gentle gesture. Sweet, even. And so contrasting to his domineering personality.

She smiled a thank-you. "What did she look like?"

"She was extremely tall for a woman. And she wore a strong perfume, spicy with hints of cinnamon. . . ."

Cailey didn't need for him to say another word. She'd smelled that perfume, a unique scent that had been supposedly custom-designed for the wearer.

The woman Lander described was—as she'd expected—the same woman her critique group had interviewed on Wednesday.

Oh yes, her name had been Monica. No, it was Monique something-or-other. Or was it Molly? Cailey couldn't remember.

Who cared? All she wanted to know was why. Why would anyone do this? And how?

Was it some kind of revenge? The woman had seemed to take the critique group's decision well. Although, now that Cailey thought about it, something had flashed in the woman's eyes when they'd given her the bad news.

Cool determination? Or perhaps something a lot more sinister?

"I know who you're talking about," she said, realizing that Lander had been rattling off details of the woman's appearance while she'd been ruminating about their meeting over mocha lattes at Starbucks. "But I don't understand how she could . . . how this happened." She glanced down at the unbound papers beside her, reading the title on the first page. "Dark Surrender." It was Mia's story she was supposed to write, not her own? Did that mean Mia or Lisa was writing hers? God help her! "And I also have to wonder where exactly that leaves me?"

"I can't answer the first part but I do have a response to the second one." A twinkle glittered in his eye, making her both wary and intrigued.

"Oh yeah."

"Sure. It's simple. You lost the wager. You're in my bed-room . . ." He turned and strode across the room, pushing open a closet door. ". . . and you have vowed to serve me," he said over one shoulder.

She opened her mouth to say something, but no sound came out. Really, what was there to say?

Serve him? She didn't suppose he meant . . . dinner.

He turned around, a thin metal bar in his fists.

Ohhh . . .

In a week, she'd written exactly twenty-nine pages of her lion erotica story, the bulk of them about the sexy Lander, the King of the Werekin. But she had also introduced the heroine, a waitress—like herself—who was afraid of cats—again, like her-self—and who tended to prefer her lovers on the dominant side.

As in Dom-inant. Ropes. Spreaders.

Simultaneously, a shiver of unease and a shudder of anticipa-tion danced down her spine. She wrapped her arms around her-self.

Lander sat beside her, his expression serious but not severe. "You belong to me, Cailey. And I expect nothing but complete submission from this point forward."

Wow. This was real? It had to be. Lander had given her all the proof she needed. There were no other explanations.

She gave her last few lingering doubts the heave-ho. Whether it was impossible or not, somehow the Rejected Critique Part-ner had set Lander, King of the Werekin, loose, allowing him to pull his creator into the world she'd created.

"Prepare for me," he whispered, his breath warming the side of her neck. "Do you know what it's like to serve a king?" His hand curled around the doorknob, he smiled. "You'll find out in less than ten minutes."

4

Out of the darkness he came, Jafari, chaos personified. Both man and god, possessing power over the elements his creation feared most—dark disorder, turmoil, mayhem.

Legend had once given him a wife, but with the loss of faith in their myth came the destruction of his kind. Now he was alone in the abyss. Abandoned by the people of ancient Egypt, the people he had created.

He wished for only one thing: to exist again.

And now someone had called to him. He was free of the shadows. Free to create new gods to serve him. New enemies to destroy.

And he would reclaim the throne that was once his.

—From *Dark Surrender*, a work in progress by Cailey Holm, writing as Mia Spelman

Cailey was the first to admit she'd never been the kind to jump blindly into a situation. She was a planner. A thinker. A play-it-safe kind of girl. Whether she was making a decision as insignificant as where to buy a new comforter for her bed or where to live, she always, always, always took the time to consider all her options. The word "impulse" didn't exist in her vocabulary.

So why was she even thinking about letting Lander tie her up? Had she lost her freakin' mind?

Yes. The answer to that question had to be yes.

The sound of her swallowing was outrageously loud, thanks to the heavy silence that hung over her head like a cloud. The telltale signs of stress were there, in ample supply: sweaty palms, racing heart, jittery nerves. Yet, something else overshadowed the uncomfortable sensations.

Undeniable fascination.

This wasn't like anything she'd ever faced. This man—this real flesh-and-blood hunk with the face of a god—was her character. Hers alone. A blend of movie stars, models, and a high school ex-boyfriend, he was a product of her imagination. This meant he was the personification of her definition of male perfection, in every sense of the word.

How often did a girl get a chance to experience a night with the world's most perfect man? Would the reality live up to the fantasy? Did she have the guts to do what she'd never risked before—close her eyes and simply go for it?

He'd given her exactly ten minutes alone to mentally prepare herself. She glanced at the clock, one of those old-fashioned, windup kind with the second hand that whirled round and round, counting the seconds with a soft ticktock.

Nine minutes gone? Already? But she still needed more time. The second hand had ticked off the last sixty seconds too quickly. Had Lander messed with the inner workings? That was so not right!

The minute hand edged up to the twelve. Time was up. Ack!

On cue, the door swung open, and Lander sauntered in, a man who knew what he expected to find. If only she knew exactly what that was.

It seemed he wasn't waiting for her to do anything, say anything, for there he was—no "Hello, how's it going?" or "Are you ready?" He simply lifted his shirt, revealing a set of chiseled abs that made her heart do a little hop in her chest and made drool pool beneath her tongue.

The shirt inched higher.

His chest was beyond perfection. And those shoulders? Swoon!

Arm and shoulder muscles bulging and rippling, he pulled his shirt over his head and tossed it onto the floor. His hands went to the waistband of his pants. Her eyes followed them, dropping a couple of inches to the bulge below. That was one enormous prominence. She could just imagine what anatomical structure had produced it.

Ohmygod, ohmygod, ohmygod! She'd forgotten. The Lander in her book had a huge cock. Thick, long, it was bigger than anything she'd ever seen up close and personal before. How would it feel to have a penis that size in her fist? Her mouth? Her other parts?

Yummy. A shudder of anticipation raced up her spine.

Her gaze focused on his hands. Tapered fingers, neatly trimmed nails; they weren't so huge they looked like paws, nor too delicate to look feminine. They were, like the rest of him, perfect. Strong. Tanned. And no doubt nimble. What would it feel like to have those fingers trailing down the side of her neck? Teasing her nipple? Gliding between her swollen pussy lips?

A huge lump congealed in her throat. She swallowed hard once, twice, three times. And then he dropped his pants, and the lump in her throat swelled.

Lander wore no underwear, and thus the object of her previous speculation was there for her to behold. Erect, it proudly jutted from a trimmed nest of tawny curls at the apex of his smooth-skinned thighs. She couldn't help staring. It was real. Oh, so real. And simply breathtaking.

Somehow, she managed to rip her gaze from his groin to peer at his face. Instantly, she felt her cheeks heat. The intensity in his eyes could easily spike her body temperature to lethal levels.

Hands up, palms flattened, she said in a shaky voice, "Whoa! Aren't we going a little fast here?"

Who was she kidding? She was profoundly happy about how fast things were progressing. His answer was a lopsided grin, to which she felt compelled to respond with, "I mean, I know what you were expecting. That's pretty obvious. But I haven't given you the green light yet."

"Sure you have."

"Then you're hearing things. 'Cause I know I said I'd serve you. In a general sense. But that didn't mean I agreed to have sex with you, which means you're this close to . . ."

Lander took a single step toward her, inspiring her to take two steps backward. "You haven't, and you won't, refuse me."

She held her hands in front of her—like that was going to do anything! "That doesn't mean you can just assume—" Her words were cut off when he grabbed her wrists in his hands and swooped them down until her arms were tucked tightly to her sides, and her throat had collapsed.

Tipping his head, he slanted his mouth over hers.

"Hey! Oh! Mrrfff . . ."

He had soft, moist lips. Oh, they were heavenly.

So were the rest of the body parts that were in contact with hers. His hard chest was pressed up against her softer one. And, thanks to the fact that his entire length was smashed against her, that thick cock of his was like a hot brand burning the skin of her stomach. She could feel his heart beating. It was thumping at a pace that matched her own.

He gathered her wrists behind her back, one of his hands cuffing them, the other lifting to cradle the back of her head. He deepened what had been a very soft, sensual kiss. His tongue teased her lower lip, and then he nipped at it with his teeth, just hard enough to make her suck in a little mini-gasp of absolute bliss.

Where, oh where had this man learned how to kiss? She had never experienced anything like this. He was a genius, using tongue, teeth, and, most important, lips, to tease and torment her. Within seconds, the mild simmer in her veins had notched up into the blistering-hot range. Not that she was complaining. No sirree, there was no reason for complaint. Quite the contrary. Especially when he did that little tickly thing with his lips. Ohhhh . . .

She was sure she'd be throwing him to the ground and having her way with him any moment now. At least, she would if she could move. But between his steely grip on her hands, and not so literal but equally tight hold on her neck, she couldn't move a muscle. Even her eyelids felt heavy and sluggish. Come to think of it, there seemed to be only one muscle that wanted to work at the moment: the one gliding into his mouth to do the tango with his tongue.

Yet, even though her entire being was focused on their joined mouths, she managed to somehow backstep with him as he walked. One, two, three steps until something bumped against her clasped hands.

Inside her head, the words, *go with it, go with it, go with it,* echoed over and over like a stuck record. What could possibly happen to her? Could she catch a disease? From a man who didn't really exist?

Get pregnant? Not likely, especially because she was still getting the Depo shot for medical reasons.

Have her heart broken? Like she'd actually let herself fall in love with a man who was nothing but a figment of her imagination.

Be physically harmed? If her story was being written by Lisa or Mia, would they be so cruel? Not if they knew what was good for them.

Break his heart? Not likely.

This was the first real opportunity she'd had to just let go and explore that side of her sexuality she'd hidden from all her previous lovers, without worrying about anything.

Just go for it. Yes, that's what she'd do. She'd kick herself for the next decade if she didn't. Maybe longer.

Still performing magic with his mouth, her fictional Mr. Perfect eased her onto her back, and she gladly let him. A happy little quiver worked up her back, starting at the base of her spine and ending at her nape.

He mumbled something against her mouth, to which she answered, "Yes," even though she had no idea what she'd just agreed to. By God, she was going to embrace this situation and take full advantage of every opportunity that presented itself. She was not going to let a little fear stand in her way.

Ohmygod! I can't believe I'm doing this.

A chill swept through her body as panic knifed sharp and painful in her belly.

Lander took that wonderful mouth of his away, levering himself over her on outstretched arms. His gaze was sharp as razors as he stared down at her. His hair, a mass of golden-brown waves, fell over a drool-inducing shoulder. "Undress."

Her heart slid to her toes. This was always a rough and awkward moment for her, the first time a new lover saw her nude. Whenever possible, she undressed in the dark. Lander's room—with the light beaming from several sources, including a bunch of candles and a pretty healthy fire in the fireplace—had hardly a shadow to hide within. Would he understand her reticence? Did he know her like she knew him? Her past? Her fears? Her anxieties?

Oh God.

"Why have you not removed your clothing, Cailey? I gave you a command." Eyebrows lowered, eyes slitted, he sat up, crossing his arms over his chest. That enormous, erect cock of his stood proudly between his legs. Despite her embarrassment over his demand, or maybe because of it, she found herself just lying there staring at him.

Damn, he was one beautiful man. How had this happened? Why?

Growling, he lurched forward, caught the front of her shirt and jerked, tearing it right down the center.

Taken totally by surprise, she screeched, grasping the torn garment and gathered the frayed edges in her fists to cover herself. Yes, she'd decided she would go with the flow. And yes, she'd wondered what it'd be like having a dominant lover. But yikes! Ripping her clothes?

The independent, do-it-yourself woman of the twenty-first century in her screamed in defiance. How dare he! The barbarian. He had no right to rip her clothes. That shirt had cost her a pretty penny. It wasn't her typical clearance-rack find. She bit her tongue before a few choice words could slip through her lips.

"You will do as I say, and you will do it immediately," he commanded, reminding her that he was indeed written to be a man who was accustomed to having people ask "How high?" when he said jump. King of the Werekin. Leader of a group of powerful beings.

And a masterful lover.

She closed her eyes, unable to meet his gaze. How would he react when he saw her scars? Like all the others? None of them had ever said anything, but early on she'd learned there would always be a reaction.

Usually it took the form of a flare of surprise in their eyes that quickly morphed into either disgust or pity.

At least she could close her eyes. What she couldn't see wouldn't hurt her.

Standing on legs growing wobblier by the second, she dropped her arms to let the ripped shirt fall off. The material skimmed over her skin, feather soft. Then, after catching on her rump, it dropped to the floor behind her. Her fingers felt unruly as she fumbled with the button on her jeans.

"Open your eyes."

She didn't want to, dammit. She'd been all warm and happy and tingly. All those pleasant sensations would be gone when she spied the disgust or pity sure to be evident on his face.

"Open them," he repeated, sharply.

Her eyelids snapped open, but she kept her gaze low, at about nipple level.

"Look at me."

I am. The chest is part of you. Let's not get picky, all right?

He grasped her chin and lifted.

Mentally bracing herself for the disappointment she'd feel at his reaction, she reluctantly lifted her eyes to his.

What she saw made her want to weep. Raw, unbridled desire simmered in those gold eyes of his. Not a hint of disgust or pity to be found.

"You're absolutely beautiful," he said, his hand slipping around to cup her nape. He lifted his other hand, flattening it on the center of her breastbone, just above the lace cups of her bra. Her breath hitched in her throat then left her lungs in a whoosh when his hand suddenly slipped down to completely cover one breast.

She arched her back slightly, pressing her tender breast into his hand, while the hand at her nape traveled down to the clasp of her bra. It snapped open, and with hungry eyes, Lander pushed her bra straps off her shoulders. She fought the urge to catch it and cover herself. Between the cougar attack, the fire, and many skin grafts that had followed, the skin of her neck, chest, stomach, and back was grossly scarred. The surface was lumpy and unevenly pigmented. It disgusted her. She didn't have to imagine what other people thought when they saw it.

She hadn't worn a swimsuit in public since she was five.

She started to explain, "When I was five, I was playing—"

He silenced her with a shake of his head then slowly turned around.

She couldn't help gasping. His back bore nearly identical scars to hers. Right down to the location of the seams where the grafted skin had been positioned.

What did this mean? As her creation, did he bear some of her scars?

"I have similar marks," he explained. "I don't know how I got them. But no longer can I despise them, now that I have seen yours. They tie us together, make us one." He turned to face her again. "You're perfect in my eyes."

She was speechless. Absolutely dumbfounded. What was there to say when a man said such a beautiful thing?

Still not 100 percent comfortable, but much more at ease than she had been, she unbuttoned her pants, unzipped the fly, and pushed them down over her hips. His gaze was like a brand, marking her skin as it was exposed.

After a glance his way, she stepped out of her jeans then tugged off her panties.

Tingles and prickles crept over her arms, legs, back. Her nipples tightened, hardening to sensitive peaks. Her pussy pulsed as her simmering blood throbbed through her veins, swelling the sensitive tissues. She clenched her inner muscles and wrapped her arms around herself.

Never had she felt so vulnerable and so . . . beautiful.

A smile spread over Lander's face, making her heart do this happy little pitter-pattery thing. A giggle bubbled in her throat. She swallowed it just as he lunged forward and scooped her off her feet. He cradled her close, carrying her with such ease, she'd swear she couldn't weigh more than a toddler. And an undernourished one at that. He plopped her on the bed and bent low, his hands planted on the mattress on either side of her hips.

"Now that we've gotten that over with, it's time we move on."

Almost every part of her anatomy gave up a silent cheer at that bit of news. Her brain, however, was a latecomer to the party. It was still stuck in Doubtville.

What exactly did he have in mind? There was the obvious, of course, but she had a feeling he meant a whole lot more than ten minutes of thrusting and a quick orgasm. He had, after all, said something about her fantasies and brought out the bondage gear.

She wondered if he might take a bit of a breather, talk a little longer?

I'm naked. He's naked. It's a little late to put on the brakes.

All too aware of how close he was, how great he smelled, and how absolutely scrumptious his body was, she slowly lay back as he positioned himself overtop of her. He wedged his knees between her legs, forcing them apart. Then, being a very naughty romance hero, he rubbed that cock of his against her wet, hungry pussy.

Naturally, she was eager to get her hands into the action. She wanted to feel his muscles strain under his velvety skin. But, being the dominant lover he was, he wasn't about to let her touch and grab at will. Oh, no, he was not.

He captured her wrists in his enormous hands and pinned them to the mattress. After sliding her a smile that nearly caused her to burst into flames, he lifted up onto all fours, straddling her torso, and reached for one corner of the mattress. The rattle of metal gave her a clue as to what he was after long before she watched him wrap the leather cuff chained to the bed around her left wrist.

Good God, she was going to melt.

He secured the other one, leaned back, and gave her an I'm-going-to-eat-you-alive look.

She whimpered, not because she was in pain, but because she

wanted him to eat her up, and more. She'd always fantasized about being in this position with a man, not really powerless in all senses, but feeling overpowered by a strong man. She knew he could do anything to her right now and she couldn't stop him, but she also trusted he wouldn't hurt her. It was beyond thrilling, beyond what she'd ever imagined.

He scooted down, placed one hand on the inside of each of her knees, and pulled them up and wide apart.

He was going to taste her down *there*.

Oh God, ohgod, ohgod, Ohhhhhhgoddddddd! The things he could do with that tongue.

In a matter of seconds, her entire body was hot, trembling, and tight with need. Which was why when a loud crash blasted into the room, followed by an immediate cessation of Lander's magic, she cried out in fury.

Then she opened her eyes and screamed in terror.

Two enormous, absolutely petrifying black cats were attacking Lander. With mouths full of sharp teeth and claws that could tear anything but solid concrete to shreds. Lander was doing his best to fend them off, but an unarmed man, no matter his size, was hardly a match for two vicious, bloodlusting creatures like those.

Which meant not only would she have to watch Lander get eaten alive—no!—she'd no doubt be the next course on the animals' menu. And tied to the bed, she was in no position to defend herself.

Cringing, she tried to scoot up toward the head of the bed, loosening the tension on the chains, hoping she could somehow sit up and free herself from the cuffs.

Unfortunately, the movement caught the attention of one of the panthers and it charged forward, its freakish yellow eyes locked on their prey: her. Instantly, she was swept fifteen years back in time, to that summer when the cougar had attacked her.

Yes, she knew very well what it felt like to be prey to a powerful animal. She'd lived her entire life remembering that moment, when the cougar had lunged at her and locked its jaws around her arm.

Not again, please!

She screamed, praying the terror would knock her unconscious long before the first bite.

5

In the midst of a horrific battle, Cailey found herself blessedly detached from the action, no doubt her psyche's way of protecting itself from meltdown. There was only so much terror any one human being could endure. This being a scene that would be absolutely horrifying even if all three combatants were human was beyond all definition of terrifying because of her cat phobia.

Nothing like being in a room with two felines determined to eat you to bring out the worst in a phobic.

Lander knocked the panther off the bed with a full body slam, mere fractions of a second before it sank its fangs into her neck.

Her eyes closed—with the hair-raising snarl of animals, rending of fabric, and crashing of overturned furniture all around her—she lay absolutely still, defenseless, waiting for the end to come. There could be no doubt how this would end if Lander wasn't able to fight those hellcats off. And that wasn't looking likely the last time she'd dared slit open an eye to check.

If only she hadn't been tied up. If only she had a gun! A big fucking shotgun. Or flame thrower. Or grenade launcher.

If only she'd plotted out her story! God only knew where Mia and Lisa would take this.

For the first time ever, she regretted being a pantzer kind of writer. Although . . .

Surely this wasn't the end of her story already, right? She'd just arrived. They hadn't done The Deed yet, and that was no way to end an *erotic* romance novel. Plus, who heard of a romance story where both the hero and heroine died after only a few chapters?

Oh hell, what if the plot was all fucked up by her coming and taking the heroine's place? Or what if Mia decided she needed to die to get over her phobia?

If I make it through this alive, I promise to always plot my books out ahead of time. I swear.

A prayer to the writing gods had to help . . . she hoped. What else could she do? Lay there and freak out? Scream bloody hell, attracting the panthers' attention so they could gobble her up faster?

She tried to remember what she'd planned to write next. There was, of course, going to be lots of hot sex, bondage, domination, all that yummy stuff. But she'd also kind of forgotten about the other parts: the not-so-yummy stuff that was supposed to force her heroine to face her fears head-on. While she hadn't plotted the book out, she'd jotted some bullet points.

Oh no.

If she was going to actually live out those bullet points, she was in for some bad stuff. Her stomach turned over for the umpteenth time but, when she realized everything had grown silent, instead of doing another somersault, her stomach whooshed up her throat.

Why was it so quiet? Was it a good thing or bad? Had Lander

fought off the attackers? Or had they finished him off and were currently prowling toward her?

She swallowed her displaced stomach and, heart banging against her breastbone, slowly lifted one eyelid a little bit.

The room was an absolute mess, but she saw no signs of either panther or Lander. Taking advantage of the moment, she scooted up again and squirmed, flipping on one side to allow herself to sit up. Her hands, still bound, pressed flat against the mattress. On her knees, she turned to face the headboard and started scrambling with the leather cuffs, releasing one wrist then the second.

Still no sign of Lander or the panthers. *Ohgod, ohgod, ohgod!* What kind of hellish thing was going to happen next?

Dizzy and feeling like she was going to throw up any moment, she wrapped herself in a sheet, scrambled off the bed, and sprinted toward the door. After pressing an ear to it, checking for sounds of fighting felines, she slowly inched open the door.

Sprawled against one wall lay an enormous tawny-coated male lion. His mane was matted with dark red blood. Was he dead? Was that Lander? Could she even think about going out there to check on him?

Hell no!

She shut the door and pressed her back against it. What to do? If Lander was dead, where'd the panthers go? Were they hanging around, waiting for her to come out of hiding? Or would they come barreling through the door again? She doubted the wooden door would keep out animals that strong, but it sure beat having nothing.

Feeling guilty for leaving Lander out there, vulnerable, she twisted the bolt, locking the door. Chances were he was already dead, but if he wasn't, she was pretty much leaving him defenseless.

But hell, what choice did she have?

Suddenly, something started clawing at the door. Driven by sheer instinct, despite the knowledge that the animal on the other side trying to get in could be Lander, she raced in the opposite direction, finding a door leading to a bathroom on the other side of the room. She slammed the door and secured the lock, then turned, hoping she'd find the unlikely: some means of escape from this hell.

She just wanted to go home!

Then again, if she were able to leave Lander's house, what kind of reception would she receive from his fellow Werekin? That old expression "Better the devil you know than the devil you don't" had proven to be true on more than one occasion in her life. This could no doubt be yet another.

Ack! She'd never been so confused in her life, or absolutely terrified. Despite her best efforts to stop herself, she sank to the cool stone-tiled floor, and knees bent, arms wrapped around them, she started crying.

Why had that bitch done this to her? Why, why, why?

Lander released a roar of agony as some of his bones stretched, elongating and narrowing. Others shortened. The change was always excruciating, but even more so when he was injured, like now. Luckily, the wounds were superficial, would heal during the change.

On the floor, he writhed as his limbs slowly lengthened. Even in his feral form, he still possessed his human mind and soul.

Thoughts of the woman on the other side of the door flashed before his eyes as he closed them against the fierce agony overtaking his body. He needed to tell her she was safe. Ached to pull her to him and smooth his hand down her back, easing her terror.

As the pain ebbed, and the worst of the change passed, he could smell the tang of Cailey's fear everywhere, especially around the door. He knew she'd opened it, at least briefly, most likely when he'd been unconscious.

Once he was again a man—the beast pushed deep inside—he pulled himself up using the doorknob. "Cailey," he called, his voice deeper than normal, weak and raspy. Could she hear him? "It's safe to open the door." He knocked. "Cailey!"

He heard a shuffle, then the clack of the lock disengaging. He resisted the urge to push the door open and charge inside, knowing he'd probably terrify her. Instead, he held himself up by leaning against the wall, and waited.

The door slowly swung in about six inches, and Cailey's pale face appeared in the opening. Her red-rimmed eyes met his. A split second later, the door opened wide enough to let him step inside. Cailey slammed it closed behind them, and he noticed how she trembled when she engaged the lock.

Her shoulders. Her hands.

The need to protect her was like the most painful, urgent impulse. He hated how much power she held over him. Despised it with more fury than he held for his enemies, including the two panthers he'd just chased off.

Some of the ache eased as she sank into him, letting him wrap his arms around her and tuck her against his body. He had been told she would fear him in his feral form. But at least at this point she wasn't afraid of him as a man. She was opening up, allowing herself to be vulnerable.

He needed to get back to her training.

If only she could be his sole focus. Unfortunately, she couldn't. Those panthers had sent him a clear message, one he couldn't afford to ignore. He needed to take action or he'd pay a dear price.

But first, he must spend a little more time with Cailey. Before he risked leaving her, he had to secure her allegiance. He had no idea how long he'd have to be away until he talked to his security team. Starting from scratch with her, after coming this far, would be an enormous setback.

Ironically, Cailey seemed to accept the situation better than he'd originally expected. And yet, despite her response, he couldn't be gentle with her, in bed or out. Not only did the situation prohibit it, but the beast within him wouldn't allow it.

He'd be hard. Push her. Force her to face everything she'd been hiding from. Take advantage of her fears, to force her into submission.

Something had changed. Despite the adrenaline pulsing through her body, giving her a natural high, the focus of her entire being narrowed to a single part of her body: the small of her back.

It was the pressure of Lander's hand. It had intensified. A lot. A small part of her thrilled at the sensation, appreciating the power emanating from his touch, and the command he would soon have over her body.

"Cailey," he whispered harshly. The hunger she heard in his voice was like a bolt of electricity zigging and zagging through her body. "It's time. To take the next step." One hand traveled lower, cupping her bottom.

Swept up in it all—the fear that still pounded through her veins, the sharp edge in his voice, the unexpected lust simmering through her body—she arched her spine, pressing her ass into his touch.

His free hand slid up her back, stopping at the base of her skull. He curled his fingers into her hair and pulled, forcing her head back. He dipped his head until his breath fanned over her lips, sweet and hot. "I must push you. Test your limits."

Blades of panic pierced her insides, the tingle in her scalp blending with a strange thrill she'd never experienced before. The hand on her ass lifted, and in the next instant, while he held her by the hair, he tore the sheet from her body.

She gasped, shocked and yet not. Scared and yet not. And

aroused beyond thought. Beyond reason. His treatment bordered on cruelty, and yet she relished the feeling of vulnerability and powerlessness it stirred in her. What kind of woman was she, that she ached for such treatment by a man?

His mouth was pulled into a tight line, his jaw equally tense. His eyes were narrow slits, focused on hers. His mouth a delectable temptation. So close. Why hadn't he kissed her yet? How she hungered for his uniquely wonderful flavor to fill her mouth, just as his glorious scent filled her nostrils.

"I'm a man now, not a lion. But the urges of the beast inside are here. I can't deny them. Especially when you're near. My senses are ten times more acute. Colors. I see colors. And smell. Oh, goddess." He inhaled, his nostrils flaring. "I smell your panic, your excitement. I taste it now. Here, behind my front teeth. Fear and arousal. Those two scents must be the most intoxicating, addictive smells in the world. I wish I could pull them in deeper, store them inside." He forced her to the bed, turned her and bent her over the mattress. "I have to possess you. You're mine. No other man will touch you." He dragged his fingers down her back, the sting of his fingernails cutting into her skin following in the wake of his rough touch. But the mild pain only intensified the thrill of being in such a submissive position, at his mercy. He kicked her feet apart, widening her stance, and her back tensed, rocking her hips back.

How long would he torture her like this? Making such thrilling promises while denying her the release she suddenly wanted so much. It felt like her insides were in a pressure cooker. Sweat trickled along her hairline. Her hands trembled as she reached behind her, hoping to capture his hips between them and steer his cock toward her wet pussy.

Fuck me, oh please. She would beg if she had to. What was left of her pride wouldn't do her a damn bit of good right now. Not when she was sure she would die if he tormented her much longer. "Lander—"

"Silence," he bit out, his voice once again razor sharp. He wrapped strong fingers around her wrists and lifted them to the sides of the bed, pinning them to the mattress. "I am your master." He licked her shoulder, nuzzled the crook of her neck. "I could break that pretty little neck of yours so easily."

His words didn't scare her. What did was the secret thrill she felt at being so overpowered. It rivaled the fear she'd felt when those two bloodthirsty panthers had come bounding into the room.

She struggled to subdue the trembling wracking her body, making her teeth chatter.

His pelvis was snugged against her bottom, his cock pillowed between her ass cheeks. It was hot, thick, hard. And she so wanted it inside her.

"You are the sweetest thing I've ever tasted," he murmured against the tingly skin of her neck. He nipped, licked, and kissed her until the entire right side of her body was coated in goose bumps. "Goddamn, I want to take you hard and fast." He released one of her wrists and backed his hips away. The tip of his cock prodded at her anus, and she flinched, terrified he'd try to take her that way. She'd never been fucked in the ass, but she'd seen pictures, videos. She'd also used a butt plug a few times while masturbating. But just the thought of something *that* large thrusting inside her sensitive opening made her tremble. She tipped her hips, hoping to give him a more appealing alternative.

His hands clapped to her hips. "Hold still," he growled. "Don't move. Not even a finger, eyelash. Nothing." His cock started prodding at her untried hole again, and despite her best efforts to stop it, she whimpered. She felt him tense at the sound. A low rumble, much like a predator's warning growl, filled the room.

Maybe he wouldn't mortally injure her. Maybe he wouldn't snap her neck or shift into his lion form and eat her alive. But she sure as hell believed he could do plenty of other things. And not all of them were necessarily pleasant.

"Do you know anything about the mating of lions?" He teased her labia with his cock.

"No," she whispered, grateful he'd moved from her anus.

"Lions mate hard and fast . . . and often." And with that, he surged forward, impaling her with his cock. The force knocked the air from her lungs in a whoosh. She bit back a cry of both gratitude and shock. Immediately, he fell into a fast pace, his rod pistoning in and out of her tight channel, hard and fast, just the way he'd said he wanted to take her.

His chest and stomach slick against her back, he reached around her, his nails raking the flesh of her lower stomach before moving lower. He found her clit with a fingertip and drew slow circles, round and round.

She tipped her head back and moaned. A bubble of heat formed in her belly. It rolled over, growing larger, spreading, until her face burned. She rocked her hips in time with Lander's thrusts, and tightened her inner muscles around him, amplifying her pleasure.

He drove into her, his fucking unrelenting, rough, wild, just the way she'd expect it from an animal. He teased her time and time again, bringing her to the verge of release and then denying her. She wanted to cry, to scream, to beg.

"Look at that pretty little ass. It's fucking perfect. Damn, I want to fuck it, sink my cock deep."

She shuddered at the thought of something that big being inside her untried hole. Surely, it would kill her. At the very least, it would hurt like hell. No, she couldn't handle that.

Still fucking her pussy, he tested her anus with a finger, dragging some of the wetness seeping from her pussy back. Instinctively, she tightened both her pussy and ass. Dark thrill spiked through her, and she couldn't help gasping. It burned as he slowly pushed his finger inside, gradually stretching her tight muscles.

No, this was so not going to happen! She flinched, but he caught her hips between his hands and held her. What had once been a pleasant feeling of having surrendered control was now a little less pleasant. She was still aroused beyond words. Her body was thrumming like a struck gong, but a shadow of fear had darkened the tone.

She was truly at his mercy. Her position wouldn't allow for much movement. Her thighs were pressed tightly against the side of the bed, and a strong hand held her torso flat to the mattress. That finger was still probing, the tip dipping inside her anus and then withdrawing.

With each invasion, the stinging eased a tiny bit until eventually, the pleasure dwarfed the pain. His finger moved deeper, and she wanted it, craved more. She tipped her fanny up, silently pleading for what her body demanded.

"Come now for me. I want to feel your pussy milk my cock and I want to smell your sweet juices. That scent drives me crazy."

He didn't have to ask twice. Instantly, a powerful orgasm quaked through her body, sending wave after wave of pure bliss through her being. Tears gathered in her eyes, not because she was sad, but because so many emotions had gripped her, she was completely overwhelmed.

Inside her gut, she just knew this was what she'd been waiting for. Searching for. A dominant lover who knew exactly what she craved.

Lander bit back a howl, slowed his thrusts, and relished the feel of Cailey's sweet pussy convulsing around his cock. The heady aroma of her release filled his nose and teased the sensitive bundle of nerves in the roof of his mouth.

What a glory this was, to fuck Cailey while the world around him exploded in vivid color and scents and tastes. It was like nothing he'd ever experienced before.

Inside, the beast fought for control, threatening to take over again. He struggled to keep it subdued, knowing Cailey—who was not Werekin—couldn't handle watching the change. But oh, how fucking painful it was, holding off the beast. His bones cracked and popped. Agonizing spasms wracked his body, delaying the release he craved.

She was so hot, her tight little pussy slick for him. Her body soft and giving. And that pink hole temptingly tight. She would learn to accept him there. He'd prepare her slowly. But for now, he would be content with the pleasure he found in her pussy.

And oh what pleasure he found there. He could feel his cum pulsing up his cock, his balls tightening. A part of him wished he could delay release, the other reminded him how thin the thread holding back the beast was. It could snap at any moment, and he would lose control.

As the spasms of her orgasm eased, he quickened his pace again. He thrust deeper, harder, a relentless drive toward orgasm. He reached around her again, teased the hardened peak of her nipple. She whimpered, the sound stirring the beast again. Roused, it pushed to the surface, nearly overtaking him. Once more, the agony gripped him. He slumped forward, leaning against Cailey's back.

He was losing the battle. He had to come now.

He threw his head back, and a roar tore from his throat. Cailey's soft flesh clutched in his hands, he guided her hips back, frantically thrusting as deeply as she could take him. He felt the twinges in his fingers and toes as they started shortening, the tingle of his skin as his lion coat started covering his neck, chest and legs.

Now! He despised the beast swallowing him up.

Now! He held his breath, sweat pouring from his forehead, chest.

Now! He wouldn't give up. No.

Oh goddess, give him the strength to hold the beast at bay. His legs were thickening, but he pulled on her hips, continued thrusting. Relief was right there, just outside his reach.

"Cailey," he called, his voice roughened by the change.

She reached back between her widespread legs and cupped his testicles. A slender finger skimmed the lower rim of his anus and stars exploded behind his closed eyes. Instantly, as the first burst of semen pulsed into her body, the beast retreated, releasing him from the change, and he was free again to enjoy the rest of his orgasm as a man.

After the heat in his blood eased to a mild simmer, he was able to think a little more clearly. And the first thought that came to mind was how close he'd come to losing control. No lioness had pushed him that close. Then again, he'd never seen such glorious colors, smelled such wondrous scents. Felt the slick heat of a woman's pussy. He'd always lived in a colorless, odorless, sensationless world. With each minute he spent with Cailey, his senses sharpened more. Sight, sound, taste, touch.

He'd never known what he was missing.

He sagged against Cailey, looping an arm around her waist and snugging her against him. He buried his face in the crook of her neck.

Damn, he'd no sooner found release than his cock was demanding more.

Swiftly, he pulled from her, yanking a blanket from the bed to cover her. He helped her to the bed, noticing her wide-eyed, wary gaze on his still-erect cock.

"I can't get enough of you. I doubt I'll ever get enough. Your body, face, scent. Dammit, the way you smell. You have no idea what it does to me."

"I'm beginning to think that's a good thing." She inched toward the head of the bed, reclining against the headboard. Her hands shook as she clutched the blanket to her chest. Her pupils were dilated so wide, the irises were narrow bands of color.

He could read her body, just as the beast could read his prey, anticipate its every move. She was struggling. He sensed the conflict inside of her. Yet, he wasn't in a position to ease the discomfort. That frustrated him, as well as hurt him. The confusion he read in her eyes made him want to leave, to make an excuse and walk away, at least for a little while.

Or tear that damned blanket away and unleash the beast.

Shit, he needed to leave. Yes, it was time to take care of those panthers.

"I'll return later, little one." His balls so tight it was painful, he gritted his teeth and headed for the door.

6

"You're leaving? Now?" Cailey couldn't believe this. Her Mr. Perfect Romance-Book Hero was no better than your typical male; ready to run out as soon as The Deed was done.

They hadn't even shared a few minutes of pillow talk. Or a smoke. Some cuddles. Not a damn thing. Granted, he wasn't rolling over and going to sleep either.

But he had to sense she was confused, not to mention a little petrified. Even she could see her hands were still shaking. She had lots of questions to ask him, and would have appreciated a few answers, some reassurance, too. It wasn't like she did this every day: sleep with someone she'd just met. Someone who could turn into a freakin' animal.

Patience had never been one of her virtues. But, fortunately for Lander, forgiveness was.

His hasty excuse wasn't his fault. It was Mia or Lisa's fault. Bitches! She glanced at the pages of Mia's story, now scattered all over the floor. Vengeance was so not her thing, though it was oh so tempting.

Lander halted just inside the doorway. "I have to go. My

enemy's ready to make his move. Those panthers wouldn't have risked coming here if he wasn't."

Obviously, he was hell-bent on pulling a quick retreat. To her surprise, her eyes started to burn.

Uh-uh, there was no way he was going to make her cry. The gorgeous, sexy, impossibly powerful and manly *jerk*. She did not get hurt by men. Ever.

It was exhaustion. And terror. Shock. That, too.

She sighed, sniffed. "Oh, yeah. Your enemy." Granted, she had forgotten about that evil-versus-good stuff for a little while. Evidently, just like in real life, pretending a problem didn't exist wouldn't make it go away.

Not that she didn't have good reason for forgetting. Lander's body would make most girls forget some things: their name, for one. And for two, any excuse they might have for not jumping his bones. "I wish I'd plotted out the rest of the story. Sure would be handy, knowing what was going to happen next," she said.

"I don't know what you mean by that: "plotted." You're talking again of a story? What does it mean? Do you know the future?"

"No, I don't." She sighed. "This sucks."

"No, what sucks," he said, his voice not quite so sharp and hard, "is having to leave you." He looked at her with some seriously hungry eyes and a shadow of a smile. His tongue swiped across his lower lip and he stepped into a pair of snug pants and shrugged into a leather vestlike garment.

After fastening the three metal buckles holding the vest closed, he strode across the room to crowd her personal space with his scrumptious bulk (yes, she had most definitely forgiven him for running out on her, already). He lifted her chin and ran his thumb across her lip. "If I had more time . . . the things I would do to you."

Promises, promises.

A happy little quiver zipped up her spine. Regardless of how scared she'd been when he'd been fucking her, she'd also been crazy-aroused—like, beyond words. Even though Lander's sexuality was harder, in a way darker, than she was completely comfortable with, she was still game for some more of what they'd done earlier. Not to mention, she was terrified of being left alone in this strange place. "Are you absolutely sure the panthers can't wait?"

"Positive."

Wanting to keep the mood light, she pushed her lower lip out in a faux pout while maintaining a playful tone to her voice. "Fine. Leave. But what if they come back? You aren't leaving me here alone are you? Without a gun or something, I'm a sitting duck."

"No need to worry. I've already set a guard outside." He kissed the tip of her nose.

He had to be kidding. A kiss on the nose? Did he honestly think she'd be satisfied with that?

"What was that?" she asked.

"A kiss." He turned toward the door.

Time for one last (desperate) attempt to convince him to stay. "No. This is a kiss." She yanked on his wrist, forcing him back around. Then she looped her arms around his neck, pulling hard, until he sat beside her and planted her lips on his.

A low rumble sounded in his chest. The vibrations seeped into her stomach where it ignited mini blazes here, there, and everywhere. Their tongues did a little dance in their joined mouths, twisting and caressing and thrusting. Meanwhile, Cailey's stomach clenched and relaxed in time with the hot blood pounding through her body.

He broke the kiss about an hour too early. "Like I said, I have guards posted outside, and there aren't any other windows or doors. You're safe here. As long as you stay in this room."

"Okay. Fine." Oh, this sucked. He was not going to be swayed, and he'd been smart enough to cover the important stuff—like her safety. She couldn't offer any other believable arguments for him staying there with her. Not to mention, she supposed it was partly her fault he was facing this trouble in the first place. She had, after all, written the bit about his archenemy, Jag.

As she watched him head back toward the door again, she didn't even offer to help him, knowing exactly how much—or rather, little—help she could be. She could barely handle being in the same room with a harmless kitten, let alone battle a pair of deadly panthers.

A part of her, however, was worried. The witch had suggested someone else was writing her story. Which meant nothing was guaranteed anymore, like (yikes!) the happily-ever-after she'd planned.

What if Lander was killed? Could he be killed? What would happen then?

"Please be careful." This time, she didn't bother hiding the fear in her voice.

"Don't worry. I'll be back soon." This time he made it about halfway to the door.

"Hey!" she called. "How about some clothes?"

"Later. Rest now. It's late." He went back to her, kissed her one last time, and left. And for the first time since arriving there, she realized how much she enjoyed Lander's company. And how empty the room felt when he was gone.

This wasn't just about being scared of what might happen, or scratching a sexual itch, or getting questions answered. He was interesting—fascinating, actually. She wanted to spend time with him, talking about stuff. Everything.

She thought about trying to fall asleep; in fact, she tried really hard for a while. But after laying there for what felt like hours (but wasn't) she gave up. Every time she heard a noise, her heart would start slam dancing with her rib cage, and she'd jackknife upright, her eyes on the door.

Instead, she gathered the strewn pages of Mia's story into a semineat stack, put them back into order, and started brain-storming what direction she wanted to take Mia and her Egyptian god. The possibilities, as they said, were endless. But before she'd written a single page, a knock sounded at the door.

She had company? Friend or foe? Couldn't be Lander. He hadn't knocked before, except when she'd locked him out.

Bedecked in a bedsheet toga, since Lander had swiped her torn clothing on the way out, she shuffled to the door and opened it a smidge.

Two beautiful women stood in the hallway, abso-freakin'-lutely gorgeous women, with perfect hair, perfect faces, perfect bodies.

She hated them. And, knowing they also turned into animals, feared them. What a way to die: murdered by a couple of shape-shifting fashion dolls.

And yet, seeing the guards standing beside them, she had to believe the Perfect Twins weren't going to threaten her in a literal sense. Figuratively, well, that went without saying. Next to them, she looked like dog meat. She'd never possessed a body like that.

At the very least, seeing these two women with their picture-perfect figures made her regret the two bags of Redenbacher's popcorn she'd eaten for dinner last night and the half-bag of chips she'd eaten at her critique group's meeting. All that salt made for some serious bloating.

A stiff smile pasted on her face, she stepped aside, pulling the door open. "Hello." She sounded far more chipper than she felt.

The two women swept past her, their movements lithe and fluid, exactly like Lander's. She guessed they were also lion shape-shifters. Both of them possessed golden-brown hair, although one woman's was a lighter shade: more blond, less brown, closer to her own hair color.

Two sets of slanting gold eyes focused on her.

If only she wasn't sporting some really bad bedhead, had at least a touch of makeup left on her face, and had something more attractive than a sheet to wear. There could be no doubt what she'd been doing with their Werekin king. Oh, ack! Could she just crawl into a hole?

Oh well. So, she would be known as the king's whore. She supposed there were worse things to be known for. She'd never entertained strangers in a sheet, but this was where she was, and there was nothing she could do about it.

Still wearing a stiff smile, an apt compliment to her makeshift dress, she closed the door and motioned toward a set of chairs in the room's corner.

Was this the were-lion's version of suburbia's welcome committee? If so, her guests had arrived empty handed. Where were the tuna casserole and cookies? Mmmmm, cookies. Her stomach rumbled, reminding her it had been a while since she'd eaten a solid meal.

Suddenly, and most definitely unexpectedly, the two women sank to their knees, arms snug to their sides, hands clasped behind their backs. "It is our pleasure to serve you," one of them said, her eyes lowered to the floor.

"Serve me?" Cailey echoed, incredulously. So this wasn't the welcome committee? These two beautiful girls were her (giddy giggle) servants? She didn't remember writing about the heroine having maids. "Cool!"

"You are too cool? Or you wish to be cooled?" the other one asked the floor.

"Uh. Neither." She wasn't sure she could get used to them talking to her toes, but then again, who was she to question the Werekin culture? If they weren't staring at her, she wouldn't be as self-conscious wearing her sheet. "I meant I'm pleased."

"Then we are pleased."

"And I'm pleased that you're pleased." Oh, this was going to be fun. Maybe Lander had left her with no clothes, no television, and no books, but he'd generously given her a couple of young women whose sole purpose was making her happy.

Hmmm . . . made a girl wonder. How far would they go?

If she didn't let loose and have some fun, she just might go crazy with fright. She was in a foreign place full of people who turned into cats, for God's sake! This was her worst nightmare.

It was either pretend like everything was just peachy, or snap.

First things first, though. She was starving with a capital "S." A tense smile spread over her face. "I'm really hungry. Can I have something to eat?"

"We have vegetables, meat—"

"Lasagna?"

Her maids screwed their faces into bewildered scowls. "We have not heard of lasagna."

She supposed it was too much to expect a bunch of cat-people to cook up some pasta. Ice cream was also probably out of the question. She wasn't very fond of vegetables. She couldn't remember the last time she'd eaten a salad, piece of broccoli, or even a baked potato. The meat sounded pretty good. Maybe a T-bone steak?

"I'd love some meat, medium well. Pink inside's good, unless of course it's chicken or pork."

"Very well." The Perfect Twins stood, glanced at each other, and hurried from the room. She made use of the time they were gone to search the room for something to wear. She rummaged through closets and dressers, trying to find something that wouldn't be absolutely enormous on her. She tried on a shirt that skimmed her knees and bloused around her body like a balloon. She cinched a wide belt around her waist. Next, she made a visit to the attached bathroom, scrubbed her teeth with a dampened fingertip, finger-combed her hair, and pinched her cheeks to give them a little color.

It was very late and she was tired, but she wasn't so exhausted that she didn't care what she looked like when the twins came back. It was a matter of pride. And pride was one thing she'd always clung to.

A little later, the twins returned with a tray holding a glass of red liquid (wine?) and a bowl of something so repulsive she immediately gagged.

What the hell? Were they trying to feed her animal guts? It then occurred to her that lions ate animals. In fact, weren't the organs like a delicacy or something?

Maybe to a lion. But that sure didn't mean she was going to eat it. Face turned, because just the sight of that red, stringy horror-movie prop was making her sick, she waved it away. "No no! I can't eat *that*."

She didn't turn around until she heard both sets of feet shuffle out and the door close.

Great. Looked like she, the girl who considered vegetable a four-letter word, had just become a (gasp!) vegetarian.

7

"They're about to make a kill," Lander whispered to Kir, his younger brother, second to the throne, and the head male of a nearby pride.

As King of the Werekin, Lander ruled over not only his own pride, but all prides, herds, and packs of shifters. His position left him vulnerable to attack, and he'd long learned whom he could trust. And more important, whom he could not.

Kir, he could trust with his life. In fact, Kir had proven so on one unforgettable occasion.

Kir grunted, muscles rippling as he stood poised in the heavy shadow of a tree, ready to attack. "I say we get them now, while they're distracted."

"No. We wait." Lander watched the panthers rush the small herd of impalas, the silver-blue light of the full moon reflecting off their sable coats. "I want to follow them a little longer, see if they'll lead us to our enemy."

Kir huffed an irritated sigh.

"What good'll it do to kill these two? Jag will just find a couple other guys looking for some easy money."

Kir sighed. "Yeah, I know. I was just looking for an excuse to feed my bloodlust. My territory's hurting for some decent prey. The lionesses haven't found a healthy herd of gazelles in months."

"Mine either," said Bourne, their youngest brother, stepping up behind them. Dryce, third eldest, was with him. Four brothers, representing all four prides of lion Werekin, the most powerful men in the world.

With great power came great responsibility.

Lander nodded. "I'm seeing the same thing here. I've sent some teams out into several territories, to gather data on animal populations. So far, what I'm hearing back isn't good. All the main prey populations are down—gazelle, zebra, wildebeest, buffalo. Something's out of balance, but I don't know what yet. The teams are looking at everything: death rates, numbers of live birth, water and food sources. I'm hoping we'll have an answer soon."

"Yeah. And in the meantime, we're stuck eating that tasteless domesticated stuff." Bourne wrinkled his nose. "The lionesses have lost the pleasure of the hunt."

"I think it's impacting us all, in ways we never would have guessed." A nearly debilitating hunger gripped Lander as he watched the panthers land a young impala. "It's still there—our nature. We're hunters, predators. The instinct to hunt is going to come out one way or another."

"Not sure I'm following you," Dryce said.

Lander forced himself to turn his back on the panthers, now huddled around a steaming carcass. "If we can't hunt prey, the darkest side of our humanity will take over. We'll kill each other."

Cailey sensed Lander had returned before she'd even opened her eyes. There was this warm, tingly sensation that overcame her. Even though she was in bed, eyes closed, and half asleep, she felt herself smiling. And when that low, rumbly voice of his added to the other sensations, her smile broadened. She opened her eyes, finding his golden-eyed gaze.

"Comfortable?" he asked.

"Very."

"My lionesses tell me you haven't eaten much."

"No offense, but your selection kind of sucks." At his raised eyebrows, she got specific. "Maybe you didn't know, but we human types like our meat cooked. Not stringy, raw, and bloody. Gag! And I'm not exactly a vegetarian, either."

"Cooked?"

"Yeah, you know. Heated. Over a fire. So that there's no blood. And the meat is warm and tender."

He wrinkled his nose. "I cannot imagine that tasting very good."

"You'd be surprised. Hey, I'm not much of a cook, but maybe you'd give me kitchen privileges? I can handle some simple stuff: frying a couple of burgers."

"Burgers?"

She sighed. She was a far cry from a Julia Child or the goddess of domestication, Martha Stewart. But hey, even her worst efforts beat eating raw rabbit food every meal. Ugh! Not only was it awful tasting, but she was starving like ten minutes later.

She wondered if the lion-people had any of the modern conveniences she'd taken for granted until now: microwave, blender, food processor. Sigh, sigh, sigh. What she wouldn't give for even a Lean Cuisine, and those weren't exactly her idea of good eating. A nice steak from Outback sounded really good right now.

A flood of saliva filled her mouth. She swallowed, hard, when Lander gave her another one of those scrumptious eat-her-up looks. My, my, her hero had quite the zip-zoomy sex drive.

And who was complaining? Certainly not her.

"What time is it? I'm really hungry," she confessed, sitting up. The covers slipped down to her waist, revealing her clothed upper body.

"A little after six. So am . . . I." His gaze narrowed slightly. "You're wearing clothes."

"Yes, of course. I had visitors. I'm assuming you know that. Was I supposed to play hostess in the nude?"

He frowned. "The lionesses are not your guests. They are your servants. . . ."

"Yeah, I understand, but still—"

"You have no obligation to play the role of hostess. They were sent to serve you."

"I got that, but—"

"Therefore, there was no need to clothe yourself." His voice became progressively sharper, more intimidating. Which was why, by the time he'd reached the word "yourself," she'd pretty much given up trying to defend her actions. He'd said he would take care of the clothing thing later. He hadn't suggested she go hunting for clothes on her own.

"Have you forgotten what I said?" he asked, prowling closer.

"Nope. How could I?" She regretted the quip the minute it slipped from her mouth.

He stopped within reaching distance, planted his feet in a wide stance and crossed his arms over his chest. "What kind of message do you think you've sent my lionesses? By wearing clothes, you have defied me."

"Gosh, I hadn't thought about that. It's so different in my world. I guess it makes it hard for me to relate to your need for everyone's total submission—"

"The life of every member of my pride is dependent upon their complete submission to their king. Should they fail, any number of things could happen. None of them are good." He sighed. "I must treat you like the other members of my pride while you're here."

"Which means?"

"You must be punished."

Her stomach dropped to her toes. What kind of punishment

did a guy who turned into a wild animal dole out? She was pretty sure she didn't want to know. Yet, her pride wouldn't allow her to drop to her knees and beg for mercy.

A huge lump formed in her throat, and her mouth dried, her tongue feeling like leather.

He couldn't hurt her, she reminded herself. She had created this man, she'd written his past, present, and future ... well, bits and pieces of it. She knew he was a good person, although flawed. And she knew he was not cruel, although he was strong and dominating. Finally, she knew his brand of domination did not include hard-core sadism or humiliation.

Even that didn't make her feel any better. There were still plenty of ways he could hurt her, some more agonizing than a blow from a whip or cane. She almost hoped he'd bend her over and strike her with a cat-o'-nine-tails.

"Take the clothes off," he demanded, his voice razor sharp. His tone let her know he meant business, and expected her complete submission. From the buzz of irritation that zapped through her body, she knew she wasn't exactly wired for around-the-clock slavery. She didn't want that.

What she wanted, craved, was sexual submission. Kind of vanilla bondage. Some fun with restraints. No real pain. No torture. And definitely no humiliation. Just intense enough sensation play to amplify her sexual response.

Unfortunately, the man before her expected so much more.

Hot and cold at the same time, she undressed, handing him the wadded-up clothes.

Coolly, calmly, he took the garments from her, turned, and strode back to the closet. After placing them in a basket on the floor and closing the door, he turned to face her. "You will remain unclothed until I give you permission to get dressed."

She bit her tongue to keep from making a sarcastic remark.

"I am not only your king, but also the man who has promised to see to your every need." He caught her chin in his hand and demanded she meet his gaze. "You must respect me, do as I say. Always." He released her chin.

She snapped her head to the side. "Okay, maybe I over-romanticized what being a lover of a dominant and controlling man was like," she grumbled. "After all, authors don't always write what they want in real life. They write what their readers fantasize about."

"What did you say?" he demanded. When she didn't respond, he grabbed her chin again. "What secrets are you keeping from me?"

She shivered. "Nothing. No secrets. You're right." More than ever before, she needed to be on her guard. Walls up, high up. She wasn't buying his excuse for demanding her submission. Something else was going on here.

This wasn't about her setting a bad example to his servants. It was way over the top. Totally beyond controlling.

Was he trying to get something from her? If so, what? Would he use her fears and insecurities against her? Use her weaknesses to manipulate her?

He pulled on her chin, forcing her to follow him. "This way."

She followed, not that she had any choice. Sure, she could knock his hand away and stand her ground. But she just didn't have the balls to do that.

You're so fucking spineless.

"I sense you don't have much experience with submission. This is why I'm going to show you a little patience. I empathize a little." He crowded her, forcing her to back up, until her entire backside was flattened against the cool, hard wall, and her entire front side against his hot, hard body.

Even though he still had his pants on, she knew he was aroused. The huge bulge in his pants was one big sign. The flames she saw in his slitted eyes, another.

He released her chin, skimmed his hands down her arms,

then wrapped his fingers tightly around her wrists. He pinned them against the wall then bent down and whispered in her ear, "Don't move. No matter what."

"O-okay."

She was ashamed to admit she was getting seriously turned on by this game. Lander's power, strength—not to mention his raw, potent sexuality—seemed to seep from every pore. She could smell it, taste it, feel it deep in her gut.

He left her then, and instantly, she missed the simmering heat that emanated from his body. He undressed, revealing he was, indeed, as aroused as she was. The tip of his erect cock glistened with pre-cum. She had the sudden urge to drop to her knees and take him in her mouth, lick away that salty pearl.

She realized a moment later that she wouldn't be given the chance.

He opened the door, and in came the Perfect Twins. No sooner were they inside the room than they were on their knees, eyes lowered, hands clasped behind their backs.

Instinctively, Cailey wrapped her arms around herself, hiding as much of her scarred body as she could.

Lander positioned himself so that the servants' backs were to Cailey as they knelt before him, and he could see her face. The cruel bastard. He was going to watch her as he did . . . whatever . . . with those two women she hated so much.

Damn him.

Their gazes met for a split second before he broke the connection. "As king, there are certain things I demand from all my subjects, including my lovers. I don't ask these things because I get some kind of perverted pleasure from causing pain."

Liar.

"I don't look to satisfy some deep-seated need to control, either."

Then why?

"I may not be a perfect man, but I don't stoop to using other people to battle my personal demons."

Because he was her hero, she wanted to believe him, and yet she realized there was plenty she hadn't yet discovered about her character yet.

She hadn't written a synopsis. Hadn't done any character worksheets or even thought deeply about his motivations, the skeletons he was hiding in his closet.

Maybe their story wouldn't be just about her—about dealing with her fears, exploring the darker side of her sensuality. But maybe the story would also be about Lander, about something he needed to deal with?

"Adria, Nevan, strip," he commanded. Within a single heartbeat, the two servants began shedding their (skimpy) clothes. A few minutes later, they were kneeling before him completely nude. Their flawless, golden skin shimmered in the flickering candlelight. And flames were reflected in their long, wavy hair, which tumbled over slim shoulders, down slender backs, reaching nearly to their perfect little fannies.

"Being master means it is my responsibility to keep all my pride members in their positions. Because when they aren't, terrible things happen that shouldn't. People get hurt."

Who got hurt? This wasn't the first time Lander had said such a thing. Cailey had to wonder whom he was talking about. Was there a terrible tragedy in his past?

He motioned to one of the twins, the one with the blond hair. "Adria."

She stood. "Yes, Master."

"Serve me." His eyes never left Cailey's face, even as that other woman, that perfect woman she despised, knelt at his feet and let him fuck her in the mouth.

Confusion and shock churned hot and painful in Cailey's stomach. She had no right to that man. Absolutely no claim.

And yet watching him fuck that woman's mouth pissed her off. He was hers, dammit. She'd created him. For her heroine. Not for that wench.

Then she turned to him, and she let him see her rage in her eyes. Could he know how much this would hurt her? She guessed he had some inkling. That was why he was doing it. To manipulate her.

Why? No, she didn't need to care why. Fuck him. She wouldn't let him hurt her.

It was simple. All she had to remember was that this wasn't real. It was just a bad dream, and sooner or later she'd wake up.

Her heart didn't belong to Lander, the man who didn't exist. It would never belong to him. Because if she let herself fall for her hero, she was signing up for sure heartbreak. It was unavoidable. He was a *fictional* character.

Her anger still boiling inside, she closed her eyes to focus. She just needed to build up those walls. They'd protected her before. They'd do so again. And if he couldn't hurt her, he couldn't manipulate her.

"Watch me."

Fuck you.

She opened her eyes, not because she wanted to, but out of reflex. She didn't want to look at him, but damn if she could stop herself. Her gaze snapped to his face, like it was attached to a rubber band. It caught on his squinty-eyed glare and held it, daring him to look away first.

He thrust his hips forward harder, forcing his cock deeper down Adria's throat. Cailey shuddered, both insanely aroused by the way he moved as he fucked that woman, but also frigid at the chill she witnessed in his eyes. Even so, she refused to look away.

It was foolish to challenge his authority, but dammit, her pride wouldn't let her drop her gaze like she knew he expected. The other women didn't look him in the eye unless he told them to. But they were servants, more or less his playthings, from the look of it.

She would never be a man's plaything. She was a person. Who yes, liked a little submission in the bedroom, but also expected to be treated with respect, both inside and outside of it. Clearly, Lander had other ideas about the kind of treatment she deserved.

His glare turned even chillier. Icy. He caught the woman's hair in his fists and pulled. His cock escaped her mouth with an almost comical pop. "Leave us."

Aw, poor baby. He didn't even get off.

Adria and Nevan scrambled to their feet and rushed toward the door, completely avoiding looking at her. "Bye, bye!" she called gaily to their retreating backs.

Spineless wenches. How could they let a man treat them that way? It was so wrong, wrong, wrong! Slavery had been outlawed like a hundred and fifty years ago, at least in her world.

She was so not buying Lander's excuse about the pride being in danger if there was no order among the members. He just wanted to keep those women in their places. If she had the balls, she'd spit in his face.

To think she'd fancied herself in lust with this man! Sex appeal still dripped from him like chocolate sauce from a sundae, but thanks to that little stunt he'd pulled, she was now immune to his charms. He wouldn't get between these legs again, oh no, he would not.

As she'd feared, the reality was nowhere as great as the fantasy when it came to Lander the King of the Werekin. He was a great big jerk in lion's clothing.

"There is no room for pride in this relationship," he stated flatly, taking one, two, three steps her way.

What relationship? The one that doesn't exist? "Does that mean you'll be swallowing yours?" she taunted, holding her ground. She'd learned a long time ago the wrong way to deal with men like Lander. To cower from them. Just like those other two women had done.

But she didn't cower anymore. She was strong now.

As a teenager, she'd been belittled, beaten down, humiliated, and made to feel ashamed of her thoughts, actions, words, emotions by a longtime boyfriend. Back then she hadn't been strong enough to stand up for herself or feel sure enough of her worth.

But those dark years had made her tough. Calloused. And quite capable of defending herself.

Her first lover had stolen her confidence, her innocence, and her trust. What worse could any man do to her?

8

Jafari charged into the room, the heat of molten rock pounding through his body in mounting waves. The woman would defy him no more. The decision had been made. He'd been given no choice. He would make it so she'd have to accept him. Or die.

He halted as the memory of her eyes, filled with pleading tears, swept into his mind. They were the color of the summer sky. A blue jay's plumage. That shade. So rare in the frigid, black world he lived in.

He remembered the scent of jasmine on her skin and the sweet flavor of her kiss. Flowers. Honey. Sweet and fragrant. How he'd missed such sensations. The silken feel of hair slipping between his fingertips. The sound of a woman's moan in ecstasy.

The fury within was overtaken by another kind of emotion. A dark passion that left him shaken. He didn't just want to possess this human, to demand her piety. He wanted her as a man wanted a woman. Her loyalty, dedication, affection.

A very dangerous thing for a god.

—From *Dark Surrender*, a work in progress by Cailey Holm, writing as Mia Spelman.

* * *

As master, Lander never took pleasure in punishing his servants. In fact, sometimes he felt their pain more acutely than they seemed to.

Particularly in this case.

It wasn't as if Cailey hadn't reacted. She had, in just the way he'd anticipated. With anger. But, because of that odd connection between them, which had recently weakened, he sensed the rage was camouflaging something else. Maybe a deeply rooted pain she was avoiding.

Over the past few moments, he'd come to believe this was his price, the one he would pay for her wondrous gift.

The witch hadn't just meant for him to drag Cailey into his world, take command of her mighty power, and later send her back to her world, depleted and powerless.

No. There was a price to pay, always. Especially when the gift was so great.

Cailey deserved to receive something from him. That something he would give her was to gently, or perhaps more forcibly, push her to face the emotions she was hiding from.

Somehow, he felt he knew her, understood her.

For example, he knew she felt it was okay to get angry. She'd given herself permission to feel that emotion. But hurt—the kind of soul-deep agony that most people experienced at least once in their lives—that, he sensed, she would not.

The witch had told him about the cougar attack that had made Cailey fearful of cats. But she'd failed to tell him the rest. This was not about any single incident, as traumatic as that attack might have been. Cailey wasn't afraid of an animal.

She was afraid of herself.

When Cailey had first arrived in his world, he'd hidden the beast within him because he knew she feared it. The beast represented all that Cailey despised. It was untamed, ruthless, cunning. A predator driven by dark instinct.

But now, as he was beginning to understand her better, he realized the beast might heal her.

"What are you feeling now, Cailey?" he asked.

"Nothing." She settled into a chair, her gaze lowered to her untouched breakfast plate.

She would lie to him again? She dared lie to him still? Even after being punished? Anger, sharp and hot, charged through his system.

He had tolerated her attitude during her punishment, because he knew he had to maintain control. But he would not, could not, tolerate her continued lying. Not anymore.

He closed the distance between them, knowing the proximity would disarm her somewhat. He stood over her, forced her to look up at him by lifting her chin with his hand. The other, he braced on the chair's arm. "Would you like me to punish you again?"

A shadow swept through her eyes but she didn't speak.

Angling lower, until his mouth almost touched hers, he repeated, "I ask you again, what are you feeling?"

"I think I've made it perfectly clear what I'm feeling," she said through gritted teeth. Her breath teased his nostrils, stirring his hunger. He knew how delicious she tasted. He ached to seal his mouth over hers and dip his tongue into her sweet depth.

"I still need you to say the words."

"Why? So you can feel all big and powerful?" she snapped, eyes slitted.

Moving closer, he whispered. "No."

Taste her. He wanted to taste her.

"So you can use my feelings to manipulate me?" she asked, a little less angrily.

"No."

"So you can hit me hard, where it hurts, next time?" she challenged, voice wavering.

There. A bit of the truth. He let a comfortable silence fall between them for a handful of seconds. Then he asked more softly, this time against her mouth, "Do you hurt, Cailey?"

"No. I don't. I never hurt. Never."

It wasn't a lie this time. She truly believed those words. He could hear the conviction in her voice. The last traces of his anger evaporated.

"Why do you suppose that is?" he asked, forcing himself to inch back so he could focus on her eyes.

She shrugged, her I-don't-care attitude not quite ringing true. "I'm calloused. At least that's what people tell me."

He nodded, captured by the shadows he saw in her eyes. "Calluses come in handy sometimes." He held one of his hands up, palm out. "Like these."

Her gaze flickered from his face to his hand then back again. When it made it back to his eyes, it had softened. Her breathing, once rapid and shallow, had slowed. And the red in her cheeks had faded to a much more pleasant shade of pink.

She was reaching for him with those eyes. Pleading for his help.

I won't fail you, Cailey. I promise. I'll gladly pay your price.

"They started when I was younger," he explained, sitting and dragging his chair closer to hers. "A mere cub."

She extended an index finger, tracing a line over the hardened skin on his palm. "They're very hard. Thick. It must have taken a long time for those to form. And they're still there."

"Yes."

"But you're a king. Why would you have to do manual labor?"

"Because sometimes it's necessary, and even a king will do what is necessary. Or rather, a wise king will do whatever's required of him."

How he liked this moment. It wasn't the most erotically charged, no. It was more . . . intimate. Touching. To his heart.

He found himself feeling something he'd never felt before, a profound joy that made his insides warm in a very different way than before.

Yes, his cock was rock hard, his balls tight. But there was something else going on, deeper. In a way, that something else made him feel vulnerable.

She pulled her hand away, folding it into her other one on her lap. "But isn't that why you have servants? To do all the hard work for you?"

He plucked up a piece of fruit and pressed it to her lips. "My servants are not slaves. They volunteer freely. Perhaps in your world things are very different between your kings and their servants. But I won't ask my servants to perform only the duties I don't care to do myself."

"Really," she said flatly, doubt narrowing her eyes. One corner of her mouth quirked into a shadow of a lopsided smile as she chewed and swallowed.

He gently lifted her hand and twined his fingers through hers. He kissed the smooth, satiny skin on the back, tracing the delicate blue lines of her veins with his lips. "You don't believe me." With his free hand, he fed her another piece of fruit.

"No. I mean, why would anyone volunteer to be someone's servant? Even if you don't treat your servants like slaves?" She looked genuinely perplexed. "You don't pay them?"

"Pay?" It took him several seconds to realize what she meant. "No. I don't compensate the lionesses for their service."

"And yet, they want to serve you?" This time, she lifted a piece of food to her own mouth. He watched her lips part, the berry slipping between them, disappearing into the sweet depth of her mouth.

"You are free to ask them when you see them next." He caught a flare of emotion pass across her face. But, like a flash of lightning, it was short lived. And then her expression returned to one of curiosity and confusion. "I believe my lionesses serve not only for the benefit of the entire pride, but also for the satisfaction and honor. I am, after all, their king."

If anything Cailey looked more confused as she continued to eat.

Could their worlds be so different that she was simply incapable of understanding duty and honor? If that was the case, it made him wonder what kind of world she had come from. All he knew about her world was what fragmented knowledge he'd gathered during those short moments before he'd captured her, and the disjointed images she sometimes sent him through that invisible mental connection. As such, he had a very limited viewpoint.

"Hmmm. If they're not getting paid to perform certain duties, how do they pay their bills?" She gently tugged her hand out of his.

"Bills?"

"Yeah. Rent, car note, insurance, utilities. We earn money at our jobs and then use the money to buy stuff, pay for things we need."

"It seems our economy is very different from yours in that respect. It's not dependent upon the exchange of currency."

"Then how do you get what you need?"

"I simply go get it."

"Yeah?" She visibly puzzled over his statement for a moment before her eyes flashed with understanding. "Oh, I get it. *You* are able to just go get what you want. Like you said, you're the king. What's everyone else do? They have to buy stuff, right?"

"No, they do the same thing as I do."

"No way."

"Again, you don't believe me?"

"Not that I'm some expert in anthropology or anything, but I don't know of a single culture—outside of maybe some tribes living in the jungle or whatever—that doesn't use some form of money to buy and sell goods and services."

"You do now."

"Weird." She blinked at him a few times. "So, if I wanted some new clothes, where would I get them?"

"From me."

"But where would you get them? Do you sew? Or would your servants make them? Where would they get the material to make the clothes?"

"The market."

"Market," she echoed, eyes flashing. "Then you buy them after all."

"No, I take what I need."

She sighed. It was a long, tired, heavy exhalation. One that punctuated the mystification he could read in her expression. "This is weird."

They were wasting time, talking about such an insignificant thing as the market. Especially now that she'd finally eaten a little.

While he enjoyed the easy comfort building between them, there were other more weighty matters they needed to discuss. He decided it was time to turn the conversation in another direction. "It is insignificant."

"To you, maybe. But not to me. I'm kind of liking the idea of just going to get what you need, without having to slave away at a stupid job to earn a few dollars an hour." Clearly, the object of their discussion was more significant to his Cailey than it was to him.

"Your world has its stresses. But I am sure it also has its good points."

"What do you know about my world?"

"Very little. Basically nothing."

She tipped her head and studied him, chewing on her lush lower lip. She pointed to their plates, both empty. "Well, let me ask you, which one would you rather live in? A place where your every need is guaranteed? Where no one goes without the basic necessities—food, shelter, clothing? Or one with exciting, convenient, and useful technologies like cell phones, laptops, and MySpace?"

"You have gone without the basic necessities? Without food?" Immediately, he sensed her withdrawal. It wasn't a physical one. But emotional. He sandwiched her face between his hands. "I know it hasn't been very long, and I realize it's hard to talk about such sensitive matters so soon, but we have been intimate physically. That means something to you. I can tell."

Her gaze finally met his. "Yeah, it does mean something." After a beat, she whispered, "How much do you know about me? How much did the witch tell you?"

"I believe only enough to help you."

"Do you know everything?"

He felt her tugging, trying to pull back, but he kept her there with gentle pressure on the sides of her head. "Everything? No. But you can tell me."

Her eyelids dropped. "There's nothing to tell."

He hoped at least one tear would escape from those beautiful eyes, but he knew none would. When she opened her eyes again, he could see the shield she'd put up. Conversation over. She'd shut down. "So which would you rather have? You never answered."

"That's an almost impossible choice to make. I've been to your world. I couldn't stay long, and didn't see everything. But I saw enough. Maybe to some, those 'convenient technologies' might be a basic necessity."

"To whom?"

He couldn't afford to delve into that territory yet. Maybe talking about his brother, the fifth brother he'd lost shortly after the curse, would draw her closer, help chisel a hole in that wall she'd erected around herself. But he couldn't take the risk.

He needed Cailey's respect, not pity. Her trust, not suspicion. "I'm simply talking in generalizations."

Her gaze didn't waver. "You're lying."

No one had ever dared call Lander Cornelius a liar. He swallowed a sigh.

This wasn't supposed to be happening this way. Cailey was his captive. The witch who'd sent him into her world had said nothing about Cailey challenging him. He was supposed to be doing that to her—not only freeing her from her fears, but also forcing her to her knees, bending her will to his, and taking claim to the magic she possessed.

Besides, he had no issues to overcome.

Frustrated, and feeling a little off balance, he released her face and leaned back, even though he knew his withdrawal would be a sign of weakness. He needed some space. To think. To consider his next move.

Cailey wasn't like any lioness in his world. She was free-thinking and defiant and had no qualms questioning him, challenging him, showing her anger. No lioness had ever dared do such a thing. In one way, he found her odd behavior refreshing, intriguing. In another, terribly frustrating. Infuriating.

Perhaps the answer was to let her see the beast. Then, she'd have no choice but to respect him.

Was she ready? Or would it be too terrifying and undo what little he'd managed to accomplish? Whatever she thought, he couldn't let her think he was shifting to punish her further.

He stood. "I think it's time you see me in feline form."

"No." The challenge he'd seen in her eyes instantly vanished. In its place were thick shadows of dark dread. She leapt to her feet. "Please. I'm sorry I reacted the way I did earlier. I was pissed. I'll admit it. If you need to punish me for getting mad, I'll gladly take whatever you dole out. Whip me. Do whatever, but please, don't do the cat thing."

"No, this isn't about your behavior, about punishment or

consequences." Or was it? Was he letting his frustration, his lack of experience with this kind of behavior, lead him to unmask the beast too soon? "You've been here. You've seen other cats."

Turning from him, she wrapped her arms around herself. "Sure, the panthers, who don't exactly inspire a greater respect and admiration for the species."

"My point exactly." He leaned closer again, not only because he was anxious to drive his point home, but also because he was simply drawn closer. Her scent was like the finest perfume, her beautiful face the finest work of art he had ever seen. And he hungered for another taste of those pretty, full lips. "If you see me in my feline form, you'll learn they aren't just deadly predators. But also graceful, beautiful animals that should be respected and admired."

She inched back from him. "B-but we're still in punishment mode, which means if you go feline on me now, I'm going to associate your cat form with bad stuff. I think I need to go shopping first, before you go there."

"Shopping?"

"Yeah." Eyes wide, she gave him the most pathetic, pleading look. Her lush bottom lip quivered ever so slightly. The motion drew his gaze and spiked his hunger. "What better association can you form between two things? Shopping with anything is always good for a woman."

"Shopping?" he repeated.

She took several steps back. "Please? Maybe I don't deserve any new clothes. I . . . didn't handle that punishment the way you probably wanted me to. But if you follow that kind of"— she visibly swallowed, searching, as it seemed, for the right word—"situation with this shape-shifting thing, I'm not going to be able to see any beauty or majesty. It's bad after bad after bad."

His insides twisted, and a sharp sensation pierced his gut.

"Fine." Flustered, he threw his hands in the air.

Who would have thought this woman could mess with his head so bad? But dammit, she was. She had. And he had to somehow get a handle on things now, before he lost complete control.

What sort of danger would a woman like this bring to his people? A woman who possessed such a great power?

"I'll take you to the market," he grumbled. "But only if you tell me of one time when you've felt some kind of pain." When her jaw snapped open, he added, "I'm not talking about a physical pain either. I mean a deep pain here. In the heart."

Her gaze dropped. Her eyebrows, too. She pressed her lips together, drawing them into a line as she visibly struggled. "I can't remember. It's been such a long, long time."

"You can remember. But you just don't want to."

"No, I'm serious. I can't remember. Oh! How about I get afraid sometimes. Like when two panthers—"

"That's not what I'm looking for."

She sighed, pouted. He wanted to kiss that fat lip. "You're so mean."

"It's either you tell me about a time when you felt pain, or I 'go feline' on you. Here and now."

"Fine! I'll think of something." She started pacing, wringing her hands. To the bed and then to the table, back and forth. "But you've got to give me a few minutes to think. This isn't something that a girl's just going to be able to come up with off the top of her head."

"That's just it. For most lionesses—er, women—it is."

"I guess I'm weird, then."

"I'll give you three minutes."

"Ack! That's nothing. You might as well give me thirty seconds."

"You had better think quickly, because you've just wasted fifteen seconds."

9

Cailey wanted to scream. To cuss. To simply get up and walk out of the room.

This was just too freakin' unfair! What the heck was this guy trying to do to her? Completely destroy her mentally? Hadn't he done enough harm?

First he'd kidnapped her.

Then fucked her.

Then fucked another woman in the mouth.

Then got pissed because she got pissed.

And now he was demanding she either fess up with some deep, dark, secret agony or he was going to change into a big scary lion.

The bitch—er, witch—who sent her here was going to pay someday for this. She'd make sure of it. And so was Mia or Lisa, whoever was writing these pages.

"Two minutes, thirty seconds." He motioned to the clock sitting on the table next to the bed. "Two twenty-five."

"What the heck? No way. You have to warn me before you start the timer."

"All right. It's starting. Right. Now." Arms crossed, he stood there, staring but silent.

Totally distracting her.

Didn't he understand some people simply didn't feel the same things other people did? Thanks to her upbringing—no mother, a tough disciplinarian of a father who loved her but was totally incapable of showing softer emotions—and a rough patch in high school, when she'd let a guy manipulate her for a couple of years, she wasn't the soft, needy kind, whose delicate little self was hurt every time someone looked at her wrong. She'd grown to be strong, self assured. Independent.

Calloused.

Those calluses had to have come from somewhere, the obnoxious voice said in her head. *And somehow he knows it. You can simply admit what he already knows.*

She promptly told the voice in her head to shut the hell up. Nothing good could come out that kind of craziness. Some things were just better left buried in the past.

Besides, the last person who'd tried to play amateur shrink to her—besides her harmless critique partners, of course—had been kicked to the curb so fast his head had spun.

What made people think they had any right to delve into her closet and poke around for skeletons? She had no Dark and Terrible secrets, at least no more than anyone else. Her closet was no more a graveyard than Disneyland.

Deep-down hurt? What the hell?

"Time's up."

"Aw, shit. Do you really want me to make something up? Because I haven't endured any terrible tragedies or anything. I wasn't raped by my mother's cousin, or abandoned by my parents and secretly raised by my grandparents. My folks aren't meth addicts or alcoholics. If you're looking for that kind of thing, you can watch those daytime talk shows. They always have lots of fucked-up people on them."

"Then you're reneging on our agreement."

"Which means you're going to change into a lion?"

"Yes." To her surprise, he lunged forward, and crushed his mouth against hers. The kiss was raw, wild, untamed, carnal. And oh so thrilling. His lips, tongue, and teeth tasted, conquered, subdued. And regardless of the panic that had swiftly threatened to overtake her, she found herself swept up in a wild, thrashing river of erotic hunger.

She more or less climbed his body, until her full length was pressed against his, her breasts flattened against his broad chest, her pubic bone jammed against his thigh. She hooked her fingers, clawing at his shoulders.

Meanwhile, as she acted like a wanton wench, like she hadn't a care in the world outside of jumping Lander's bones, inside she was a jumble of mixed-up thoughts and emotions.

How could she react to him this way? He'd done so many awful, detestable things she should hate him, not lust after him like he was the last fucking man on earth. She should be pounding her fists against that enormous chest, not rubbing her breasts against it, the friction making her nipples harden to sensitive peaks. She should be kicking him in the balls, not gyrating her hips against his thigh like a bar whore.

Should, should, should. Shouldn't, shouldn't, shouldn't.

There she was, and there was no denying what she was doing. A part of her was absolutely sickened by her behavior. The other side, one she perhaps had never seen before, cheered her on.

Who the hell was going to judge her now? Who would know? Who gave a fuck?

She turned off her brain and surrendered to the delicious sensations swamping her system. Tastes, touches, and smells. She was aware of his strength, felt it in the ease in which he lifted her off her feet. Even in the way his hands touched her ass as she wrapped her legs around his waist.

He turned, and then she was sandwiched between the wall

and his bulk. Yes, this was most definitely a wonderful position to be in. Nipple to nipple. Mouth to mouth. He captured her wrists in his fists and pinned them to the wall, leaving her to support herself with her thighs. She pinched them tighter, which increased the contact her pussy made with his scrumptious abdomen.

"Yes," she murmured into her mouth.

"Are you afraid now, my little Cailey?"

"No. Not at all."

"Good. I want you to remember this as you watch me change. The way I touch you, kiss you. Fuck you." He released her hands, shoved down his pants, and before she knew it, the head of his cock was prodding at her slick passage. He gripped her hips in his hands, holding them stationary and thrust his pelvis up, driving his cock deep inside.

Grateful for the sweet invasion, she wrapped her arms around his neck, clinging to his bulk. He wasn't gentle as he fucked her. And she didn't want him to be. Harder. Rougher. That's the way she wanted it.

Oh, what this man did to her! With each upward thrust, he rocked his pelvis forward, which created the most delightful friction against her clit. Perfect pressure. Perfect rhythm. In no time, every nerve in her body was aflame. And liquid heat was pulsing through her body, carried by her pounding heart.

"Take your release, Cailey. Take it now." He thrust harder, their bodies coming together almost violently. "I can't hold out much longer."

His hands still supporting her bottom, his cock buried deep in her clenching pussy, he turned and walked them to the bed. Down she went, landing with a bounce. Not missing a beat, he lifted her hips and drove into her. The angle made the head of his cock stroke that magical spot inside. Added to that, Lander leaned back, giving him access to her clit, and started stroking round and round.

She was lost to her pleasure in less than ten gasping breaths. Aflame in convulsing heat, she bucked her hips up, welcoming his cock into her pulsing pussy. He fucked her harder, making what was already a mind-blowing orgasm even more amazing.

And then he suddenly withdrew from her. There was a loud thud. Strange sounds emitted from the side of the bed.

Dizzy and still tingly from scalp to toe, she drew her legs together and rolled onto her side. She opened her eyes when she heard a low rumble. Instantly, she snapped them shut again.

Either a lion had just sneaked in, gobbled up Lander, and was standing there, deciding whether he had room in his full belly for her, or Lander had gone feline.

Either way, she was freaking out.

Completely frozen in terror, she kept her eyes closed and swallowed the rising contents of her stomach over and over again. In her head, she was screaming. In reality, she was absolutely silent. In her head, she was inching toward the other side of the bed. In reality, she was lying there like a pig on a spit, waiting for the DONE button to pop up on her chest like a fucking Butterball turkey.

Move your ass, dammit! Move. Now. A finger. An eyelid. Something!

She heard the animal walking, the heavy padding of his paws striking the floor. From what she'd seen, the lion—who she really didn't want to think of as Lander—was enormous with a thick golden-brown mane framing his face. In her mind's eye, all she could see were those sharp teeth. Framed in black cat lips. And those hard, cruel, yellow eyes.

Her worst nightmare come true.

She concentrated on breathing first, only because her spinning head made her realize she hadn't inhaled in a while. Then, her brain's supply of vital oxygen restored, she cautiously inched toward the opposite side of the bed.

In response, the lion reared up. His two front paws landed on the mattress, his weight making her roll toward him.

Instantly, she recalled that scene from *Jaws*, where the boat tipped back and a man slid into the gaping mouth of the shark. She was so not going to be eaten alive!

Not today. Not ever.

Did she know for a fact that Lander the Man could control Lander the Lion? Or was it possible that once he changed, instinct took over and his human mind, his very soul, left him?

God, she could only hope it didn't.

Fighting the effect of gravity, she logrolled across the bed. In her head she knew there was no way in hell she could roll, crawl, or sprint faster than that enormous, clawed, toothed beast, but that didn't stop her from trying. She said a little prayer, crossed herself—something she hadn't done in decades—and made a break for the bathroom.

The beast leapt through the air and landed directly in front of the door.

"Shit!" She whirled around, searching for a place to hide, but none could be found. This wasn't a cave, but a cage. There was only an attached room with a nice, thick, steel door.

And of course, there was no gun hanging over the fireplace either. She didn't even have a knife. Hell, right about now, she'd be damn grateful for a nail file. Or even one of those little cans of mace.

She was alone, defenseless, vulnerable. And beyond petrified.

The animal opened its mouth, emitting a roar that sent a tsunami of terror rushing through her system. The lion did another one of those leaps again, high into the air, and landed a few feet away. It just stood there, staring at her with those awful yellow eyes, just like the mountain lion had when she was little. Sizing her up. Waiting for her to move so it could attack.

Oh god, ohgod, ohgod!

She couldn't help it. A shriek ripped from her chest, blasting up her throat. Tears spilled from her eyes, blurring her vision. "No, no, noooo!"

Her stomach clenched into a horrific spasm. Stars glittered

in her eyes as she dropped to her knees, heaving. A second later, as she sensed the lion prowling closer, closer, she was grateful for the darkness that blocked out the stars, the lion, the terror.

Yes, the darkness.

Her prayer had been answered.

"Dammit, Daisy, quit licking me. Bad dog." Eyes closed, Cailey knocked her obnoxious beagle away and rolled onto her stomach. She reached for the blanket, but felt only an uber-soft fur pelt beneath her.

What the hell? She didn't have an animal skin rug in her room. And Daisy'd died about thirty years ago.

Oh yeah. She wasn't at home. She was in the lion's den. About to become cat chow.

Immediately, she snapped to. Alert, her heart kick-started by a surge of adrenaline, she opened one eye. "Ohthankgod!" she blurted.

The enormous cat was gone. Lander the man was back. And it appeared she still possessed all vital parts of her anatomy.

"Come with me." His eyes sparkled as he gazed down at her. His jaw was tight, but his mouth was quirked up in a sexy demi-smile. He was on hands and knees overtop of her, his thighs straddling her legs. She had the impulse to wrap her arms around his neck and pull, until his weight crushed her.

She needed to be held, feel safe.

"Where are we headed? Please tell me I'm not going to be introduced to more felines. I haven't recovered fully from that first time yet."

"Oh, no. Not yet." He kissed her forehead then trailed little licks and nibbles down the side of her face.

Mmmm. She was starting to feel a little warm and toasty inside. The heat was overtaking the chill of terror. The fear that had wrapped its icy fingers around her deepest parts and gripped them so tightly she couldn't breathe slowly loosened their hold.

"I'm taking you somewhere pleasant." More heat. He kissed the crook of her neck, laving her skin with his tongue.

Despite a crop of goose bumps that popped up all over the right side of her body, yet more warmth gushed through her.

He straightened up, then stood, her wrists in his hands. Up she went, on legs that weren't as sturdy as normal—not that she could blame them—across the room, toward the door that led to white nothingness.

She halted just inside the door, waiting for him to open it. "But I can't go out there. I tried, remember?"

"I think you can now."

Did that mean she could go home?

As if in answer to her question, he added, "The witch told me you're able to go anywhere, once you're ready. I think you're ready now."

This was so confusing! Weird rules that made no sense. Lander having oral sex with a servant. This whole story was screwed up. Was it because of Mia or Lisa, or the witch?

"Who made up these rules?" she grumbled.

Doorknob in hand, he grinned, pulling. "I don't know." He stepped to the side, motioning for her to proceed past him.

She poked her head out into the corridor. It looked pretty much like a normal hallway—darkish, lined with closed doors—although the décor was sort of strange. Had a medieval feel to it, like Lander's bedroom. And the walls looked like they were solid stone. Reminded her of an old castle.

It was surprisingly warm out there, for how cold the corridor looked. The odor of damp dirt and old something else hung heavy in the air. And the floor and walls were cool to the touch. The only sources of light were the occasional lit torches protruding from the walls at regular intervals.

Now she could see why Lander might appreciate technology. It seemed his world was not as advanced as the real one. Not even close.

She could just imagine his reaction to a Corvette, a television, or a computer.

"This way." He caught her wrist, stopping her from moving farther down the hall. He opened a door, and motioned her inside the dimly lit room.

A dungeon. Like the kind she'd seen on the Internet. There, in the corner, hung what looked like a sex swing. And there was a cage in the other corner. A tall wooden racky thing over there. And in front of one wall sat a low bench with a cross behind it. Along the remaining wall ran shelves full of smaller items. Below the shelves hung a variety of whips, ropes, and leather straps and restraints.

The warmth he'd stirred with those kisses was gone.

Once again, cold tendrils coiled inside her, like icy swirls of blowing snow kicked up in a blizzard. Maybe she'd fantasized about this sort of thing once or twice . . . okay, a lot more than that. But still. Really doing those kinds of things? Yikes! Not to mention, she had a terribly low tolerance for pain. So any extreme stuff was totally out.

Would he even give her a safe word? Ask what her limits were? Or was this real bondage, not bondage play?

She wasn't going any farther until she knew what to expect, regardless of the fact that Lander was pressing rather firmly against the small of her back, steering her toward the corner with the sex swing.

She planted her feet and leaned back into his hand, using her weight to keep him from propelling her forward. "Uh, hang on a second."

"There's no reason to be afraid."

Easy for him to say. She supposed he wasn't planning on letting her chain him up and smack him with a paddle. Ouch!

For some reason—and not the obvious one—that notion made her scowl. She was so not into dominating a man. Particularly a man who was as big and powerful (and absolutely scrumptious) as Lander.

Whether it was the giddy relief after having survived meeting his feline form, or the sexy vibe of the room (or just plain insanity) she was feeling warm and toasty—and tingly—once again.

Maybe he gave off some kind of chemical pheromone or something? Really, how did this make a bit of sense otherwise? She'd been seriously pissed at him after what he'd done with Adria. Then so scared she'd literally passed out. And then, after being led down here, to the wild world of S and M, more than a little nervous.

Now she was feeling like a kitten sunbathing in a sunny window. She could practically hear herself purring.

How freaking crazy was that?

Pheromones. Yes, that had to be it. He was pumping out some magical, super-duper, heavy-duty man-lion sexy hormones. And she was simply unable to resist. It was a chemical thing. Yeah. That was it. That was her story, and she was sticking to it.

"I didn't hurt you when I turned."

"Yeah. Well, I thought that was just because lions don't eat dead prey," she said over her shoulder.

He leaned closer, until her entire backside was resting against his frontside. "If that were true, I'd never eat. The lionesses do most of the hunting for our pride. We males rarely kill what we eat."

"That, I suppose, was intended to make me feel better?"

"Can't say I'm not trying." He pushed her a little harder this time, and she let him lead her across the room.

Leery, she stopped a good ten feet from the sex swing. "I'm still not sure about all this."

"It's meant to be a reward." Laughter in his eyes, he stepped around her, motioned toward the sex swing. "You are going to accept your reward."

"Reward? For what?" Slightly confused, she sank down, settling her bottom in the swing. Rewards, prizes, that kind of thing was good. She'd received the occasional reward. Never had she been disappointed when one was offered.

Then again, never had a so-called reward been associated with whips and chains.

Granted, she wasn't denying she liked the whole dominant-lover thing. It was exciting. Particularly when the guy was built like a god. But she'd never imagined herself mixing with the latex bodysuit crowd. That was what this kind of bondage dungeon was all about. Hard-core domination. Sensation play. Pain. Endorphins.

All she was looking for was a firm hand, gentle restraints, and a little naughty talk during sex.

When he lifted her hand and tied it with a rope suspended from a metal ring screwed into the ceiling, she asked, "Aren't we supposed to talk about this first? You know, discuss the rules. Limits. Safe words. I've never done anything like this before, but I've read about it in books."

"There's no need. I don't intend to test your limits today." He tied the other wrist then knelt, lifting one of her knees to position her leg.

Maybe he was telling the truth, but she had to be sure. "I think we need to talk about it anyway. I ... uh ... have some concerns. ..." Okay, she was trying to have a rational discussion here. Not easy when she was naked, her hands over her head, her one leg tied, her pussy and breasts out there, open, accessible, exposed. "I ..."

Her face was getting mighty hot. So were a few other parts of her anatomy. She pretended she wasn't melting inside like a candle left in a sauna. Or at least, she tried to pretend.

He tipped his head to smile up at her.

Was it like a hundred degrees in here or what?

"What do you want to tell me, Cailey?" He ran a flattened

hand up her shin and over her knee. It rested for a moment there, then continued to inch slowly up her thigh. "Do you want to tell me how you want me to take control? To tie you up? Make you feel exposed and vulnerable?"

"Uh . . ." *Yes.*

That naughty hand, that wonderfully naughty hand, moved another couple of inches north. "Or do you want to tell me how turned on you get by having me watch you get fucked by a dildo? That sweet, hot pussy taking a big dong."

"Oh."

"And we should talk about those nipples, too. Can't forget them. Let me guess: it drives you crazy if they're pinched just as you're about to come."

She couldn't speak anymore. Her throat had imploded.

"Finally, there's this sweet little ass of yours. You've never taken a man there. It scares you. But I know you've learned to relax. I think you've been training yourself. That pleases me, Cailey." He slid his finger into his mouth, moistening it, then pressed it against her anus.

After a quiver, she opened to him, taking his finger to the knuckle. He dragged another finger over her clit. A shock wave shot through her, like a jolt of electricity. She arched her back, thrusting her breasts toward him. A puff of air huffed from her mouth, and she tightened the ring of muscle around his finger, holding him inside.

Good God, this man knew how to reward a girl!

She couldn't wait to see what other rewards he had in mind.

10

Sweet goddess, he was going to lose control. The sight of Cailey, her body open to him, her swollen lips glistening with her juices. The scent of that sweet honey slicking her passage. The sound of her little gasps and moans. And the sensation of that tight ring of muscles gripping his finger.

The beast was right there already, waiting for that moment of vulnerability as he found release. But for Cailey, he needed to keep it contained right now.

Dammit, he'd have to deny himself. But that didn't mean he would deny her.

A reward was what he'd promised. A reward was what she would receive, no matter how much it tormented him.

He fastened her other ankle in the leather restraint, careful to tighten it only enough for her to feel it. As long as she felt the slight weight and pressure of the cuff, she would be satisfied. He knew she wouldn't try to break free.

He sensed it was the sensation of being restrained that excited her most. Just as it was the awe of her submission, the amazing trust she had in him, that sent wave after wave of thrill through him.

His balls ached something fierce, the weight and pressure of his cum like the force inside a shaken bottle of champagne.

Later. Focus on Cailey, he reminded himself. But damn, his balls hurt.

He asked, "Do you masturbate, Cailey? What makes you hot?"

"Sometimes." She sounded breathless. He could see the slight tremble of her legs and arms, the quiver in her stomach muscles. Her pupils, once pinpoints, expanded to nearly cover her entire irises. It thrilled him, to witness the effects of her desire.

Her nipples. Jutting out to him, an invitation to taste.

"Tell me, what do you do when you masturbate?"

She licked her lip then sucked it into her mouth.

"Tell me."

"I can't tell you that."

"I want to hear you say the words. I want you to hear yourself."

"Why?"

"Because I know what that will do to you."

She sucked in a small gasp, releasing it unevenly. "I touch myself."

"Where?"

"On my bed."

"No, where do you touch yourself? Here?" He skirted her folds, swollen and engorged from arousal.

"Yeeessss. There. And my clit."

"Your clit. How do you touch your clit? Do you rub it hard? Soft? Do you like fleeting, teasing touches? Or more firm ones?"

"Semifirm."

He pulled at the tissues hooding her little pink pearl and pressed against it. "Like this?"

"Ooooh, yes. Circles."

He slowly circled over the hard nub with his index finger, using his free hand to grab the dildo and lube he'd placed within reaching distance.

"Do you fuck your pussy with your fingers? Like this?" Still circling over her clit, he pushed two fingers into her. The slick tissues gripped him, soft and wet, hot. A blast of desperate need hit him in the gut. Dammit, this was fucking hell.

"Yeeessss."

He could see the insides of her thighs tightening as his fingers fucked her, bringing her closer to completion. It would probably kill him, but he had no choice. This was her first reward, and he would make it nothing less than mind blowing. To do so would make things progress so much easier from this point on.

Of course, a quick release, while being satisfactory, would be a far cry from mind blowing. He knew bringing her to the verge several times, withdrawing, and finally giving her that relief would make her orgasm much more powerful.

The trick was in reading her body. Carefully. Looking for the signs and following the instincts of the beast. He'd have to loosen his hold on the beast, to let him come to the surface. A bit of a risk, but worth it.

He closed his eyes, envisioning the feline within him. It was always there, most often waiting in the darkest recesses of himself, eyes glowing brightly in the shadows. He called to it, visualizing the lion prowling out from within a cage, moving with stealth and power closer to the light, closer to the surface.

As it came forward, he felt his senses heighten even more.

The scent of Cailey's arousal intensified, musky sweet and oh so tempting. He tasted her in the air. He heard her every gasp, and even the racing thumping of her heartbeat. His mouth watered. Body tensed.

Hunt. Stalk. Take.

He bent down between her legs and pulled in a deep breath through his nose, wishing he could hold that fucking beautiful scent inside forever. He didn't want it to fade. Couldn't stand the thought. He opened his eyes to the sight of her wet lips, dripping with sweet juices, and he knew he had to taste her.

"Lander?" she whispered, her voice quavering.

"Have you ever had a man kiss you here before? Any man but me?"

"No. N-never."

Her answer satisfied the part of him that ached to possess her, to make her his forever. It was a part of himself he'd never known existed until that moment. He'd always shared his lionesses with the other males of the pride. Jealousy, the need to possess exclusively, was one emotion he'd never experienced. He wasn't sure what to do about it.

He parted her labia with his fingers, pulling them wide to expose her clit and the rosy opening to her vagina. He swirled his tongue over her clitoris, slowly, round and round, then after a couple of minutes flicked hard and fast.

"Oh God, Lander. Ohgod, ohgod, ohgod."

He changed back and forth. Slow then fast, adding a couple of fingers into her vagina. Pumping in and out. He knew the moment when she was about to come. It was a scent, one that nearly ripped the beast from him. He threw himself backward, a moment before it was too late. Cailey cried out. Her hips bucked up, her ankles and wrists pulling at the restraints.

"No!"

He would do it again and again, bring her to the verge of release. And then, after what would surely be nearly excruciating torment, he would give her the release she had earned.

It would be a sweet reward, for both of them.

This was a reward? In whose book? Surely not hers.

Three times now Lander had brought her to that magical

crest—twice while she'd been in the swing and now once on the bench. Just as she'd been about to tumble into an orgasm, he'd withdrawn from her, jerking her back from the peak.

She was so frustrated, she wanted to scream. But she wouldn't. He had already warned her. If she did, he wouldn't let her come. And dammit, after going through this three times, she knew there was no orgasm for her until he decided.

Ironic, she'd been so anxious to submit to a man, just like this. She was tied up and vulnerable, completely under his control. It was her ultimate fantasy. Yet, she wasn't exactly overjoyed by how things were going. At least not yet.

Looked like he was going for round four.

At this point, she wasn't sure she had the energy to do this again. She felt weary, and yet the blood pulsed through her body in scalding waves, demanding the release Lander had denied her three times.

She whimpered when his finger found her sensitive clit once again. The bastard knew exactly how to touch her, how fast to move that finger, how much pressure to use, how much lubricant. He went for a slender dildo this time, and for the briefest moment, she hoped he might bring her to a swift climax with it. He slicked it up with lots of lubricant and teased her anus with the tip.

Oh God, did he know what he was doing to her? This was so unfair! So cruel.

She hated him.

She adored him.

"Show me how you take this in your ass. I'll go slowly."

Slow wasn't how she wanted it. She wanted to be fucked hard and fast. Yes, oh yes. She nodded and he eased the dildo's smooth, bullet-shaped tip into her anus. She pushed against the invasion, and slowly, just as he'd promised, it inched deeper inside.

"Oh yes, ohyes, ohyes," she murmured, over and over as

she took the toy deep inside. He stopped thrusting in, leaving the flared end outside, and the ring of muscles closed around it, holding it in place. "Fuck me, please."

How she adored the feeling of a thick cock inside her pussy, while her ass was full. It was beyond words. She knew it wouldn't take her long to reach that place again, the warm, pulsating place where everything centered on that spot between her legs and tingly heat radiated through her body, so intense she could practically taste it.

He unfastened the restraints binding her ankles, then forced her knees back. She quaked as he knelt between her legs, his cock in one fist.

"You've been such a good girl, Cailey. You've earned your reward. I won't stop you this time. Take it." And with that, he thrust inside, filling her completely.

The air huffed out of her lungs when he seated himself fully. And it leaked back in, reinflating them. Oooh, so good. So absolutely right. He fucked her slowly at first, and she relished the sensation of his thick cock gliding in and out of her clenching tissues.

Fucking had never felt like this, so beyond words. Wonderful didn't begin to describe the sensations zooming through her body with every inward thrust of his thick rod. Every time he pistoned in or out, his cock grazed that special place inside her, the one that intensified the sensations. Within moments, she was breathless, every muscle in her body knotted so tightly she wanted to cry.

She opened her eyes, just needing to look at him, to register this once-in-a-lifetime moment in her memory, for always.

God, he was such a beautiful man. His body all thick and big and powerful. The most gorgeous man she'd ever met, let alone slept with. And he was looking at her like she was Miss Universe.

"Cailey, oh, fuck, little one. My sweet kitten." He reached up, pinching her nipples hard enough to send waves of pleasure-pain through her body. And she was there, at the magical place, and her body spasmed around him. He groaned into her mouth, gave one final thrust and withdrew his cock from her quivering body.

He released her arms from the restraints that had held them out to the sides, and sitting on the floor, pulled her onto his lap. He held her, the dildo still in her ass, for a long time. She clung to him, grateful for the closeness, the feeling of safety. He touched her so tenderly, stroked her hair, her shoulders.

This guy was just too good to be real. If only he *were* real.

Finally, he gently lowered her to a thick fur spread on the floor and pulled the toy from her anus.

She hoped he wasn't going to leave her again. Not yet.

He set the used toy aside and eased onto his side, facing her. His eyes were full of emotion as he looked at her. She couldn't help smiling. Such a tender moment. No words needed to be spoken. She sensed what he was feeling.

"Lander, I . . . that was . . ."

A knock interrupted what was going to be a very heartfelt, genuine, if not a little awkward, declaration.

In rushed a large man Cailey had never seen before. "My king. I apologize for interrupting you, but there's news. Your brother Kir is missing."

Lander jackknifed up. "No."

11

Lander let a mighty roar rip from chest, blast up his throat, and echo off the distant mountains.

He'd grieved before. But not like this. His brother. Murdered. For no reason but to get at him. Vengeance.

Jag, that fucking bastard and his fucking agenda.

On his knees, he reached down to gather Kir into his arms. As he moved, a tiny flash of light caught his eye.

What was this? A small, glittery object caught the silvery light of the moon a second time. He plucked it up and stood, inspecting it closely.

He recognized the item immediately. And yet, he couldn't understand how it could have ended up out here, miles from the city.

Answers. He would get them. As soon as he could.

He dropped the item into his pocket and knelt beside his brother again. Even though his brother's body had already been partially spoiled by the local scavengers, starving for lack of food, he couldn't leave his brother there where he lay, fodder.

True, it was the way things were meant to be. But there was only so much insult this man could take.

Kir. Dead.

As king, Lander had trained himself to show no emotion, particularly the kind that could reveal weakness, vulnerability.

Duty, honor, obligation; the well-being of those who relied upon him for protection. These were far more important than anything else.

Kir. Dead.

Dammit. The bastard, Jag, had still managed to discover a vulnerability in his king. Kir was the one person Lander might have given it all up for: the throne, everything.

Rage was building within him, gathering momentum. His eyes burned as tears threatened. No emotion, dammit. He scooped Kir into his arms, staggered to his feet. Focused on each breath he inhaled and each step he took, he rushed past two lionesses.

His enemy had known what this would do to him. Drive him into a trap.

"My king," one of the lionesses said behind him. "You cannot bring the deceased into the city. The risk of disease."

He knew the risk. Just as he knew he could not allow all the members of his pride to be exposed to potentially lethal infection. There were few medicines to protect them, and therefore the many laws governing the treatment of the dead had to be strictly enforced. By everyone.

"I will not bring him inside the city walls." He didn't stop walking as he talked. "Kir's body will be purified. By fire."

"Very well." The lioness shifted into her feline form and raced ahead of him, no doubt intent upon preparing the fire.

With the recent decline in lower species of animals, they'd abandoned ceremonial burning, hoping to help the struggling carnivore species to survive. Their world was a complex cycle of death and life, each level supporting the other. But Lander would be damned if he'd let his brother's bones be picked clean.

A white pillar of smoke reached to the clouds in the distance. The fire had been prepared.

He walked the distance to the city wall, talking to his brother's spirit, apologizing for his suffering and vowing to provide for his wife and children. Later, overwhelmed with grief, Lander said a final good-bye, vowed he would make sure Kir had not died in vain, and, climbing up onto the raised platform behind the fire, tossed Kir into the churning center.

Then, unable to watch the angry tongues of flame lick at his brother's body, he turned and entered the city's main gate. As he pushed through the crowded streets, passing lionesses, cubs, and the few males who called his city home, he could think of only two things.

First, finding a way to make this right.

And second, finding out what Cailey had to do with his brother's death.

If anyone could possibly wear an emotion on the outside, like a huge neon sign hanging around his neck, that was Lander. And the emotion he was wearing: frigid fury.

Cailey saw it everywhere, from the way he walked to the ticking muscle on his jaw. And his eyes, oh God. Was that rage directed at her?

What could she have possibly done to make him so furious?

For the first time since arriving in this strange world of cat-people, she was absolutely petrified of Lander. She jumped up from her seat at the table, sending her breakfast and a plume of loose paper scattering through the air, and dashed toward the bathroom door: the closest exit. But before she had the door open, Lander had caught her from behind and hauled her around to face his rage-filled face.

She shuddered, that glare turning her blood to ice. "W-what's wrong?" Over and over, she kept asking herself what she could have done to make him so angry. She'd spent almost her entire time there, in that room, isolated. And when he'd left her yesterday afternoon, nothing had been wrong between them. At least, she hadn't sensed anything. Although she'd worried when he didn't return to her last night.

He held her arms so tightly, they throbbed. "Make it right. Now, witch."

"Witch? I'm not a witch. What're you talking about?"

"My brother Kir." He hauled her across the room, totally unaware—or unconcerned—about the fact that she wasn't exactly keeping her feet beneath her.

"I don't know your brother. What's wrong with him?"

Lander stopped, stared at her for a handful of agonizing seconds, and then said, "He's dead."

Cailey's heart literally screeched to a halt. Lying beneath Lander's fury was a much more powerful emotion: love. And the kind of profound loss that only someone who'd suffered such a thing could relate to. She should have recognized it before.

But that still didn't help her understand why Lander thought she had anything to do with his brother's death.

"I'm so sorry, Lander."

"No. You can't feel pity, or sorrow. There's no need." He started walking again, dragging her (naked!) down the corridor to a set of narrow stairs descending down to a tiled landing below. "You just have to fix it. Do whatever you must to undo this."

He wanted her to undo Kir's death? Tripping along behind him, she used her free hand to steady herself against whatever surface she could, including Lander's back when nothing else was in reach. "But I can't."

"You must." Practically running, he continued through a door and outside into a narrow street crowded on both sides by two-story wood and stone structures. Painfully aware of her nakedness, she wrapped her free arm around herself and avoided looking at anyone.

People stared at her as she and Lander rushed by. She could feel their eyes on her.

"There are some things nobody's able to do, Lander. Please stop. Please."

He didn't stop. Instead, he just kept rushing through the crowded streets, through clusters of women, children. She was absolutely mortified, ashamed beyond words. And ready to cry.

"Lander," she said, yanking on his arm. She wasn't going to be pulled along like a toddler. Shamed in front of so many people. "Stop!"

He stopped, oh yes he did. But she wasn't particularly relieved. In fact, in about three skittery heartbeats, she wished he'd go back to galloping through the crowded street to God only knew where.

Once again, she found herself practically cowering in terror.

"I'm scared," she admitted, hoping it would disarm him, throw him off balance, make him think before he did something terrible. "I'm ashamed. And confused. And naked."

The air practically sizzled between them. Silent, he stood too close for comfort, staring down at her through slitted eyes, his mouth pulled into a hard line. "The witch told me you can change the past."

She shook her head. "She said what? How could I do that?"

"She said all I had to do was gain your submission, and your power would be mine. You willingly submitted to me. So now you must do as I say."

She stood gaping at him for who knew how long.

First, had all that romance earlier been a ploy? Some kind of demented way to supposedly gain power from her?

If so, what power, and exactly how could this transfer of power work?

The only thing she had was her writing, the stories she wove. If Lander was able to dominate her, he could make her write whatever he wanted? Was that what the woman had meant?

That kind of made sense, except for one small detail: their critique partner reject hadn't given her Lander's story to write. She'd been given another story to work on.

Had the woman made a mistake, meant to give Cailey her own book? "I wish I had magical powers. I really, really do."

"Liar," he spat. "You do possess magical powers, and I have seen the proof. With my own eyes. Colors. I see colors where before I couldn't. I smell scents. Taste flavors. All of this, you have done. With your magic."

"No. I haven't. It's not me. I don't know how—"

"How can I believe you. You've done nothing but lie to me since coming here."

"Hey, I have not." Granted, she'd told him a few white lies, more like harmless little fibs. She'd told him plenty of truths, too. "I said I don't know your brother. That was the truth."

"Then how did this end up next to his dead body?" Lander crammed his hand in his pocket and withdrew it. Cailey watched his fingers unfurl, revealing one diamond stud earring. An earring that looked a whole lot like the one she wore in the third hole in her left ear—a vestige from her semirebellious teenage years.

"An earring? It's not . . ." Of course, she smacked her hand to her ear, searching for the jewelry that she fully expected to be there.

It wasn't.

Had she taken it out last night?

"It's not mine."

"It most definitely is. No lioness in this city possesses anything like this."

"Someone's framing me," she reasoned.

From the doubt on his face, she could see he wasn't buying that explanation. But she didn't have any other to offer. Truly, she was stumped. And more than a little pissed. Who was trying to cause her trouble? Who even knew she existed? Before now, she'd been sequestered in Lander's bedroom like a prisoner, being served by the same . . . perfect . . .

Bitches!

Were they jealous? Of her? Was that why they'd put her earring next to Lander's dead brother? To get rid of her? She could only imagine the penalty she'd pay for killing a king's brother.

A life for a life?

Shit, maybe it was better for Lander to think she *could* change the past. It might be her only hope of saving her ass. At least until she could prove she was being framed. "Okay, okay! I'll do what I can. Just please, take me back home. This is humiliating, being hauled down the street like this. Please."

"Very well." Lander did an immediate one-eighty, heading back in the direction from which they'd come. "You will do your magic immediately upon our return." He halted, suddenly, and Cailey practically crashed into him. "If you fail, you will pay a dear price."

Just great. How the hell would she get herself out of this?

"An earring?" Bourne asked, motioning to the tiny trinket Lander held in his fingertips. "That is what was found."

Lander ran his thumb over the polished surface and, staring into the gem's sparkling depth, nodded. "It's hers."

Dryce, standing at the door, crossed his arms over his chest. "Your guards have also located a witness who reported seeing the foreigner outside of Kir's house the night before last."

Impossible. Or was it?

Lander fisted the diamond, almost thankful for the pinch he felt as the facets bit into his skin. "Run me through the time line again." He didn't want to believe what his brothers were telling him. Or the evidence that was mounting against Cailey faster than snow in the mountains in the deep of winter. But at the moment, that evidence was pretty damning.

Bourne flattened a piece of paper on Lander's desk, a brief

time line. "We approximate Kir's time of death at two o'clock yesterday morning. You left home just after midnight. Cailey was alone."

"With a guard posted outside the door," Lander pointed out.

"Your lionesses reported bringing Cailey a meal about an hour after you left. You returned a little after three o'clock, finding her where you'd left her. You then went to bed, rising at five."

Lander fingered the edge of the paper. "But the guards would've seen her leave. What about Kir's movements? Did anyone see him leave his house any time after Cailey was supposedly seen outside it?"

"No," Dryce answered, walking across the room and settling into a chair in front of Lander's desk.

"So are we thinking Kir died at home?" Lander placed the time line on the corner of his desk and stood. His nerves were too on edge for him to sit. He needed to be up, moving. To work some of this fury out of his system. It was that or go crazy.

Dryce steepled his fingers under his chin. Nodded. "All the evidence supports that theory."

Pacing, Lander asked, "Was anyone else seen near his house at that time?"

Bourne shook his head. "No."

Lander needed to talk some of this through. The time line worked, but other pieces of the puzzle didn't fit as well. "Okay. So Kir didn't leave home, at least not alive. And yet he was discovered outside the city walls, miles away. Regardless, Cailey could be telling the truth."

Cailey had suggested she was being set up, that someone had planted her earring by Kir's body. He wanted to believe her story was more plausible than the one the guard was trying to sell him.

"Telling the truth about what, Lander?" Bourne asked.

He trusted his youngest brother a great deal. But he wasn't

ready to tell him everything he suspected. Not yet. "Question: how could a woman Cailey's size remove Kir's body?"

Dryce swiveled in the chair, facing Lander. "We don't know. But at last report, a team was searching Kir's house, gathering more evidence. We should hear from them soon."

Lander dragged his fingers through his hair. "And how long has Kir's body been in the desert?"

"We're guessing he was placed there shortly after he died. Within hours."

Lander shook his head. "That means Cailey would have had less than two hours to get to Kir's house, kill him, sneak him out of the house, deliver him to the point where he was found, and return home. Never mind the fact that such a feat would be difficult for someone your size. Someone who knows his or her way around the city. As far as I know, before yesterday morning, Cailey had not left my bedroom. She'd never met Kir. I've never taken her to his house. How would she know where to find it, how to reach the city gate, or for that matter, how to get home?"

"You said she can do magic," Bourne stated stiffly.

Lander's heart literally stopped beating. "Yes, there is that." How could he have forgotten? If she was powerful enough to change the past, present, or future, surely she possessed enough magic to transport a man and herself a couple of miles.

Once again, doubt snuffed out hope.

Cailey might have killed his brother? But why? How?

"Has it been determined how he died?" Lander asked.

Bourne pulled a page out from the neatly stacked papers he'd set on Lander's desk. "Preliminary report suggests a knife wound to the chest."

The words stung, the pain like a blade to his own chest.

But the question still remained: why?

Why did anyone kill? Self-defense. Revenge. Fear.

Fear?

Maybe if Cailey had killed his brother, she hadn't done so at his house. Perhaps he'd caught her by surprise, and, terrified for her life, she'd defended herself. "Has it been determined whether he was in feline or human form when he died?"

Bourne leafed through the papers. "No. I'll talk to the doctor and see if he can tell." Bourne moved toward the door, but before he'd opened it, a knock sounded from the outside. He stepped aside and pulled it open, revealing the visitor, one of Lander's elite guards.

"My king." The guard bent a knee, bowing. "I have a message." He handed Lander a sealed parcel, then stepped back to await a response.

Lander broke the seal and opened the neatly folded paper enclosing a stack of written papers. Page after page described in detail what was found at Kir's house. Blood: possibly Kir's. Hair: also, from the looks of it, Kir's. Articles of clothing belonging to a lioness. Another piece of jewelry, owner not identified. Footprints in the blood on the floor. Handprints.

Lander sighed, dismissing the messenger. He was trying to avoid the inevitable, but if anything told him that would be impossible, that damn list did. Whether he wanted to or not, he had to go to Kir's house and see the evidence for himself. He had to determine for sure whether Cailey was telling the truth.

Or whether the worst had happened: he'd invited a killer into his city.

What have I done?

By seeking the power to end all his people's pain and tragedy, had he brought the very source of it to their doorsteps?

12

A man who'd lost everything rarely survived such loss, at least not without desperately clinging to whatever scraps fate might pass his way afterward.

Jafari could accept such failing in a man. But when the one in question was a god, the being who had created the very vessel all mankind's future rested upon, it was humiliating to be so weak.

Jafari despised his eyes for wanting to look upon the woman. He despised his body for being so quickly and completely aroused by the mere thought of her. He despised his mind for being so intrigued by her every word, thought, and gesture. He despised his soul for surrendering to her.

She filled the inky shadows of his world with luminous radiance. The empty chill with warmth. She made his world complete. But more shockingly, she made him more than a god.

She made him human.

—From *Dark Surrender*, a work in progress by Cailey Holm, writing as Mia Spelman.

* * *

Three days. Two nights.

That's how long it had been since Lander had rushed out on Cailey, after demanding she raise his brother from the dead.

Three days. Two nights.

That was how long she'd paced the floor, trying to figure out how to fake her way out of her promise.

To her knowledge, there'd been only one man who'd ever been resurrected from the dead: the guy whose birth everyone celebrated on Christmas day. Outside of divinity, and the occasional horror-flick monster or paranormal romance character, no one came back from the dead.

Shit, shit, shit!

At least Lander had been gone for a while. Not that his absence helped her. In a way, it made things ten times worse. Instead of getting this whole thing over with and facing the consequences (which she didn't even want to imagine), she was left to freak out in isolation.

But out of desperation (distraction was a good thing), she had finally turned to Mia's story and began writing. She was about a chapter into it when the brainstorm to end all brainstorms struck her.

Could it work?

If the pages of their stories were some kind of wire or tether, tying the friends to their stories and to each other, could they somehow communicate to each other via those magic-imbued pages?

Hell, it was all she had.

She scrawled as quickly as she could, roughed out a scene in which a messenger went to Mia's heroine, pleading with her to save the king's brother in the book she was writing. When she was through, she set the pages aside.

And finally, after three days and two nights of panic, she slept.

* * *

"We have enough now to arrest her and charge her with murder," Bourne stated grimly.

Lander slumped into the nearest chair, the weight of the decision looming over him so heavily, he literally felt it bearing down upon his shoulders.

Regardless of the damning evidence, which was now even more substantial than an earring and a smudged footprint, he still had a hard time believing Cailey had done such a thing. Slaughter a man nearly twice her size with a knife, remove his body afterward, and then return home before she was missed? Not only did the nature of the crime seem so contradictory to her nature, but it was logistically hard to buy. Unless—and this was a huge unless—she had either she used magic or had help.

"You say she is from a foreign world," Bourne reminded him.

Lander dragged his fingers through his hair. He knew what his brother was suggesting. It was the only way any of this made sense. Sort of. "She is. I know this for a fact. I traveled there, by magic."

"You brought back the magic."

He heard the anger in his brother's voice, which not only annoyed him, but also shamed him.

Their people had little respect for magical arts. For good reason. It had been a curse that had made them the way they were—sometimes men, sometimes beasts, the two warring within their bodies. Always. Fighting for control. Magic had also made them orphans.

So, when he'd told his three brothers that he'd been contacted by a witch and offered a great gift, they'd been pessimistic about the whole thing. First, they questioned whether the so-called magic was real. And once he'd convinced them it was, not only did they not believe the gift would be for their benefit, but they suspected some great tragedy would befall them if Lander dared bring it into their world.

He'd felt the same way in the beginning, until the witch had told him she gained nothing from his decision, either way.

Finally, against the council of every man he trusted, he traveled to Cailey's world and brought her back. Because he feared for her safety, he'd kept her confined to his house.

What his people feared, they tended to destroy.

What if his brothers had been right? What if Cailey was the one to be feared, not the other way around? The voice in his head continued to deny that possibility. No. She couldn't kill anyone, not even out of terror. Or with magic.

And she was definitely not an agent of his enemy. No.

She was being framed.

Dammit, who was doing this to her? To him? Now what should he do? The evidence was more than enough to convict her. Yet he was sure she was innocent. Let the trial continue or release her?

What an impossible decision to make, between the justice that every member of his pride would demand and a magic none of his fellow pride members could even conceive of.

The power to change the past. Shape the future. Maybe even lift the curse. And bring back those they'd lost. Brothers. Parents.

Then again, if what Cailey said was true? What if she didn't possess any magic? Or what if she could not surrender it to him?

But that led to another question: why would the witch lie, telling him Cailey did have such a power, especially if the witch had nothing to gain by his decision?

So many fucking questions, and no one to answer them. The witch had disappeared upon his return home with Cailey. And because she had sought him out, not the other way around, he had no idea how to find her.

Cailey more often lied to him than told the truth. He'd get no answers from her.

And his remaining brothers, Bourne and Dryce, his trusted council, looked upon magic with jaded eyes, more hostile than accepting, and definitely more willing to believe the worst than the best. They couldn't be objective.

"My king. What is your decision?" Bourne asked, stiffly, his posture communicating all too clearly what he believed should be done.

Lander shook his head. "I don't believe she killed Kir. It could be planted. All the evidence."

"The footprints?"

"If someone borrowed her shoes."

"Her scent?"

"Transferred from a personal item."

His brother dropped to a squat before him. "May I have permission to speak honestly?"

"Yes." He knew what Bourne would say, but he would not deny him the chance to speak the words.

"I understand why you brought the foreigner here. I don't agree with your decision, but that is not my place. You've got to see the witch lied. I suspect she was sent by Jag, and you might have willingly escorted a dangerous assassin within our walls. Surely you've considered that possibility."

"She's no assassin."

"The evidence says otherwise. Why can't you even consider it? If it were anyone else, you would."

"Because I know her. And I want to believe she's innocent. And that she does possess a magical gift. A power. Just think of the pain and anguish we could spare our people. The witch said—"

"Oh yes, the power to change the past. To release us from this damnable curse and shape our future. Bring back our brothers. Could it be, the future she wishes to create might be one where Jag is king and your bones are picked clean by the scavengers in the desert?"

Lander lunged to his feet, shoving past his brother. "No. No, no. no. The witch told me Cailey's power is used only for good."

"Then ask her to use it. Force her to use it." His brother sneered. "If she's found guilty of murdering the king's brother, she will be sentenced to death. Is there any greater reason for her to call upon her great powers than the basic need to preserve her own life?"

Bourne was one cruel sonofabitch, but he did have a point.

It sickened Lander to even imagine Cailey, terrified, locked in a tiny room with several lionesses. With her fear of their kind, he imagined that would be horrifying. Not to mention dangerous, since she would lack any form of self-defense against a lioness in her feline form.

No, he couldn't allow her to be arrested.

"I'll hold her in my house." He stopped before the fireplace, now filled with ash and a single charred log. His insides felt as volatile as the fire that had once burned there. Emotions churning. Thoughts thrashing.

"You know the pride won't accept that, once word is out that she is to be tried. They'll not only be confused by your seeming betrayal of the law, but also angered by your lack of respect for your brother."

Lander's back stiffened and rage flared anew within him. How dare his brother question his love for Kir! He kept his back turned to Bourne, his glare focused on the pile of ash in the fireplace. "You know I loved our brother. More than anything."

"Then you must allow the law to be carried out."

"She is not a lioness."

"You can have her held in a solitary cell. When she is facing conviction, she'll use her power if she has any. At least you'll learn the truth: whether she's a murderer or a witch . . . or both."

Lander scrubbed his face. His eyes burned from the lingering stink of blood and death in Kir's bedroom down the hall. He took a long look around Kir's living room, at the portraits hanging on one wall. Dammit, how he missed Kir's cocky, annoying voice, and that wicked twinkle in his eye.

Bourne was right. If Cailey wasn't arrested, his pride would more or less abandon him, and any hope of protecting them would be lost. No doubt Jag would be there to lure them into a false sense of security, underhanded deceiver that he was. And then, who knew what might happen. Already, life had become harder for them. He didn't want to imagine what it could become with a man like Jag leading them.

"Very well." The moment the words slipped from his mouth, the beast overcame him. He charged from the house on all fours, lifted his head, and roared his curses to the moon above.

Once again, duty had forced his hand. And most likely by the end of the day tomorrow, Cailey would be taken from him. The agony ripped from his throat, taking the form of yet another echoing roar.

Until this moment, Cailey never would have suspected Lisa— the critique partner who was normally so down to earth and practical—was such a sadistic bitch. It was bad enough she'd turned Cailey's having-kinky-sex-with-a-lion-man story into one of her typical murder-mystery-slash-suspense stories. But now she'd gone too far.

When Cailey got home, there would be hell to pay.

She knew she should be petrified. And she was. But she was even more pissed.

First, there'd been the message, delivered this morning. Four words were scrawled on a piece of paper: *Sorry, no can do.*

And then shortly after noon a group of man-lions hauled her out of Lander's home with her arms bound behind her back. They took her to jail. Arrested! She was being arrested for the murder of Lander's brother.

Just how the heck did they think she'd managed to do such a thing when she'd been outside his house only once?

Lisa, you are so going to pay for this.

A couple of days ago, she'd figured out who was writing her story. When she sat down and thought about it, it had been so simple. First, not only had Lander's story shifted directions, heading into Lisa's territory, but also she knew, since she was writing Mia's story and there were only three girls in their critique group, Lisa had to have received hers.

At least, if one of them wasn't going to end up with her own story. And because that witch was such a bitch, Cailey just knew she wasn't going to let that happen.

Lisa, you have no idea what you've done.

Lander had looked at her like she'd suddenly grown two heads, horns, and a tail. Did he really believe she could kill someone?

At least this time she was wearing clothes. The thigh-length, translucent robe he'd handed her wasn't exactly substantial but it did semicover the bits that needed concealing most.

"I'm innocent," she'd muttered as she was tugged past him. "I swear. I-I just need a little more time."

He met her gaze for roughly a second then turned away.

So much for any hope of him clearing this up for her. How the heck would she get herself out of this shitty mess? Grrrr!

It wasn't Lisa's MO to write her heroines out of trouble by using magic, but maybe, just maybe she'd show a little pity?

Naw, that would be too easy.

In the glaring light of day, Cailey had been marched down the crowded streets, her captors surrounding her on both sides and behind. They created quite a spectacle for the many people out and about.

Not only was she mortified beyond words (once again), but also her anger was edged out by a serious case of fear for her safety. It seemed that Lander's people didn't exactly share America's innocent-until-proven-guilty attitude toward suspected criminals.

Gosh, would she even get a trial, she'd wondered? Or had they already convicted her?

Lots of golden cat eyes glared at her with hatred, and what little anger she'd had simmering under the surface turned to frigid terror. She'd never felt so despised. Hated by a pack of people who sprouted claws and fangs whenever they wanted.

"What's going to happen to me?" she asked one of the guards, the one who'd treated her the most gently, which wasn't saying much.

"You'll be tried in our court. The evidence against you will be presented. And a judge will determine whether it's enough to convict you."

She supposed it was a good thing that there would be a trial, although as she tromped through packs of glaring cat-people, she doubted it would be a fair one.

"How long before the trial?"

"We have very little crime in our city. As a result, your case is the only one on the docket. It's scheduled to begin tomorrow morning."

"Wow." She supposed that was good and bad. Good because she wouldn't be sitting in a prison cell for months, waiting. Bad because if she was convicted, her story could be cut short in a big way.

Lisa had better not be thinking of straying from romance with this story. At least in romance, it was highly unlikely a heroine would be put to death for murder. Or gobbled up by pissed-off cat-women.

Hardly made her feel any better, though.

All this raw hatred was getting to her, even though she wasn't exactly the people-pleasing kind. She wanted to defend herself, right there in the streets; to shout out her innocence, despite the fact that no one would believe her.

What about Lander? What was this doing to him?

She missed him so bad it hurt. The image of his chilly mien

as she'd been led out of his house was like a brand in her brain. It wouldn't go away, no matter how hard she tried to push it out.

This just sucked. On so many levels.

Lisa, I hate you.

After suffering one humiliation after another—a strip search! Ack!—she was escorted to a courtroom that looked a lot like the one back at home. The last time she'd been in court, she'd been sitting in the jury box, listening to a case about a suspected drunk driver. It was a whole other thing being in the defendant's chair, particularly because she didn't have a smooth-talking defense attorney working for her.

She was on her own, left to defend herself.

The judge, a middle-aged man with more white hair than brown, read the charges to her and asked how she pleaded. Naturally, she said, "Not guilty."

The next day, one piece of damning evidence after another was presented to the judge, by a detective for the local police. By the end, even she was convinced she'd killed Kir.

Things were looking bad.

Not to mention, she'd learned something interesting about these people. They absolutely despised magic. Anything associated with magic: people, things, places. She didn't have the whole story, but it was obvious some big tragedy had happened because of magic. And now, since it seemed everyone knew she had been magically brought to this place from some foreign world, she was to be feared and despised.

It was like the Salem witch trials all over again. There was absolutely no hope for her. She was going to lose this trial in a big way.

Her stomach hurt. Her head hurt. By the time the prosecutor, or whatever he was called in this place, had wrapped up his case against her, she was ready to throw up.

Only one thing would have made her feel better, less isolated and vulnerable. One thing that didn't happen. Or rather, one person who didn't come.

She kept waiting for Lander to show. Surely, he'd want to know what was happening during the trial. Never mind the fact that he'd been sleeping with her, or that he'd brought her here to this weird world of shape-changing people and lack of technology. The deceased was his brother.

To her surprise, however, he didn't show. Not for any of it. Not even when the verdict was read a few hours later: guilty.

Or the next morning, when she was sentenced—to death.

God, her story was totally out of control! Never, never, never would she put another romance heroine through hell.

That was, *if* she lived to write another book.

13

He'd finally come to see her. At least it was before she'd been executed, not after. Was there any chance he was going to actually help her?

She took in his glare, the stiff way he was holding his body, the crossed arms and ticking muscle along his jaw.

Nope.

"You must use your magic, Cailey," he said.

Not much of a greeting, but she supposed they were well beyond. "Hi, how're things hanging?"

What would it take to convince him she couldn't do magic? Her death?

Once again, she was reminded of those witch trials, back in the sixteen hundreds, when they'd tried women by tying them to heavy rocks and throwing them in rivers. Sink or swim, they lost no matter what.

"There's no magic."

"You would rather lose your life than relinquish your magic?" he shouted, for the first time losing that calm, cool, and collected demeanor she'd found so damn irritating. And it finally registered with her how desperate he was to believe she could do magic, and at least one reason why he'd let this trial go so far.

He was forcing her hand. Too bad she didn't have four aces. More like a two, five, six, and eight.

Her eyes were burning now, threatening tears she'd held back for days. The humiliation was bad. The terror horrible. The uncertainty excruciating. But the desperation she glimpsed in Lander's eyes was a hundred times worse than all those put together. If only she could bring his brother back from the dead.

But Lisa wouldn't write the story that way. She knew that, as much as she knew Lander loved his brother with the kind of fierce devotion she'd never seen in anyone before.

"Lander, if you're waiting for me to do some kind of spell or make something happen with magic before you stop my execution, I'm going to beg you to believe me. I. Can't. Do. Magic."

"The witch. Why would she lie?"

"I don't know. I wish I did, because if that's why you brought me here—to get some kind of power from me—then it's all a huge mistake. And I don't know where we go from here."

"I don't believe you." He turned and walked away, and angry tears slipped from her eyes, streaming down her cheeks, along the sides of her nose. Some gathered along her upper lip, salty and hot.

"You don't want to believe me," she said to his back. "I can understand that. But what I can't understand is how you could stand watching me be put to death for a crime I didn't commit and a failure I can't control. I thought you cared about justice, even if you don't care about me."

The bastard didn't stop walking.

The dam broke and a surge of tears gushed from her eyes.

Why was Cailey being so stubborn? What did she stand to lose by using her power? This made no sense. She was facing certain death if she didn't revive his brother and turn back the events of the past few days. Outside of self-preservation, what possible reason could she have for withholding her power?

"Anything?" Bourne asked as Lander entered the room where Bourne and Dryce had been waiting.

Lander shook his head. "No. She's still denying she has any magical powers."

Dryce shook his head. "She'll die by sunrise tomorrow."

"I told her, but she's still claiming she's innocent, despite the evidence presented at court, which was very convincing . . . at least on the surface."

"You still doubt the witness?" Bourne asked, looking wounded.

"No, I don't doubt him. I just doubt the evidence. Nothing was presented that couldn't be put there by someone else, someone with an agenda."

Dryce looked thoughtful, scowling, arms crossed, genuinely confused. "And why would anyone—with an agenda, or not— want Cailey dead?"

"Don't know. Outside of the obvious: the fact that our citizens think all magic is the work of the cursed."

"It is," Bourne snapped. "Look what this magic has done to us, to Kir."

Those words were like a knife in Lander's gut, but as always, he struggled to maintain an emotion-free mien. Lander knew Bourne blamed him for Kir's death.

Bourne's anger was driving a wedge between them. Sadly, Lander's list of trustworthy friends was growing shorter by the hour.

Had this been his enemy's hope? Had Jag seen an opportunity to create dissention from within, to weaken the king's power and influence within the pride?

That made a whole lot more sense than Cailey murdering his brother for some unknown reason and disposing of the body single-handedly. He could tell—both from her reaction to things and his own pride members—that she had never been in the city before. That made it close to impossible for him to believe she could have committed the crime.

Now, as far as the issue of her supposed powers went, that was a much more painful truth to face. As the trial progressed, it became harder and harder to believe she possessed the power he so much wanted her to have.

No magic?

His brother would never again walk upon the earth alive.

He had lost yet another—his dearest—family member, friend, and ally.

Forever.

Another officer stepped into the room, his face grim. "The foreigner is being taken to the courtroom. Because of the nature of the crime, and the relation of the victim to our king, the judge has ordered her sentence to be carried out immediately."

Cailey was about to give her life for nothing. The woman he realized meant more to him than any lioness he had ever known.

Maybe her magic was of a different sort? The kind that only he, as a man who could never allow himself to show emotion, would appreciate.

The thought of losing her forever, another tragic loss on the tail of the first, sickened him.

Lander leapt to his feet and raced past both men. He had to stop this now, before it was too late—regardless of how it would look to the pride. This was one risk he had to take.

The corridor leading to the courtroom yawned long and wide before him, and it seemed to take forever for him to run in human form down its length. He shoved past two armed guards at the door and bolted into the room, just in time to see Cailey kneel at the feet of the man licensed by the court to take her life.

"No!" he shouted as the executioner raised his arms, the long silver blade flashing over her head. The entire room stilled, and hundreds of sets of eyes turned to him, widening with recognition. Several seconds of shocked silence followed. "As king it is my right to pardon anyone of any crime."

The judge frowned. "As you wish, my king." He motioned to the guards and they helped Cailey to her feet, unbound her arms. A rush of frantic whispers followed as those expecting to witness the death of a convicted murderer, a dangerous foreigner, realized their king had indeed freed her.

He wanted to take the trembling woman into his arms and comfort her. But first, he had to speak to these men and women, to try to help them understand why he would do such a thing.

He walked to the front of the room, feeling the hundreds of curious stares following him. He turned and faced them, meeting their gazes one by one, until he'd made it across the entire room. Cailey's was the last he met. "You may not understand my actions today, but as your king I am within my rights to pardon this woman. In my eyes, she has committed no crime against our pride, against me personally, or against my family."

If a blade of grass had struck the floor in that room, it would have been heard. Silence sat heavy in the small space. His control over the pride hung in the balance, slipping through his fingertips.

He continued, "You may think I've made a terrible mistake, and that by freeing this woman I will put you and your families in danger. But I swear, I have done what I know is best for the pride, for your safety and well-being."

"She is your concubine," someone shouted from the rear.

He was shocked. Who would dare speak to him with so little respect?

If this was Jag's ploy, it was working. Before today, he'd never had a member of his pride speak to him with such a tone.

He took several slow, deep breaths before continuing, "She is not my concubine. She is—was—my captive. I brought her here against her will to perform a duty for me. For all of you."

More silence.

"But she is not my captive any longer. I expect you will treat Cailey with respect, should you meet her on the street. She is a guest of your king, an ambassador from another land. And as such, she deserves to be treated with the same respect as any visitor to our city."

More silence. He'd known this was going to be hell, but he'd had no idea how bad that hell would be.

He sighed. "Anyone who disrespects Cailey Holm will be arrested for treason."

Once again, the room filled with shocked whispers. Lander took Cailey's hand and led her out of the building. She walked beside him, silent, her delicate little hand tucked in his the entire way home. As expected, the instant they stepped into his house, she walked into his arms and doused his shoulder with her tears.

If ever Cailey had been ready to drop to her knees and kiss a man's feet it was now. She'd come so close to the end, she was sure every cell in her body was twitching in celebration of being alive, particularly those in her head, which had been this close to being separated from the rest of her. Beheading, in this place, was evidently the only way to off a convicted murderer. And here she'd hoped for a more pleasant, gentler death, like being put to sleep with drugs or something. She should've known better, considering this world's somewhat barbaric ways.

Oh, who cared? She was alive! Yayayayayay! She'd officially been pardoned. And Lander had made it clear to one and all that if even a hair on her head was harmed, their asses were his.

Despite the celebration going on inside her body, in another way her mood was still very somber. Now was not the time to put on the dancing shoes. There were some things she needed to tackle with Lander. Like this whole magic thing: did he still believe she could do magic?

And his grieving for his brother, assuming he had finally

come to accept the fact that she couldn't bring him back. She sensed Mr. Stoic was this close to crumbling.

Lastly, she needed to deal with her lingering shock over how far Lander had let things go before interceding. Did he truly care about her or not?

They were now in the room she'd come to call home, and she was consuming her usual vegan lunch. Since that first night, she'd stuck with what was safe: veggies and fruits. The so-called kitchen in Lander's home was no more than a room with a sink and counter. No cooking instruments whatsoever.

Lander was sitting at the table, staring at nothing, silent. The crack in his veneer was getting wider. So was hers. She pushed her mostly empty plate away.

"Should we talk now?" she asked, breaking the thick silence between them.

"About what?"

"What happened back there. You saving my life. Yeah, that."

"You don't have to thank me. I did what was best for my pride. What was just."

Just.

That almost disappointed her. Did he do nothing for his own sake? Because he wanted it? Or because he was driven to by emotion? Outside of the naughty stuff, that was. "So you barged into my execution and proclaimed my innocence because it was the *right* thing to do?"

"Yes."

Hmmm. Where would she go from here?

She wanted to hear him say it was because the thought of losing her had driven him to a desperate act. A part of her believed there was more involved in his decision to step in than pure logic. Mostly because of the way the people in the courtroom had reacted. They were confused. Pissed. For a man who lived to maintain the respect of his pride members, it was a risky move to make. "So, do you still think I have magical powers?"

"No," he said coolly. "If you did, you would've saved your-self."

An arctic chill zigzagged through her body, making every hair on her nape stand on end. "Then you did let that trial go that far—to the point where seconds stood between life and death—just to test me?"

He didn't look at her. "I had to know the truth."

Okay, her mood had just turned sourer than a Sour Patch Kid. No, it wasn't sour, it was a freaking inferno of fury. Like Mount Vesuvius during the big eruption. All the emotions she'd bottled up inside since arriving at this godforsaken place came bursting to the surface. Whoosh.

Her heart started hammering against her breastbone, her hands shook, blood pounded in her ears.

In her head, she knew they'd talked about this after the trial, but for some reason her emotions overtook her anyway. She could see herself reacting and yet couldn't stop it.

"You let me be dragged through the city streets, humiliated, put through a sham of a trial, humiliated some more, hated and convicted, and nearly put to death just to see if I'd use some stupid magic to save my ass? You. Bastard."

"I had no other choice."

"No other choice? I should kick you in the 'nads." She jumped to her feet and ran to the door, throwing it open. Driven by confusion and rage, she sprinted down the hallway leading to the front door and shoved past two guards to leave the building.

Out in the city streets she dashed, among glaring, distrustful lion-people. She was instantly inspired to turn tail and head back inside. But she was too pissed to do that yet. So she just ran. And ran. And ran. Until the air heaving in and out of her lungs felt sharp as razors, and her legs were twitching, her head spinning.

She hated this place. She hated this story. And she especially hated that jerk of a heartless man she'd created. Many times, she and her critique partners had said if ever they were given the chance, they wouldn't want to live with the heroes in their favorite romance novels. They were too domineering. Controlling alpha assholes.

If this didn't prove that theory, nothing did.

That was it. Cats of all kinds sucked. She'd never look a feline in the face again with anything but contempt.

Men sucked, too. Especially dominating, controlling ones.

Maybe she'd even give up writing romance novels. She couldn't stomach the idea of writing another love story starring a manipulating jerk.

She'd known Lander had let her be arrested to see if she'd do her little magic act. He'd pretty much admitted that while she was still in the courthouse. And she'd suspected he'd let it go farther because of the magic. But to actually hear him admit it—that he'd waited until seconds before her death. And that he hadn't stopped the execution because he cared. . . .

How little she meant to him, that he'd be that willing to risk her life for some stupid, made-up magical power.

Her body was all jumpy and jittery, thanks to the adrenaline pumping through her bloodstream. She kept walking, distracting herself with thoughts of how she'd get herself out of this hellish place and back to the safe, relatively catfree reality. She was done with this. So, so done.

That damn book. She needed to finish writing Mia's stupid Egyptian god story. Which meant she had to go back to Lander's. Grrr.

Fine. She'd go back. She'd just ignore the jerk, spend all her time writing, until she'd finished the stupid book. Normally, it took her a few months to write a novel, but that was with real life getting in the way. If she just wrote from sunrise to sunset, she figured she could get it done in a few weeks. She could ignore one jerky lion-man for that long.

Doing a one-eighty, she ran smack dab into Adria. The one

who hadn't exactly been the nicest to her. "Are you following me?" she sneered, "Did Lander send you?"

"No. I was worried about you. In case you didn't realize it, the pride isn't exactly ready to welcome you with open arms. I was afraid you might run into someone who was willing to risk Lander's rage to eliminate the danger you represent."

Now, that was quite a one-eighty for Adria. Or was it? Had Cailey misread Adria's quiet demeanor as hostility? Believed the worst because she was so jealous? "I noticed your people have this thing against magic. Will you tell me what that's all about? To me—nothing personal here—but your anxiety's a little over-blown." Ironic, that coming from someone who'd once been so terrified of a five-pound kitten, she couldn't walk into a pet store without breaking out in hives.

Adria looked surprised. "Lander hasn't told you?"

"No, I guess he hasn't . . . had the chance."

"Then I will." Adria looped her arm through Cailey's and started leading her back home. And Cailey suddenly felt less alone, lonely, and despised. "We were once a gentle and peace-loving people. But we weren't content with what we had. We wanted more. Medicines to cure our sicknesses. Technologies to make our lives easier. So when a group of witches came to us, promising all those wonderful things and more, our king—Lander's father—signed a contract with them, not realizing what he'd done. The spell was cast, and a great many gifts were given to our people. Machines like nothing we had ever imagined. Drugs to cure the worst illnesses. But when the time came to pay the price for the spell, our king refused.

"The witches were enraged. Not only did they take back most of the gifts, but a second spell was cast. A dark spell, caus-ing our natures and our very souls to be split into two. The na-ture became the beast. Our soul became our human form, and we were damned to live this way for all eternity, one battling the other."

Fascinating. Cailey hadn't written this backstory yet, and it touched her in a strange and unexpected way. For one thing, it made her realize what a huge risk Lander took in speaking out on her behalf in the courthouse. It also made her realize what a huge risk he'd taken by bringing her here in the first place.

Aww, hell. She was starting to see there was probably more to this stuff than she'd seen before. Which meant she might actually need to talk to Lander and listen to what he had to say.

Shit. That was bound to be one painful conversation. And she was so not into pain, in any form—mental or physical.

"So, it's kind of a big deal that Lander used magic to bring me here?"

"A huge deal."

"And I'm kind of taking my life into my hands by walking the streets, since this tragedy didn't happen so long ago, and all magic is bad?"

"Exactly."

"Thanks for coming after me." Cailey inched a little closer to Adria's side as they walked, even more aware of the looks she was collecting on her way back to the relative safety of Lander's house. That guard, the one she'd fought past, she was now extremely grateful to see at his post. In fact, she even apologized to him as she approached.

He acknowledged her with a nod and stepped aside to let her into the building.

Adria left her when they located Lander in his lush library-slash-office off the main corridor. It was dark inside the room, save for the flickering gold light coming from the fire in the fireplace and the wavering illumination of a few candles positioned on the few horizontal surfaces that weren't filled with books.

The room made her feel cocooned and safe. A comfy couch sat in front of the fireplace, flanked by a couple of chairs. Lander was sitting in one of the chairs, his legs stretched out in front of him, ankles crossed, a glass in one hand. He lifted his head when she entered the room, and she saw something flare in his eyes. It was the closest she'd seen in a while to an outward display of emotion.

The air felt heavy, pressing down upon her shoulders, head, limbs. Her legs were a little wobbly, too, as she crossed to the sofa and settled into its uber-soft cushions. This time, she didn't speak. She waited.

For him to find the words that needed to be said.

He started with two words, two beautiful ones at that, "Forgive me," and she knew in her gut that this was the beginning of healing, for both of them.

14

If he didn't release the emotions building inside, Lander knew for a fact he'd do something he'd regret, something that could put every member of his pride at risk.

There was one person he wanted to trust, one person he wanted to risk sharing those emotions with.

Cailey.

His face a mask, hiding the grief that burned clear to his soul, he set down his wine, stood, and charged at her like a furious rhino. But to her credit, she didn't run. Instead, when he threw his arms around her and crushed her to him, she relaxed into his desperate embrace. And she didn't move, even though he was sure he'd held her that way for at least an hour. He simply dropped his head, burying his face in her fragrant hair, and let the tears come.

There were no sobs. In fact, his throat had closed so tightly, he struggled to breathe. There was simply a cascade of hot, salty droplets from his eyes. A silent river of torment, of loss, rage, and frustration. He didn't release her until the tears had dried up again.

She, however, didn't retreat as he'd expected. Instead, she

looped her arms around his neck and tipped her head back, reddened eyes narrowed to slits, lower lip trembling.

He cupped her precious face. "I don't deserve it, but I ask you to forgive me. I didn't release you only because of justice. . . . I . . ."

She pressed a fingertip to his mouth. "I understand now. I know why you needed to believe I could do magic. How desperate you were to have your brother back."

His head dropped until his forehead rested against hers. "But I should never have let my wants, no matter how overwhelming they were, override my respect for you." The agony of his loss gnawed at his insides. It was the most excruciating pain he had ever endured. Nearly crippling.

"But don't you see? That's why I can forgive you." She sandwiched his face between her soft hands and ducked down to meet his gaze. "Because what you did, you did out of love. For your brother. And then, you stood in front of your pride and said those things about me. . . . I had no idea how much that meant, not until Adria told me."

"I . . ." Goddess, could he say the words? "I need you, Cailey. I don't show emotion to anyone but you. I can't. I'm so alone. So lonely and closed off."

A tear ran down her cheek. "Lander. Oh, God." She tightened her hold on him, flattening her body against his. And of course, the beast within him reacted, sending currents of vibrating heat through his body.

Not now.

She swiped at the tears dripping from her jaw. "You trust me that much? To let me see you like this?"

"Yes." He swallowed once, twice, three times. He had never spoken the words he was about to say, to anyone. Not a lioness. Not his brother. No one. "I need a sanctuary. A safe place where I can let go and just . . . feel. I hadn't realized you were my sanctuary until the moment I learned I might lose you."

"I'm . . . overwhelmed." She sniffled, ran her hand across her face, rubbing away the glittering wetness gathering along her upper lip and cheeks. "No, make that totally and completely honored. A man as strong as you, trusting me with your secrets, your pain and vulnerabilities."

"If I don't, I know I'll make a mistake, act on my anger. That's what my enemy wants. I think that was why you were framed. It's all meant to be a distraction, a way to separate me from the rest of the pride. But I can't talk about this with anyone. About my frustration. My fears."

She nodded, compassion softening her expression, her eyes. "I know what you mean." She released his neck. One of her hands swept down his arm, then caught his hand. She pulled him toward the bed. "Everyone needs someone who understands them." She hesitated for a moment, and her gaze dropped for a split second before lifting again to his face. "I want to tell you about my stuff, too. I think you'll understand me better than anyone. I didn't realize how much I was searching, too. For someone who would understand me."

He sat beside her, grateful she'd decided to speak first. He wasn't ready to talk about Kir. The emotions were still too raw.

Cailey sucked in enough air to inflate one of those enormous parade balloons. Then she released it, slowly. She could hardly believe she was doing this—talking about the things she had long ago vowed to never mention to anyone again.

For her, talking about stuff did nothing to make the pain go away. It just brought the hurt closer to the surface, where she could feel it. That was why therapy hadn't worked. That was why she'd decided nothing would work.

But now she wasn't talking to cure herself. She was talking to put Lander at ease, to make herself vulnerable to him so he'd feel more comfortable doing the same with her. Not that he hadn't already. He'd cried. Sort of. There'd been lots of tears, but no sobs or words of grief.

It was still something. An enormous step in the right direction.

Granted, the step in the right direction would also carry them both to some major heartbreak when she was finally able to go home. Lander wasn't going to follow her there. He was the king, a ruler who loved his people more than anyone or anything.

But she couldn't think about that right now. For one thing, she still wasn't convinced she'd ever be able to leave this world. A tiny part of her didn't want to go.

God.

She swallowed the boulder that had taken residence in her throat in the last millisecond. "I want to tell you about the day I was attacked."

Lander nodded, his expression full of respect and compassion.

"My father and I had taken a trip out west when I was six, after the fire. This was supposed to be the trip of a lifetime, a celebration after a really rough year. We drove in a rented camper, one of those fancy numbers with the kitchen, bathroom, the whole nine yards. I looked forward to the trip for months."

The words were coming easier than they ever had. She was grateful. More than grateful. She was shocked.

"We were in Montana, hiking in a rocky area, and then all of a sudden, it was there, this enormous cat, hunched low, ears back."

Images from that day flashed through her mind, crystal clear, like a video montage. She felt her body tense, adrenaline pump through her veins, the hairs on her neck rise. Her heart thumped hard and heavy against her rib cage, and cold sweat coated her forehead. It was like she was living it all over again.

"I'm here, little one." He squeezed her hand, the sensation bringing her back to the now, back to safety.

She gave him a grateful look. "My father told me not to move, but I was too petrified to listen, especially when it looked at me with those weird eyes. I turned around and ran toward my dad, screaming, which I've come to learn triggered its hunting instincts. I felt the weight hit me from behind, the agony of sharp claws tearing at my skin. The crushing pain. The bite. My arm."

Tears were streaming down her face now as the memories flooded her mind. She'd always heard the body had no memory of pain. But that was a lie. Hers did. She felt all those sensations now, almost as intensely as the moment they'd happened.

"Afterward, it didn't matter what size the cat was; once I saw that look in its eyes, I panicked. They're predators by nature. I'm prey. Maybe it makes no sense when we're talking about a five-pound kitten but that's the way I see them."

He didn't say anything, just pulled her onto his lap, tightly against him. Strong hands caressed her back, cradled the back of her head. A voice rough with emotion murmured comforting words, "It's okay. It's over. I don't blame you for being afraid."

"The worst moment was when I realized that even my father—the man who controlled everything around him, including me—couldn't restrain a wild animal. I was completely at the beast's mercy, and no one was going to change that. A soulless animal would decide whether I lived or died. No one or nothing else."

"Then it released you."

"Yeah."

"It showed you mercy."

"Not hardly. I was a mess. I spent a week in the hospital, recovering. Broken bones. Lots of stitches. More scars. A concussion. I slammed my head on a rock when I fell down." She dragged in a gulp of air and blew it out. "Whew. I haven't talked about that in a long time. It's hard."

"Thank you for sharing with me."

"Yeah."

"Was that when the walls started going up?" he asked, quietly.

"No," she admitted, meeting his gaze. "The first bricks were laid a couple years before. When my mother died. One hurt after another built them up over the years. Things my father said or did, and sometimes the things he didn't say or do. A really messed-up relationship I had with my high school boyfriend. Later, a coworker I thought was my friend, who had me fired. Life's hard. I was homeless for a while. Alone. Scared."

They sat like that for a while, arms encasing each other, breathing in and out in synch, as if they were two pieces of one being. Slowly, gradually, the heat radiating from Lander's body warmed her chilled skin. The warmth seeped inside. She could feel it move through her bloodstream, pulse up and down her arms and legs. Eventually, it gathered in her belly and between her legs.

She wanted to hear what he'd been about to say. But now, thanks to the emotional roller coaster she'd just ridden, she also craved something more carnal, a physical release of all the emotion still bottled up inside.

A sensation buzzed up her spine, like a charge of electricity. And it seemed Lander felt it, too. He inhaled, audibly, and tightened his hold on her. His touch changed from a gentle, undemanding caress to a firm, hard possession. He nuzzled her neck, his searing breath tickling her skin and giving rise to a coat of goose bumps.

It was happening again; that chemistry was cooking up some serious heat. And she was grateful for the chance to just lose herself in a world of erotic sensation.

Even if it was only a temporary escape from the pain.

15

Ahhh, the way this man touched her. With just the right combination of soft sensuality and hard, carnal hunger. Cailey closed her eyes and just soaked it all in.

Sometimes his hands skimmed over her skin, like a soft breeze in summertime. Other times, they clawed and pinched. Spanked and held. She'd never realized how significant the way a man held her was, not until now.

Again, it was all about feeling a sense of possession, a loss of control and vulnerability. To her, those were as much a turn-on as a porn movie was to a man. Maybe more so.

It couldn't be an accident that Lander knew exactly what she craved in a lover. He was revealing things about herself—at least sexually—she'd never consciously acknowledged. Like how much she wanted to be dominated. How incredible pissed-off-slash-making-up sex could be. And how little control she really had over her emotions.

She'd thought she could be all he's-not-mine, he-can-do-whatever-he-wants.

She'd thought wrong.

This had progressed way beyond the point of empty sex, already. She had feelings for Lander. Some pretty hefty ones. Damn, these things happened fast!

Lander interrupted her philosophizing by flipping her onto her belly on the couch and giving her rear end a firm smack. The sound echoed through the room. The sting registered in her brain a millisecond later. In reaction, her spine tightened, tipping her pelvis down, into the cushion. A gush of heat surged to her pussy. She buried her face in the leather and whimpered. Then, because the burning had already faded, she rocked her hips the opposite direction.

Yes, she wanted more.

"You enjoy the feel of a hard hand on your ass, don't you, my kitten?"

"Yes," she mumbled.

"Hmmm?"

She turned her head. "Y-yes."

"How much?"

"More than I ever guessed."

"Ask me."

Oh God, this was a sexy, naughty game he was playing. She loved it. Loved, loved, loved! Why didn't real men do this stuff? Was it true what they said, that the heroes in books could never be real? That they were the figment of a woman's imagination, with only the good parts and none of the bad?

She'd like to think not. Lander wasn't perfect, although he was pretty great.

She inhaled, relishing the scents of leather and man she picked up from the couch's cushion. "Please, Lander, spank me again."

"What's it do to you, kitten?"

"Makes me really hot. Like crazy hot."

"Very well." There was a moment of silence, and Cailey tensed up all over, sure he'd smack her any second. Forget about the sweet agony of the strike; that anxious, tense anticipation—heart pitter-pattering—was cranking up the heat to epic proportions.

Once again, she heard the sharp slap before she felt the pain. Delicious. Stinging. Not so excruciating she couldn't take it. Nor too soft. What a wonder it was, to have a man who knew everything about his lover. The absolute wonder.

That was it. She was ruined for the average man. Forever. No other man could possibly compare to this one and his magical hands.

"Tell me, what are you thinking?" His hot breath tickled her nape. Teeth scraped the side of her neck. Once again, she found herself covered in goose bumps.

"I'm thinking you're absolutely the most amazing lover ever."

"Is that so?" There was laughter in his voice, and a little touch of something else. Flattery?

Every man loved to have his ego stroked. "I swear. Oh my God."

He rolled her over onto her back, turned her so her feet rested on the floor and wedged his hips between her legs. That bulge she was so fond of rubbed against her wet tissues. She was oh so grateful for the friction, although she would have preferred it if the bulge was unclothed, along with the rest of Lander. As great as those clothes looked on him—they reminded her of the leather gear she'd seen some men wear at the Renaissance festival—she was anxious to feel his velvet skin gliding over hers, his chest to her nipples.

"Mmmm." His voice was a low rumble, not unlike the heavy purr of a cat. And for once, she wasn't totally turned off by the similarity of the man to the beast. Rising to his feet, he leaned over her, lapped at her neck, slow licks from the crook of her shoulder to her earlobe.

He studied her for a moment with those bizarre golden eyes

of his, and she just lay there, a little bit breathless, a little bit dying, wondering when he'd gobble her up.

He was so powerful. So beautiful. So perfect. For her.

"Lander," she whispered.

"It's the beast." His voice was gravelly, lower than it had been a few seconds ago. "Trying to hold it in. Really trying hard. But that smell. Oh, goddess."

"Smell?"

"Your arousal." He dropped to his knees again. His head was at the level of her navel. He audibly inhaled, his nostrils flaring. "Damn, that scent." This time, when his gaze met hers, it was full of raw desire. Something wild flickered in his eyes. And then he pulled her knees wide apart.

She thanked every deity known to mankind as he parted her folds and licked her pussy. Slow swipes to her clit, one, two, three. Then four quick thrusts inside her vagina. Then he added his fingers into the action. Two of them, no, three. They thrust deep inside. He found that spot inside her, the one that made bursts of white light explode behind her eyelids.

Her heartbeat thumped in her ear, and she rocked her hips back and forth to the rapid beat. She'd been on the receiving end of oral sex in the past, but this, oh God. This was beyond . . . beyond. His tongue flickered over her clit with exactly the right amount of pressure, and at exactly the right pace.

Release came out of nowhere, like a bolt of lightning from a cloudless sky. Hot and powerful. It blazed a path from her pussy up to her face, singed her scalp, then did a U-turn and charged straight back down again.

But he didn't stop. He continued tormenting her hyper-sensitized tissues, throbbing, pulsing, with tongue and fingers. A second orgasm followed on the heels of the first. More pulsing heat.

Her brain was a molten puddle in her skull. Her bones had

softened to wet sponges. And every drop of wetness in her body had burned off, like water droplets on asphalt in August.

Minutes later, twitchy, giddy, sprawled on the couch, she opened her eyes to give him a grateful smile. He hadn't taken his pleasure this time. Had only given.

She knew why the second he leapt to his feet and staggered toward the door, one hand pressed to his chest, the other shielding his face from her.

"No." His voice was a low growl, not wholly human. "Not now. Reward." He threw himself at the door, but by the time he reached it, his fingers had shortened and arching claws were curling from their tips.

Cailey watched in horror, and fascination, as the man who had just given her the most amazing pleasure ever, turned into a lion.

Unlike the first time, she couldn't tear her eyes away. Instead, she watched his face. He'd closed his eyes, but she didn't need to see them to know how terribly agonizing the change was. It was there, plain to see on his face.

She could hear his bones cracking, snapping like dried twigs. And in her gut, she could practically feel the burn of his muscles twisting and stretching as his limbs changed shape, his torso lengthened. It was almost a relief when the thick fur coat sprung from his skin, like speeded-up video footage of grass growing. The thick tawny mane covered his neck and back of his head. His scalp tightened, pulling his ears up to the top of his head.

And then he was a lion. Standing very still in the middle of Lander's library. Its eyes opened, its gaze met hers. And she sensed Lander the man was inside there.

She wasn't as petrified as she'd been before, although it wasn't like she was ready to curl up next to it and take a nap either. There was still a little terror. Her fear took the form of a racing heart rate and shallow breathing that made her light headed.

But this time, she wasn't ready to run away, screaming. Even when he opened his mouth for a big, growly yawn. Or maybe that was a yawny growl?

Either way, she was scared, but not so bad she couldn't handle it. She stayed put, never taking her eyes off the lion. Off Lander. It—no, *he*—paced back and forth, and she wondered what he was thinking—*if* he could think.

He edged closer, hesitant, almost like he didn't want to scare her. Closer. Closer yet. Until—yikes!—he was within touching range, if she leaned forward and reached with her arm.

Most definitely within leaping range.

She'd seen how far that animal could jump. But jump he didn't. Or lunge. Or even bare his teeth. Instead, he just stood there with those yellow-gold cat eyes, watching her.

Did he want her to do something? Say something? Wasn't it enough that she wasn't freaking out, racing from the room, like she probably should be?

A memory of the cougar attack flashed into her mind, unwanted. Her body reacted. It felt like a kick to the gut. Oomph. Out went the air from her lungs, and she was gasping again, scrambling on the couch, clawing at the pillows.

This animal wasn't the cougar. And she wasn't about to be mauled. It was Lander. He wouldn't hurt her. He couldn't hurt her.

Dammit, why wasn't the self talk working?

Panic took over, sending her heart into a full-fledged gallop. Her stomach clenched. Nauseous. She couldn't breathe. Was going to pass out. Away. Escape. Now.

Sitting sideways, she scooted backward, feeling behind her for the couch's armrest.

Everything was okay. Those teeth weren't going to sink into her flesh, crush her bones. It was Lander. Lander, King of the Werekin. A character she created.

He couldn't hurt her.

Fuck, why couldn't she talk herself out of the panic?

At the edge of the couch now, she did a fanny spin, swinging her legs over the side. They barely supported her weight as she sidestepped around the desk, her attention zigzagging from the lion—still standing where he was—and the door. With each step she took, she expected him to rocket her way, all sharp claws and teeth and hair and muscle.

But he didn't. And then she was in the hallway. Alone. Safe. It took a while for her hands to stop shaking, her heart to stop racing. But slowly, the terror eased.

What a fucking chicken. She shook her head. It was hopeless. Absolutely freaking hopeless. She'd never get over her irrational fear. Why? Because it *was* irrational. And by definition irrational meant unreasonable. Unable to be reasoned with. Beyond her control. And thus beyond her ability to change.

Mia had been so wrong. *Nice try, girl.*

So much for Mia's grand plan for curing them all.

Cailey heaved a disgusted sigh and resigned herself to the fact that she'd be living with this stupid fear for the rest of her life. The trauma had simply been too much. The scars too deep. At least in her case.

Gosh, what if Mia and Lisa had been kidnapped into their stories as well? She couldn't help the little (evil) laugh that burst from her throat. Now that would be some poetic justice, particularly for Mia, Miss Freud-Wannabe. Was she having sex in water with her Egyptian god? Right this very minute? She bet Mia was just about dying, if so.

Ha. And ha! Serves you right.

And Lisa. She wondered if her two hunky ex-cops were running their guns all over her.

In a much better mood, she inched open the door.

Lander was nowhere to be seen. Bummer. He was probably as disappointed in her as she was in herself. He'd done everything—outside of immediately changing back into a man—to make it easy for her. Still, she couldn't handle it. Couldn't stand being in the same room with him.

And the worst part was, he hadn't talked to her about his brother, the pain of his loss.

Oh, that just sucked! She'd felt so special when he'd told her she was his refuge, the person he wished to share all his secrets with.

Maybe he'd decided she wasn't strong enough. Unworthy.

16

Jafari cradled her in his arms, feeling the life draining from her
body, yet powerless to stop it. Lost in agonizing grief, and blind
with rage, he cursed all creation.

Again, that which he'd made had turned on him. But this
time it had been much worse. Because now, he wasn't isolated
from the world. He was a part of it. He'd willingly stepped into
his own creation and allowed it to become a part of him, to
change him.

And look what had happened.

He loved this woman. And like everything he'd ever loved,
he was destined to lose her.

—From *Dark Surrender*, a work in progress by Cailey
Holm, writing as Mia Spelman.

It was perfect.

Lander gave the lioness an approving nod, accepting the garment she'd offered. Cailey would be thrilled with his gift. Or so
he hoped. He did know her in the most intimate way, but even
he had doubts when it came to her personal tastes in some

things, clothing included. But he knew one thing she would greatly appreciate. And as much as he would like to take her on her "shopping" trip as she was, he knew that was not practical. For one thing, he knew he would not appreciate the other males in his pride seeing her completely unclothed.

No, she was his. Today, he would mark her. In public.

He found her in his room, waiting patiently. He'd had the lionesses bring her food and drink, so she wouldn't be hungry or thirsty. He had plans for her. Lots. Starting with their trip to the marketplace.

Cailey could hardly call the translucent nightie Lander presented her—gorgeous as it was—appropriate streetwear. But since she'd taken one jaunt through town a few days ago in a robe no less transparent, she knew females in this world tended to dress on the skimpy side. Actually, a more fitting descriptor might be slutty.

Regardless of the fact that women outnumbered men at least ten to one, it seemed the males dictated the females' dress code.

At least she wouldn't be frying in the heat. During the day, this world was hot, hot, hot. Like, desert hot. The air was dry, thankfully. So at least she wasn't feeling like she was walking in a steam room as they left the cool interior of Lander's home.

She'd been here for almost a week now. And not once had she seen a motorized vehicle, a computer, a television, microwave. No power wires, phone wires, or electronic appliances. Also interesting, she noticed as they walked—this time, they were taking it at a much more leisurely pace—the streets, building exteriors, air, were so clean. Everything smelled fresh, like mown grass and spring flowers.

Perhaps the scaled-back lifestyle had its benefits, although after about a half hour of walking, she was totally ready for some motorized transportation. A moped, even, would be acceptable.

At least this time she wasn't being glared at as she walked down the street, although she didn't miss the looks Lander gathered from his citizens, some wary, some much more friendly. Women and children, and the occasional man, greeted him as they walked. It took much, much longer to get from point A to point B than it ever would have if she was walking on her own.

Not that she was complaining. No sirree. This girl hadn't spent a minute in the gym in years. As a result, she was hurting a bit after a few blocks. The frequent stops for Lander to acknowledge his loving citizens gave her a chance to catch her breath.

But soon enough, they reached what she guessed was their destination and she quickly realized the marathon walk had been worth it.

Oh, the joy! It was like an enormous outdoor craft fair, with booths full of gorgeous clothing, food, jewelry, decorative items for the home. And the best part: she could simply take whatever she wanted. With only one condition. She could only accept what she genuinely needed.

Lucky for her, the needs list was looooong.

It was a dream come true for a girl who'd never gone on a limit-free shopping spree.

She started with clothes. She needed everyday clothes, and one or two special outfits for going out. Oh, and some warmer things for the cooler temperatures at night. Then she moved on to shoes, jewelry to coordinate with the special-event outfits, and some flowers to cheer up Lander's uber-masculine décor.

Lander just stood by her side, smiling, with some adorable little twinkles in his eyes. Ever since he'd broken down and cried, he'd shown more emotion around her—both good and bad. Just like now. He looked . . . genuinely happy.

And she was feeling genuinely happy.

He hadn't exactly talked about things—his brother's death, the trial, his feelings about her. But she knew in her heart how he felt. She was patient, was willing to wait until he was ready to talk.

Finally, Lander took her to a special shop at the very end of the row. Inside, she found a plethora of bondage gear, whips, paddles, leather restraints, clothing, blindfolds, and masks. Lander went straight for the collars.

Some were utilitarian—wide, black leather, with a single silver ring in the front. Others were more decorative, with pretty jewels dotting the surface and strings of beads draping from the bottom. Lander reached for one of those.

It was absolutely gorgeous. The leather collar was about an inch and a half wide, split vertically into the center so that the halves were held together by a large silver bejeweled circle at the center of her throat. From the top of the circle dangled three strings of clear crystals, and from the bottom three strings hung a smaller crystal-encrusted circle. On either side of that circle were another five strings of crystals.

He took the collar from the shop owner and, turning, placed it on her neck, saying, "No one will mistake you for my concubine again. You are my sanctuary. My blood. My soul. And my friend."

"Lander." She'd been collared, claimed. Lander cared for her. He'd said those sweet words, "My soul." That meant everything. It made this the most perfect moment in her life. "Thank you."

It took three men, in addition to Lander, to cart all her goodies home. She scrambled to put them all away, then enjoyed an early dinner with Lander, hoping he would be taking her to the dungeon for some one-on-one time afterward. He'd already warned her he needed to leave home a little later, to "handle some important things," whatever that meant. She assumed it had to do with his brother's death and the whole winning-the-pride-back thing that he clearly hadn't fully accomplished yet. He hadn't told her, but she knew many of his people saw her as a threat, and by default that made him suspect as well.

How long would it take for one man to overcome an entire culture's fear and prejudice? Longer than it took her to conquer her own?

God, if that was the case, they were both in for a long, frustrating struggle.

When she finished her meal, Lander pulled her into his lap and told her about his life as a prince. Quietly, he recounted the story of the time when he had foolishly gone outside the city walls, against his father's command, and nearly paid the dearest price of all for his mistake.

One brother dead. His other brother, Kir, had been severely injured, both protecting him against an attack. At the time, Jag had been a trusted friend of their father's. But from then on, the brothers knew who their enemy was. There was nothing Lander could do for Jared. But Lander had vowed to someday pay Jag back for what he had done.

He had never found the opportunity to do so.

This time when Lander cried, he wasn't silent. He held her and wept for the brother he had never thanked. The favor he could never return. The hatred he had for his enemy. And the grief he felt at the loss of Jared and his parents, mother and father both victims of a disease that had taken too many lives over the years.

Finally, when the tears had dried, Lander eased Cailey from his lap and stood, announcing they would be heading to the dungeon within an hour. He expected her to use the time to prepare herself for him.

Slipping into the role of newly collared sex slave, she said, "Yes, master," and solemnly headed for the bathroom for a soak in the tub. Within minutes, Adria and Nevan, her maids, rushed in to help her, baskets of grooming aids in their hands.

It took a little getting used to, having two women overseeing the grooming of her most private parts, including *there*. But the uber-smooth skin was worth it in the end. They helped her out of the bath, wrapped her in a thick towel, and then sat her in a chair and began the painstaking task of fixing her hair.

Drying and curling hair without the aid of electric tools was something of a challenge. And since Cailey's was thicker than the average girl's, hers was probably even harder. But they managed, with the use of the fire bellows and a funky curling iron they heated over the fire. Some makeup, the collar put back in place, and she was set free to check out the results in the bathroom mirror.

She hadn't looked that good ever, not even for her high school prom. And a week of vegan meals was doing wonders for her figure. Whenever she was able to go home, she was tempted to take her maids along. They worked freaking miracles.

And she just might make the vegan thing permanent.

While she was admiring Adria's and Nevan's handiwork, a messenger, a female she didn't recognize, arrived, announcing Lander was awaiting all three of them in the dungeon.

Her heart did a happy little hop in her chest. She had a feeling this time would be special, different from the others—not that she was complaining about her more recent experience. Heck no.

She proceeded to the dungeon, Adria and Nevan following behind her, a naked-women parade that would have been somewhat comical in any other setting. But in this one, it was nothing but exciting, thrilling.

Cailey's heart wasn't beating, it was fluttering. Her fragrant skin was quickly becoming slick with nervous sweat and her hands were trembling just enough to annoy her. She hid them behind her back, fingers laced, as she entered the dungeon.

Lander was standing in the rear of the room, facing the door, totally nude—just the way she liked him—with the exception of a couple of thick leather bands circling his biceps. His hair was mussed, his chin and cheeks stubbled with blond whiskers, giving him a wild, dangerous look.

And his eyes, those golden eyes, were gobbling her up.

Man, she was one lucky girl. She wanted to giggle but she didn't. Instead, she followed the lead of her two maids, who were now flanking each side of her, dropping to their knees.

She'd never had a master-slash-slave relationship in real life, but she'd read about them. Granted, her reading was limited to fiction. Probably not the most reliable source for realistic portrayal of anything, BDSM included. But at least it was something. And it had taught her that a collared slave was expected to act like a slave.

On her knees she went, and she dropped her head and placed her shaky hands on her thighs, mirroring Adria and Nevan's posture.

For the briefest of moments, she wondered what the other women were still doing in the dungeon. She hoped this visit wouldn't be a repeat of the last, with Lander being serviced by them. She might (still) have absolutely no claim on the man. He could fuck whomever he wanted. But the possessive side of her (the one that had never existed before Lander) did not like to share. Period.

While she contemplated an adequate plan for dealing with him doing stuff with her servants, he approached.

Good grief, he was huge, particularly when she was on her knees, so low to the ground.

And the adjective applied to both him as a whole and certain parts of his anatomy.

She was getting some of that! Yeah. Who cared about those other girls? They were nothing to him. Had he cried on their shoulders? Listened while they confessed their worst fears? No. That was because he might share the physical part of himself with them, but he reserved the other parts—the ones that mattered—for her.

"Cailey."

She loved the way he said her name, the way his voice dropped to a husky murmur by the end. She lifted her head. "Yes, master?" And she realized at the same time that she was falling in love with the man.

"Today, I want you to learn how to serve me properly, like your servants have learned. I am no longer demanding your submission in order to gain any magical powers. Instead, I'm doing this for you. I sense you need to submit to me, that you are curious and maybe a little unsure of some things."

"I am." Was he reading her mind or what?

"I will not harm you, but I will push you, partially because the beast drives me to. And partially because it's what you are seeking." He motioned to Adria and Nevan. "They will show you. Do what they do, follow their lead."

She nodded.

Lander left the room, leaving her to wonder what exactly he had in mind today. Would he fuck Adria and Nevan first, showing her how he wanted her to behave? Would it end up becoming a foursome, with all three women serving him in some fashion? She felt her expression darkening.

Then, Lander swept into the room with not one but two beautiful men trailing behind him.

As if her curiosity hadn't been piqued before! More guys! Naked ones! Nude, yummy men.

Would it be one for each girl? Or all three for her? Boy, did that last thought make her feel naughty. And more than a little guilty.

A heat wave zoomed up to her cheeks. The skin was scorching hot by the time Lander looked her way.

She decided she wouldn't kill Lisa when she got home, regardless of that earlier nonsense.

"This is Calder and Slade, two key members of our pride," Lander introduced, speaking directly to Cailey. "I have marked you as my own. These men will only do what I allow them to. There is nothing to fear."

Ha! She wasn't exactly scared, but she didn't bother telling Lander that. She figured if he got a smidge closer, he'd figure that out pretty quickly, with that uber-sensitive nose of his and all.

Lander walked around her, stopping directly behind her. The other two men approached the ladies on either side of her, their ruddy, erect cocks bobbing as they walked. She sucked in a deep breath as they crowded her and the two maids, their groins right there, a little above eye level. The scent of man filled her nose. It was by no means a bad thing.

"Service me," Calder growled, and Nevan opened her mouth, taking his thick cock deep into her throat. Cailey literally sat there, transfixed, as her maid was fucked in the mouth.

She'd watched her share of porn, and she wasn't ashamed to admit that what she'd seen was titillating ... for about five minutes. And then it became repetitive, boring. This, unlike watching porn, was live action. Titillating it was. Would it become boring? She had to say, these two man-lions were way better looking than the goony guys starring in the porn she'd watched. Yummy.

Look at those abs. Chiseled perfection. Legs bulging with muscles and smooth skinned. Her gaze slowly climbed north, halting at a chest that almost (but not quite) rivaled Lander's.

The other man, Slade, cleared his throat, and Cailey swiveled her head to see what he was going to do.

He motioned Adria to a nearby kneeler, and she got all giddy, expecting she'd be in for a hot show. She could imagine herself in the place of either woman, taking Lander's thick rod into her mouth, swirling her tongue round the ridge circling the thick head, or bending over the kneeler, muscles tense, waiting to see what he'd do next.

While Calder continued to fuck Nevan's mouth, mere inches from Cailey's own, the other man found himself a dildo and proceeded to torment Adria until she was literally quivering with the need for release.

Cailey got a little quivery, too, especially when Lander squatted behind her, his bulk crushing against her back, and reached around her sides to fondle her breasts and toy with her nipples. Then he nibbled her neck and she couldn't help whimpering.

This was the strangest, most erotic situation she'd ever been in. Oh, God, what this man could do with his fingers.

I love you, Lisa! Big kiss to you! Mwah!

Sadly, Calder decided to take the action a little farther away from Cailey and Lander. His cock escaped Nevan's mouth with a naughty little pop, and he helped her to her feet, leading her to the bench Lander had used the first time he'd brought Cailey to the dungeon.

That bench held some terrific memories for her. Oh yes, it did. And she saw it was going to hold even more after tonight.

Her blood sizzled as she watched Calder fasten Nevan into the restraints. He, too, went for a dildo, and whenever the maid failed to do what he asked, she was tormented to the brink of insanity.

These man-lions were beyond cruel. But in a most wonderful way.

A moan from the direction of the kneeler drew Cailey's attention back to the other couple. She watched as Slade dragged the kneeler, repositioning it so that Cailey had a clear view of Adria's backside. Then he parted Adria's ass cheeks and oh so slowly pushed that dildo into her anus.

Cailey gasped.

Lander slid a hand down her stomach, then cupped her sex, teasing her slit with his fingers.

She dropped her head back and let out a strangled little mewling sound.

"Mmmm, how wet you are, kitten. Open those eyes. Watch. Because you will be next."

She'd closed her eyes? Oh. So she had. The images inside her head had been so clear, she could have sworn they were open.

But when she did indeed open them, she discovered the kneeler had been abandoned. Adria was now being bound in ropes, her breasts bulging from the tension of her restraints. More ropes circled her waist and arms. Slade lifted the bound woman onto a table, parted her legs and then, standing at the edge, thrust roughly into her pussy.

It was Cailey who cried out.

Both maids were being fucked now, one sitting upright on the bench, legs stretched wide apart, the other lying on her back. Cailey watched them from behind, watched the muscles of the men's back, shoulders, legs, and asses clench as they drove into the women, over and over.

"Do you like watching my men fuck, Cailey?" Lander whispered in her ear. "You're so hot and wet. Are they doing that to you? Or am I?"

"Both," she answered, breathless. She dragged in a ragged gulp of air and let it out in a huff. She could swear the air in the room had thinned, the oxygen depleted somehow.

Her eyes shuttered out the erotic scene before her, cocooning her in a world of swirling colors and carnal heat. Lander's fingers were slowly driving her insane, caressing her folds, teasing her clit, breaching her opening but not filling her. It was agony, ecstasy. Both. She didn't want it to end and yet she did.

Lander's fingers stilled. "Open your eyes and watch."

Now, when she opened them, she discovered the women were off to one side and the two men were fondling each other's cocks. They kissed, their open mouths positioned just so she could see their tongues stroking, stabbing.

Two big, strong men. Touching each other like that. Oh, God, it was nuclear-reactor hot.

She'd been to a gay bar, once. She'd seen gay men kissing. But for some reason, this was different. These men projected an aura of raw power and strength, no doubt due to their underlying feline nature. So it was fascinating watching two very strong, very masculine men handle each other sexually.

As well as blistering hot.

The sizzle in her blood upped another hundred degrees or so as she watched them stroke each other's cocks. Slow motions, hands cupped, gliding up and down thick, hard shafts. Her mouth watered watching that sight. Her head went all floaty, too. And her pussy—empty!—pulsed with hunger.

When, oh when would Lander fuck her?

His fingers started exploring again. One hand went to work on her left nipple, tugging the aching tip then pinching. A bolt of pleasure-pain zigged through her body. Once again, she heard herself gasp and moan.

Lander called to the maids, who rushed to him. They helped her stand on legs as wobbly as molten gelatin and led her to the sex bench.

"Watch them," Lander whispered into her ear, motioning toward the two kissing men.

She nodded, and while Adria and Nevan strapped her legs wide, she watched Slade bend over and take Calder's thick cock in his round, muscled ass. She literally whimpered when she watched Calder's rod drive into Slade's hole with the first thrust. She could swear her heart was about to bust through her rib cage. And the fever burning her up was probably enough to cause permanent brain damage.

Enough was enough. She was ready to come. She had to come. And by God, Lander was going to let her come.

"Please, Lander." She wasn't above pleading. Not at this point. She was beyond caring about the whole role-playing thing now. Only one thought echoed through her head. Over and over. *Relief. Now.*

"Soon, kitten. Watch first."

She wanted to cry. She wanted to scream. Instead, she swallowed the roar of frustration that sat like a bowling ball in her throat and focused on the amazing sight before her.

Why was it so important for her to watch? As beautiful and arousing as this was, what was the point?

In about ten stuttering heartbeats, she learned what the point was. The two men—still fucking—started to change, just like Lander did. Thick, tawny hair covered their bodies. Their limbs shortened. A darker mane sprouted over their necks and shoulders and then she was watching two male lions fucking.

The one on top bent its head down and bit the side of the other's neck. A teeth-rattling roar echoed through the room, and Cailey's blood turned cold, despite Lander's touches to her pussy. Her entire body went tight as fear swept through her, displacing the desperate erotic hunger.

She turned her head, shutting out the terror, hoping the image of those enormous cats would fade if she closed her eyes.

Lander knelt before her, teasing her anus with a fingertip, her vagina with another. "Keep watching."

That was the last thing she wanted to do. But when she turned her head again and forced open her eyelids, Lander rewarded her with a single stroke of a finger in her pussy. A single bolt of heat blazed through her.

"Yes, that's it. Watch and you'll get your reward. It's almost over."

"Just don't leave me."

"I promise I won't. As long as you don't look away." He parted her labia and lapped her pussy, starting at the bottom and moving up toward her clit. Slow, lazy swipes with his tongue. That produced slow, yummy waves of warmth in her stomach.

This was weird beyond words but who was she to complain? She was watching a scene out of Wild Kingdom—not exactly the vision of her erotic fantasies—while Lander performed oral sex on her.

And shock of all shocks, she was loving it.

The lion on top stopped moving, and she wondered if they were done. It climbed off the back of the other and the two turned to look at her. She tensed again, but then Lander thrust two fingers inside her, filling her pussy, and the frigid chill of fear was promptly replaced with warm wanting.

So what if two lions were in the room with her? She didn't have to worry about them. She could just pretend they weren't there and enjoy the magic Lander was performing on her body. Yes, that's what she would do.

She stared blindly at one of the lions while letting Lander's tongue, lips, and hands drive her completely wild. Then Adria handed him a small butt plug and a bowl of lubricant. In her position, her anus was accessible. She hadn't forgotten about his promise to train her to take him *there*.

Her pussy tightened around his fingers and she felt a rush of liquid heat coating them as he slowly dragged them out and then thrust them back in.

His moan was more a low rumble than a human vocalization. But it was sexy all the same. So was the sensation of him massaging her anus in slow, gentle circles.

"That's it. Relax, kitten." He continued to stimulate the outside of her anus while licking her pussy. He fucked her vagina with his tongue then worked up to her clit and flicked the tip of his tongue back and forth. The little jolts of pleasure from the stimulation to her clit only added to the pleasure of his intimate touches to her ass.

He pushed the tip of the plug into her anus. It slipped inside and instantly, the ring of muscles tightened, pushing it back out.

She quivered and tried to relax, but even though she'd had a finger, a butt plug, and even a dildo in her anus a few times, she wasn't completely used to things going in instead of out. She did know one thing, though. The sensation of having something inside her rectum was intensely erotic. Naughty.

"That's it. Relax and open to me, like you're opening your pussy." Lander continued to massage her anus and once again he pushed the tip into her anus.

She relaxed and the slender plug slid deeper, deeper. Ohh-hhh. It was a wonderful thing. She didn't want her body to push it back out.

"Yes. Now, I'm going to fuck you."

Those words were the best she'd heard, ever.

Lander shuffled forward on his knees, his hips between her thighs, placed his hands on either side of her waist, and slowly inched his thick cock into her pussy. His eyes, those molten golden eyes, met hers.

She swore that if pleasure could kill a girl, she was on her way to a swift—and most wonderful—death.

In and out, oh so slowly. She felt every wonderful inch of him. And the added fullness in her rectum added another layer of pleasure to what was already one of the most amazing moments in her life.

His gaze drilled her with the same intensity of his cock's intimate probes. Instantly, she felt vulnerable and open. Once again, she sought the isolation of the darkness. She closed her eyes, but he growled, "Don't shut me out."

She dragged her heavy eyelids back up and met his possessive stare. She literally saw those eyes go hard as his pleasure stole his control. His expression turned feral. Jaw tight. Eyes slitted. Face flushed. The muscles of his shoulders rippled beneath his smooth skin. The struggle she sensed—man against beast—only spiked her desire to even greater heights.

His fucking grew more possessive, more demanding. Instead of taking her as a man, he pumped into her hard and fiercely, like a beast. And her body reacted to the change. Just like that she was trembling, hot and cold at the same time, and on the verge of orgasm.

Yes, oh yes. This was what she craved, what she had to have. This raw, wild fucking by a man who was barely human.

She let herself go, let the heat of her orgasm sweep her away. As she sighed in gratitude, Lander's voice joined hers in a duet, his guttural groan a compliment to her higher-pitched moan.

Oh, yeah, that was one song that she wouldn't mind playing in her head over and over again!

17
_____

She was surrounded. By lions. With claws that could tear her innards out. Teeth that could crush her bones.

And yet, she wasn't terrified out of her mind.

Had Lander's brand of positive reinforcement worked? Had Mia, the wannabe shrink, been right?

Right after she'd come back to earth after that ahhh-mazing orgasm, she'd opened her eyes to find all four of their fellow dungeon inhabitants had turned into lions. They sat on either side of her, the males on her right, the females on her left. Their golden eyes, the same shade as Lander's, focused on her.

One of the males batted a paw at her leg, which was still bound, and shock of all shocks, she wasn't ready to jump out of her skin.

One of the females leaned against her other leg, and much to her amazement, she smiled at the sensation of warm fur gliding down her shin.

Lander was literally purring as he withdrew his cock from her quivering flesh. "In their eyes, you are their queen."

That was a little strange to think about, since not long ago every man, woman, and child in this place had considered her some kind of threat to their lives. Now she was queen? Talk about a complete turnaround in the Gallup Polls. Things sure did change quickly around here.

"I'd be content not to be lunch."

Lander's chuckle literally bounced around inside her chest. It was the strangest kind of tickly sensation, and she almost started giggling.

"I promise you, no one wants to eat you . . . except for me." His wicked eyebrow waggle let her know he was not speaking in literal terms. "Are you okay?" Dropping onto his heels, he worked at one of her ankles, releasing it from the cuff.

"Yeah. I am. I really am."

Then one of the males gave a little roar, and she flinched. Her heart kicked into high speed and she felt her body stiffen.

Oh no. She'd spoken too soon. Damn it all.

"Relax, kitten." Lander massaged the sole of her foot. It was heaven.

She closed her eyes and concentrated on the pleasant sensation of strong male hands working out the tension in her foot. Ankle. Calf. He was moving higher, and she wasn't complaining.

"That's it. Concentrate on breathing slowly."

She concentrated, but not on breathing. Instead, she focused on his voice, his touch, the lingering scent of sex on her skin. Those were a whole lot more pleasant than thoughts of inhaling and exhaling.

It worked. The pace of the thudding heartbeats slowed a bit. And the lump of heavy concrete congealing in her stomach was breaking up.

One of the lions rubbed against her again, and she felt that heavy lump in her stomach lurch into her throat.

"Relax." Lander's hands smoothed up her thighs, fingers splayed. He rubbed at the knots forming in the tops of her legs, making them tremble. "Think of them as your protectors. Your guardians."

Guardian lions, not guardian angels? Well, hell. Why not?

While she struggled with some mental gymnastics, Lander freed her other leg. Then he went for her wrists.

"You're free now, and I'm here. They want you to touch them. To acknowledge them. Can you?"

Ack. She hadn't bolted for the door when they'd gone all kitty on her. Wasn't that good enough? Did she really have to touch one? "How about next time," she suggested, eyes still closed tightly. This was so much easier to deal with if she didn't look.

"Please, kitten. Don't do this because I'm asking. Or because they want you to. Do it because you can and you want to. This is it, your chance to overcome the fear that's been shackling you tighter than any restraint I could possibly put on you."

He was so right about that. And she could admit she was sick and tired of letting some stupid fear—and a handful of unpleasant physical sensations associated with that fear—hold her down.

She had wanted to be a vet once. Yes, she'd been a kid then, and kids do dream of becoming lots of things when they're little. Spacemen. Firemen. Ice skaters. Princesses. But her wish to be a veterinarian had been much more than a passing fancy. Her father had been a vet, and she'd watched him work. Admired what he was able to do for animals. As long as she could remember, that was what she'd wanted to do, too.

Even now, the ambition to work with animals was there, inside her, screaming for satisfaction. A need, more than a wish.

She'd even taken several years of school, but the first day of her internship she'd dropped out. Her father was so disappointed, she was too ashamed to show her face to him. Her life's center had been yanked away, her hopes, everything. She'd literally reeled with the pain and confusion.

Without her lifelong dream, what was there to look forward to?

This was the first step. If she could get past her fear of cats, then she could go back, finish. Finally have her life back. Go and face her father, and show him she was the strong woman he'd raised her to be.

Maybe Lander had kidnapped her against her will, but her fear had held her hostage a whole lot longer than he had. No doubt about it, her phobia was the most merciless master she'd ever submitted to.

No longer!

Eyes still shut, she reached to her right, knowing one of the female lions was over there somewhere. Her hand met with something warm and soft. Fur over bone. A head, she supposed.

God, all she wanted to do was yank her hand back. But she wouldn't let herself. No. No, no, no.

She let her fingers travel over the top of the lioness's head, once again concentrating on pleasant images. Lander. Naked. That one was a winner.

A pleasant flush of warmth eased the chill of her fear. Hmmm . . . maybe this wouldn't be so bad.

"That's the way. Yes." Lander continued to encourage her with a soft voice, prodding her to move closer to the lions, touch all of them, let them crowd around her, nuzzling her legs with their huge heads. Over time, she managed to open her eyes.

She scratched them behind the ears. So soft. A low, rumbling humming sound filled the room, both from Lander and the other lions as well.

Finally, she nodded. She breathed easily. There'd been no panic. No terror. The cycle had been broken.

She was elated. No, beyond elated. She couldn't imagine anything feeling better than this. She was free!

Unable to stop them, Cailey let the tears gush from her eyes. She'd long ago given up on getting over her phobia. Let herself become content to let her fear dictate her career. Where she lived. What side of the sidewalk she walked on.

For a person who was terrified of felines, the world was fraught with danger. The streets around her house. Her friends' and relatives' homes. Even the local bookstore she used to haunt, whose aged owner decided to bring her ancient tabby in to keep her company.

Could it really have been so simple?

"Oh my gosh. I think I'm over my fear. Thanks to you."

Lander looked proud. "Excellent."

"Is it gone for good?"

"I hope so." His smile was blindingly brilliant in a California beach dude kind of way. Deeply tanned skin against uber-white teeth. Could a man be more gorgeous? Seriously? "I have to leave you for a little while."

Now, that was a definite downer. She'd already come up with some ideas on how she wanted to celebrate her newly cured status. It wasn't every day a girl got over something as huge as a lifelong phobia.

And yet she knew that Lander didn't leave her unless he had to. It was probably some super-important lion king thing he had to do.

She supposed the celebrating could wait until later. She wanted to get in some writing anyway. She was suddenly inspired to write Mia's big phobia Black Moment, when she'd finally face up to her fear of water.

That was going to be a fun scene to write. Full of tension and deep emotion. Terror. Awe. Discovery. Maybe even a little sex.

Uh huh. She was inspired.

* * *

He finally had them where he wanted them. Those fucking panthers would pay for what they'd done. For attacking him in his own fucking home. And for killing his brother and trying to frame Cailey.

"I'm still having a hard time believing Adria was a part of this." Bourne said.

Lander's body was so tight, his scalp burned. Every muscle pulled to its limit. His heart hammered against his breastbone. His blood burned his veins. He could literally taste the hatred, bitter and acidic, in his mouth. "Me, too. But I gave her a chance to explain, and she didn't deny anything."

"How exactly did you find out she was the one who'd framed Cailey?"

Lander clenched and released his fists as he walked, staring straight ahead. "It took a while to piece together the clues. Obviously, it had to be someone who moved freely in and out of my home. Someone I'd never suspect. Someone who both had easy access to Cailey and her personal belongings and looked enough like her to pass for her on the street. Adria was all those things . . . and, as it turns out, a lioness who had once believed she would be my queen."

At his side, Dryce said, "I'm sorry. She's served you for so long. I never would have suspected her."

Lander looked back, over his shoulder, and then continued forward. There was no room for error today. No more blood would be shed. No lives lost but the panthers'. Had he missed anything? "I wanted Adria to deny it when I confronted her. I needed her to. But she didn't. She just wept and asked me to show her mercy by granting her a swift death. No trial."

He'd done just that, and a lioness he had genuinely loved and respected lay in the desert, her carcass picked over by scavengers.

Those fucking panthers would be joining her soon.

The building before them was a ramshackle structure, ravaged by time and the elements. Years ago, this place had looked very different, the house and barn huddling in the center of a crop of towering trees. But after the curse and the subsequent banning of all magic, his pride had abandoned the buildings outside of the city, seeking new lives within the city's walls. Hundreds of homesteads like this one dotted the landscape now, a sad reminder of the life his pride had lost.

Hidden behind a wide oak, he motioned to his men, calling them forward. One with Dryce on his right, Bourne and another two on his left. "Are the men in back ready?" he asked Dryce.

Dryce nodded. "They should be. Although we can't move into position until they give us the signal."

"How many do we have?"

"Four more at the rear of the building," Bourne answered.

"Excellent." He was well covered. In addition, he had the element of surprise working for him, since the panthers were feeding and wouldn't be ready for an attack.

His plan had worked. It had just taken some patience. He'd planted the prey, knowing the nature of the panther. Once they'd hunted, they would move their kill somewhere they felt safe to feed.

His men had followed them here, and then Dryce had sent for him, letting him know it was time.

Adrenaline pounded through his body as they closed the distance between themselves and the building. Lander leaned against an exterior wall. "Things are such a mess right now. It'll be one thing taking these fuckers down. But if I'm going to sleep at night, I need to stop Jag—for good."

"He's slimier than a slug, but I have some men working on him. We'll get him." Bourne rested a hand on Lander's shoulder, as if he felt the need to comfort him, and Lander realized he might be showing some vulnerability even now.

Had his relationship with Cailey changed him? Made him

more willing to show his weaknesses to others? That could be bad or good, depending.

Bourne continued, "You still have the support of most of the pride, and now that it's been confirmed that Cailey had nothing to do with our brother's death, she's actually gained a lot of ground with the lionesses."

"Good." Lander nodded. "It bothered her, the hatred she sensed from them. She's sensitive in that way, which was why I had such a hard time believing she'd kill anyone in the first place."

"You were right." Bourne caught a flash of light and nodded. "Okay, it's time. Ready to take down a couple of panthers?"

Senses alert, body poised, Lander ran around to the door. "Yes. Been ready since they busted into my bedroom."

"Dammit! Hounds of Hades!" A crushing blow to the back of the head nearly knocked Lander to his knees. A second, to his upper back, had him seeing stars. A moment later, the pain came in a white-hot wave. It blazed down his neck and socked him in the gut. The world faded, the colors he'd grown accustomed to seeing since he'd first touched Cailey dulled to shades of gray again. Sounds grew muffled.

A male screamed.

Dryce? Bourne?

No, he couldn't lose his two remaining brothers.

Lander retched and then staggered to his feet. The world dipped and spun as he tried to walk toward a pack of lions nearby. They were huddled over something, someone. He prayed he hadn't lost another brother to his enemies.

The beast within him was awakened by the emotions surging through him, the rage and frustration, desperation. Once again he was flat on the ground, this time completely overtaken by the agony of the change.

He just wanted it over so he could stop those fuckers from harming his brother.

Every second felt like a lifetime. And then it was over, and he was the beast.

Dryce! His cries of frustration and rage came out as an echoing roar. Adrenaline masked the pain of the blows, bites, and claws as he fought his way through the pack of enemy lions. Finally, he was through.

As he feared, Dryce lay on the ground, bloodied and unconscious.

Was he too late?

A split second later, something hard struck Lander's head. The world around him closed in, like a black tunnel. And this time he couldn't fight his way back out.

"I have terrible news." Nevan's eyes were bloodshot and teary, and for the first time since Cailey had met her, she looked shaken.

Instantly, Cailey began to panic. She jackknifed out of bed so quickly her head spun. "What? What's wrong? Is it Adria? I haven't seen her . . . Where is she?"

"It's a terrible tragedy. Absolutely awful. Oh god!" Nevan cupped her shaking hands over her mouth. Tears streamed from her eyes.

"What?" Cailey literally shook the stunned woman, petrified and desperate to hear details. Did it have something to do with Adria? Lander?

A fire started in her gut.

Nevan swiped at her nose with the back of her hand. "Our king has been defeated. He and his brothers are being held by Jag and his army. Jag is claiming the throne."

"Where? Do you know where they're being held?" Cailey raced to the closet and threw open the door.

The crying woman shook her head. "It doesn't matter. There's nothing we can do. A lioness is forbidden to interfere in any way with issues surrounding the lions and their positions of power. The strongest leads the pride. That's the law."

"To hell with the law," Cailey shouted, yanking out the most substantial pieces of clothing she owned. "What about what's best for everyone? Is Jag the kind of lion you want to lead you?"

Nevan stumbled backward a step. "No."

"Would Jag be the kind of ruler Lander is?" she asked, yanking on a whisper-thin top.

"No. No one would be the kind of ruler Lander is, outside of perhaps his younger brother, Dryce." Nevan slumped into the chair in the corner of the room and covered her face with her hands. "But there's nothing we can do."

Cailey stepped into her knee-length skirt, then stood over Nevan. Bewildered, frustrated, terrified, she was driven to do something, anything. But what? She needed help. "Are you really going to stand by and watch a man who doesn't deserve it take power?"

"I cannot interfere. It's forbidden."

To hell with that. Shoes. She needed shoes. "I can't just sit here."

"You must."

"The hell I must." Determined, enraged, and ready to scream, Cailey pulled on her shoes, then ran toward the door.

"Where are you going?" Nevan called after her.

Cailey paused just outside the doorway. "I'm not following some stupid law that makes no sense. I'm going to find a way to help Lander . . . or die trying."

Nevan pushed to her feet. "Please. You can't!"

"Who's going to stop me?" Cailey dared Nevan with the iciest glare she could muster, in the midst of total panic. "You?" She hurried down the hall, toward the stairs.

Nevan followed. "It's my duty—"

"Fuck your duty."

"But how will you help him?" Nevan said, still behind her. "You don't even have claws."

Cailey stopped in the center of the staircase. She whirled around, pointing. "Hah! That's where you're wrong. I do have claws. They're just not the kind you have." She hooked her fingers and pawed at the air.

Nevan caught her wrist, scoffing. "Well, honey, if you think you're going to fight through a pack of panthers with anything but three inch lion claws, you're in for a terrible shock."

As much as Nevan's tone rankled, Cailey knew Nevan was right, dammit. She had no weapon. It would be suicide to go running into the melee.

But it wasn't like anyone was offering to help her. And with a world full of animal-people who each possessed what weapons they needed naturally—enormous teeth and claws—there was no use for man-made ones. She would be hard pressed to find even something to use as a club. Never mind the fact that she needed something a whole of a hell lot more effective than that. Like a high-powered, semiautomatic rifle with a scope.

She dropped to her butt on the stairs, suddenly lacking the strength to stand. Covering her face, she let the tears flow.

Oh, it was so fucking weak to be crying like this. Now, when Lander needed her to be strong. But she couldn't charge to his rescue by herself, unarmed. That was way too stupid to even think about.

"I'm sorry," Nevan murmured, sitting behind her.

"No, you're not. If you were genuinely sorry you'd help."

"That's not true. Listen." Nevan shuffled around her, then pried at Cailey's fingers, pulling them away from her face. "You know our king very well. You know how he demands our respect. For both him and his laws. All of them, even the ones we might not agree with. He asks this of us because he is an honorable king, who wishes the best for everyone."

"Yeah, I know."

"And you also know that he'd never put himself above the law. He'd rather die than have his lionesses break his law and come to his aid. Why?"

"Because he doesn't want you to be hurt. Or worse."

Nevan nodded. "Exactly."

"It's still not fair."

"No. It's not. But it's the way our king would expect it."

Cailey closed her eyes, and instantly images of Lander swept through her mind. "I still can't sit here and do nothing."

"Then come with me. You might not be able to help our conquered king, but perhaps it'll make you feel better to assist the lionesses in preparing for the new king."

Oh, yippie.

When Cailey didn't stand up to follow her right away, Nevan tugged on her hand again. "Please. This is going to be a painful shock to many of the lionesses and they respect you. Your strength and love for our king will help."

"It's not exactly what I'd hoped for."

"Maybe not, but it's the best you can do. For all of us."

Resigned but far from content, Cailey followed Nevan out into a deserted street. They wound through a maze of roads, finally arriving at a narrow townhouse that looked a lot like Lander's, the only difference being the lack of ornately carved woodwork on the building's front.

"It's been a long time since there was a change in leadership among our people," Nevan explained, opening the door for Cailey. After Cailey stepped inside, Nevan shut the door and stepped around her, leading her down the narrow hallway, past a steep staircase and several closed doors. "But according to tradition, the lionesses meet with our coven sisters and prepare for the new king."

"Coven sisters? As in witches?"

"No. There are no witches anymore. Witchcraft was outlawed many years ago, after our people were cursed."

"Lander and Adria have both mentioned the curse. Can you tell me more?"

"It was a terrible tragedy." Nevan sat at a wooden table, indicating a nearby chair to Cailey. "Not so long ago, witchcraft was common in our city. In fact, all lionesses practiced the magic arts to some degree. But sadly, we became dependent upon magic, failing to find nonmagical ways to do many things. So when we were cursed, and the very thing we depended upon most became outlawed, our people suffered terribly."

"That's very sad."

"It doesn't matter anymore." Nevan shook her head. "There's nothing that can be done to remove the curse. Some of our people fear magic now. Some detest it. And others secretly hope our future kings will slowly allow it to return. Several lionesses have tried to convince our king to change the law. But he refuses."

"Obviously he feels it's best for everyone. Right?"

"Yes, I'm sure he does."

Why did Cailey have the feeling there was a *but* coming after that last statement?

"But this is one opinion I don't share with our good king," Nevan added.

Yes, there was. Suddenly Cailey felt uneasy. Did that mean Nevan wanted the law to change? Enough to help another man kill her king?

Oh God! Had she just walked into the den of her enemy? The one who'd framed her for killing Lander's brother?

"Where's Adria?" Cailey rose to her feet, bracing her hands on the table.

"I haven't seen her since yesterday. Are you uncomfortable? We can wait for our coven sisters in the front room."

"Yes. That sounds good." She assumed, as the name suggested, the front room would be toward the front of the house, close to the door.

Although she wasn't 100 percent sure she was going to need to make a hasty exit in the near future, she was all for being closer to the exit. Just in case.

That niggling uneasiness grew to an overwhelming impulse to leave when Nevan's coven sisters showed up and immediately started talking about plans for the future.

Whether their seeming disregard for Lander was due to some kind of cultural thing or they were part of a plan to get him out of power wasn't clear. But what was crystal clear was that Cailey did not share their attitude about this whole thing. Not at all.

They were planning a freaking welcoming party for the new king! Hello! She was like . . . in love . . . with the current one. Who was hopefully still alive. She was not about to haul out the confetti and party tunes, even if the guy taking his place had not been an underhanded creep.

While her hostess was busy planning the new king's coronation celebration, Cailey slowly headed for the door, hoping the lionesses would be too busy to notice she was gone before it was too late. She had no idea where she'd go, assuming she was successful in escaping, but there had to be somewhere better than this. Surely, Lander had some loyal followers somewhere, planning to rescue him. How would she find them?

She took one, two, three steps. Once she was out of the parlor—out of sight—she moved quickly toward the house's front door.

Yes! Success! She opened the door and ran, hard and fast. She didn't look back to see if anyone was following. She just pumped her arms and pushed herself to go faster.

And then something huge, like a freaking Humvee, slammed

her from behind. She hit the ground so hard her lungs collapsed. Instinctively, she curled into a ball, struggling to drag in a breath.

Whatever had hit her—whoever had hit her—yanked her to her feet. Dazed, her vision obscured by twinkling stars, she glared at her captor. Nevan.

These lion-women might look all small and dainty, but they were like freaking football players. All muscle. Crazy strong. And sneaky as hell.

"I can't have you out here running loose. Something unfortunate might happen."

"I was thinking the unfortunate thing might happen if I stuck around."

"Perhaps." Nevan's smile was empty. "Or not. That depends on you. So far, things aren't looking promising."

"Why are you bothering with me?"

"Because I made a promise to my king." Tightening her grip on Cailey's arm, Nevan turned and started walking, dragging Cailey along like a stubborn toddler.

"Well, if you ask me, you're taking this promise a little too seriously."

"I'm not asking you."

"Didn't think you were."

Cailey supposed it was time for Plan B.

Too bad she didn't have a Plan B.

She struggled to come up with something as she walked back to Nevan's house. The streets were still eerily empty and silent. It was as if the whole world had retreated inside. The lives of the city's inhabitants had screeched to a halt.

Was everyone planning for the crowning of a new king? Or mourning the loss of Lander?

Was Lander dead?

All of a sudden, the tears threatened again. She covered her mouth with her cupped hands, trying to hold the emotion inside, like she used to.

He could already be dead.

Lisa, what the hell did you write? Please tell me you know it's totally not cool to kill off the story's hero! Think, Cailey, think! You're in one of Lisa's stories right now. What do her heroines do?

18

Cailey had read enough of Lisa's books over the past several months to know that Lisa was not the kind of author to take shortcuts in a plot. There'd be no convenient resolution of this situation. No miraculous solution that would present itself to her, all wrapped up with a nifty little bow like a birthday gift. Nope. If she was truly Lisa's heroine now, she'd have to think and act like one.

Which meant she'd have to be brave and use her brains.

When a girl was in the midst of panic neither was easy. But she'd have to try.

Immediately after returning to Nevan's house, she was escorted to a smaller room at the rear of the house and threatened with being locked in like a rebellious teenager if she tried running off again.

She really bristled at being talked down to. Before today, Nevan had been the nicer of the two maids. The woman had done a complete one-eighty.

Even though it sickened Cailey to listen in, she tiptoed back out into the hallway and eavesdropped on the lionesses' plans, hoping someone would mention whether Lander was still alive or not. After about an hour, she finally had the news she'd been waiting for: he was alive, and he wouldn't be executed until morning.

The sun was hanging low over the horizon, so there was time. *If* she could come up with a stinking plan!

But it had been hours since she'd been dragged by the ear—not quite literally, but more or less—back to Nevan's place and sent to her room like a misbehaving child. She'd done a lot of fuming, pacing, and thinking, but still had no clue how she could help Lander.

But, knowing Lisa, she was expected to do something. And not only was she to do something, it would have to be big. The kind of thing she wouldn't have had the guts or knowledge to do at the beginning of the story. This was the story's Black Moment, when all hope was lost and things were their bleakest.

Damn if Lisa wasn't a great plotter! Too good. She'd written Cailey into a tight corner and left her no shovel to dig her way out.

Grrr!

Cailey slid to her butt, pressing her back against the wall. She covered her face, trying to hold back another wave of tears. Could she be any more frustrated and scared?

Think, girl! Think. What have I learned? What sort of vulnerability could I expose in myself for the love of my life?

God, he was the love of her life! Lander. A man who had been formed by her imagination.

Now was not the time to expend valuable mental energy on contemplating that one.

Learned? She'd learned not to be afraid of cats. She'd learned lions had soft fur, along with those sharp teeth and claws. They were intelligent. And the lionesses worked together.

Their culture was very different from the more isolated lives of her world, where a married couple lived alone in their home, relying only on each other for their needs—more or less.

And what sort of vulnerability could she expose? Could it be the obvious?

She'd been afraid of cats for years. What if she put herself in a position of relying on them? No, doing more than that, what if she actually took on some of the characteristics of the animals she'd once despised?

Hmmm . . .

Still, how would she do that?

"We must go for a hunt," she heard one of them say, and it was then that an idea struck her. Hunt.

Brilliant. And insane.

What if she rallied the lionesses, suggesting they hunt Jag instead of some poor deer outside the city? They could surround him, driving him toward her . . . or the other way around. Yes, that would be better.

She'd be the bait, driving him toward the waiting lionesses. Then they could do their thing with him. No male could stand up against four or more lionesses.

That could work.

Granted, there were a lot of things that could go wrong. They could refuse. He could have a bazillion guards, who would tear them all to pieces. Or he could simply fail to fall for the bait and gobble her up.

But, knowing their culture, he probably wouldn't be expecting it.

Yes, it sounded exactly like the kind of plot that Lisa would write. That had to be it.

Determined she'd get at least as far as convincing a couple of lionesses to go along with her plan, she pushed to her feet and hurried into the room. Better to get this insanity over with before she talked herself out of it.

"I have a plan," she announced from the doorway. "And I'm looking for a few brave lionesses who aren't afraid to bend the law a bit to come with me."

Her big announcement was met with stunned silence.

Undaunted, she continued, "I realize Lander has drilled it into everyone's head that the law must come first. But dammit, I love the man, and I refuse to let him sacrifice himself to a creep who doesn't deserve to be king. This isn't just about what's best for Lander. It's also best for all of you, everyone who will have to live here once Jag's in charge."

More silence.

Sheesh! What was it going to take to change a few minds?

She met the gazes of every lioness in the room. "Don't any of you care what happens to your king? He's a fine man, an honorable one who is ready to sacrifice his life for you. Doesn't he deserve your help? I mean, I realize you all operate by instinct, that the beast inside you pretty much rules your behavior. But there's got to be some humanity in there, too."

One of the lionesses nodded and Cailey immediately caught the woman's gaze with her own. "Listen to your human heart. If we work together, I think there's a way we can stop this from happening."

"The law is the law," Nevan said, standing and delivering a wicked glare at Cailey. "We must follow it. That's what our king wants from us. Our complete submission to his leadership."

"No, I believe he wants your submission to the human inside of you. The laws he has created were there to help you hold onto your humanity. It's slowly slipping from you all."

"That's a bunch of nonsense," Nevan scoffed. "We all still possess our humanity. But it's the beast within us that makes us strong. Look at you. You've lost all trace of the beast your people once were, and you're weak. Defenseless."

"Don't underestimate this girl."

Nevan found that seriously funny. Cailey didn't bother trying to set her straight. She figured there'd be plenty of opportunity to do that, shortly.

"So you won't help us. No biggie. Go back to your party planning. I don't need you." She looked at each of the other lionesses, made eye contact with every one of them again. "But for those of you who wish to find a balance between the beast and the human, follow me. I'm off to save a man who doesn't deserve to die."

Without taking a second look, she lifted her chin, turned and left the room, hoping, praying, there'd be at least a few lionesses following her out of the building—and not to tackle her. If there wasn't, she wouldn't stand a chance at helping Lander, and her romance novel would end up a tragedy.

Once outside, she turned back to the house, holding her breath as she watched the door. It wasn't until she saw the first lioness follow her outside that she inhaled. Three more came after her.

She had the help she needed.

God help her, she was about to throw herself into the lion's den. But she could do no less for the man she loved.

This was it. The end of his reign, and sadly, the loss of hope for his people.

Lander had fought hard for them, tried to help them conquer the beast. Once Jag was in power, their humanity would be pretty much lost, and the curse would never be lifted.

Dammit!

He pounded his fists against the wall of his prison cell until they were bloody and bruised. This fucking curse, cast upon his people for acting like animals. Outside of Cailey's nonexistent magical powers, the only way to break it was to somehow get his people to turn their backs on the beast within them. It was an impossible task. He knew that now.

He stared out the window, into the deep night. He wondered

where Cailey was, if she was safe. He knew she'd be terrified without him, but he'd tried to escape, to return to her, and he'd failed.

Yes, he'd failed everybody. His brothers. His people. Cailey.

He wouldn't even get the chance to tell her he loved her. But, he supposed, that was probably for the better. Because if the situation were reversed, and she was facing execution, knowing she loved him would make the pain of losing her that much more unbearable for him.

Yes, it was better for her not to know. She might not grieve as much.

He turned from the window, wishing the night would pass quickly, and hoping that once he was gone, Cailey would find her way back to her world safely. That had been his final request to Jag, the price Jag had paid for the crown. As the new king, it was Jag's duty to see it done.

Then, a sound drew him to the window. It was a tapping. Soft but rhythmic, most definitely intentional. Who would come to him? Why? The law was very plain in this regard. No one was permitted to interfere in any way in issues of leadership. When the king was defeated by another male, the members of his pride were to welcome the new king.

Who would dare disregard the law?

Furious, he peered out the window.

Cailey.

He was torn between fear for her safety and fury for her disobeying. He'd left her in the care of a lioness he trusted and respected a great deal, knowing she'd be kept safe and helped through this temporary time of adjustment. He'd never expected this, although he probably should have.

"What are you doing here?" he shouted through the thick, hazy glass.

"Getting you out."

"What? No!" She couldn't help him escape. A defenseless

woman. What kind of insanity was this? "Go home now, back to Nevan. Before you're hurt. You must."

"No."

He ached to touch her, to shake her, to drag her against him and force her to listen. He pressed his hand against the cool glass and reached to her mentally, through that invisible connection. He felt her pain, tasted her fear. "Yes, dammit! I can't watch you get hurt. Or worse."

She shook her head, her eyes gleaming with defiance. "No."

"Jag will take you home after my execution. It's been arranged."

"I don't want you to be executed." She pressed her hand against the thick pane of glass separating them from each other.

He closed his eyes and prayed the glass would fall away and he could feel her soft hand in his, warm and delicate. Smell the sweet scent of her skin. Taste those trembling, plump lips one last time. *Leave. You'll be safe. It's time for you to go home.* "This is killing me, Cailey. I didn't want it to end this way."

"Me either. That's why I had to come, Lander. I couldn't just sit back and celebrate your enemy's victory."

He pressed his forehead to the window. "It's the way it must be."

Again, she shook her head. "Bullshit. I love you. I'd rather die than let you be executed." She stood, her face a mask of determination.

He knew that look.

"What are you going to do?"

"I'm going to show you exactly how much I love you. I'm going to become a lioness. For you." And then she dashed to the center of the street and shouted, "Jag! You spineless coward. Why don't you come out here and show me what you're really made of? I'm what you want. My magic will not only make you a king, it'll give you more power than you could ever dream of. But to get the power, you have to come out here yourself."

Lander yelled, "No!" but he was powerless to stop her. As he watched, his heart in his throat, Jag in human form skulked out into the street, coming around behind Cailey's back, hands raised, poised for attack.

The beast within Lander quickly took power, before he could mentally warn her. Within seconds, he was on the ground, writhing in pain, his bones and muscles taking their feline shape again. By the time he had shifted and bounded back to the window to check on Cailey, it was too late. He could see the shadowy figures gathering around her, hidden from her view. Felines on all fours. Jag's guards, no doubt.

An instant later, he roared as the figures leaped from their hiding spots, bounding toward his beautiful, delicate woman. But he watched, stunned, as the felines attacked Jag instead of Cailey. Before Jag's guards could come to his rescue, he was knocked to the ground. His shrieks of pain turned Lander's blood to ice. He watched as Cailey ran out from the center of the melee back toward his window.

She pounded on the glass. "I'm coming for you now."

He tried to stop her, but his human voice was trapped beneath the beast's, the connection between their minds severed. He roared again, clawing at the window.

Cailey turned and ran around the side of the building, and he couldn't see her anymore.

He spun around and ripped at the door with his claws, desperate to protect her from his enemies. But the door had been built to hold in his kind. Many before him had tried the same thing. Grooved scars cut deep into the surface but didn't go through.

She would be dead long before he broke out of this room. The woman he loved more than anything.

The woman he had surrendered his throne for.

19
―――――――――

"The choice is yours. Stay or leave?"

Cailey staggered backward.

What the hell? A second ago—literally a heartbeat earlier—she'd been this close to rescuing Lander. Then everything went blinding white. And now she was in that weird white place again, and the woman her critique group had rejected was with her. Monica. No, Monique. Whatever her name was.

Cinnamon. There was that scent again.

"Make your choice," the woman demanded. "Quickly."

Cailey stood in that nothing place for at least ten seconds, totally dumbfounded. Now? She had to make her choice right now? What about Lander? Was he okay? What would happen to him if she decided to go home?

After that first conversation with this strange woman, Cailey had thought that sooner or later she'd face this decision. Recently, however, she'd begun to doubt this time would ever come.

So much time had passed since that first day. She'd pretty much learned to love her new home. Maybe it wasn't perfect but there were some very good things about this place. She certainly loved the man who resided here.

The man of her fantasies.

Dammit, how could she leave him? Surely there'd never be a real guy who could compare. He was beyond perfection. He was her soul mate, the one person who fit with her. Who understood her. Who had knocked down her walls.

If she went home, she'd leave him behind. What kind of happily-ever-after was that? None that she'd want to read about, let alone live with.

Besides, she hadn't told him everything yet. She needed to thank him for all he'd done for her. To let him know how much he meant, and how grateful she was that he'd trusted her to be his sanctuary, his refuge.

There were so many things between them she needed to tie up. It had been such a short time. No, no, no. She wasn't ready to go. Not yet.

"I need more time. Please."

The woman shook her head. "Your time is up, Cailey. You must choose."

Cailey stared down, into white nothingness. What now? Stay there with Lander? Or go home? "Is Lisa still writing my story?"

"No, she finished at exactly the same moment as you finished Mia's."

"But I didn't finish. I didn't know how I wanted it to end. So shouldn't I go back and write the final pages?"

"No. You've written all you need to."

Grrr! "Can you at least tell me how Lisa ended my book?"

"She didn't write the final chapter, either. You will each write your own happily-ever-after."

Well, that part sounded okay. "Doesn't a happily-ever-after imply the hero and heroine will be together in the end?"

The witch shrugged. "That depends."

Cailey glanced around. Where was the door back to Lander's world? "Give me a pen and paper. I'll write it right now."

"It's not going to work that way."

"Then how does it work?" Cailey wanted to cry. Or scream. Or just shake this mean woman and maybe smack her, too. "Can I just say, this being-a-romance-heroine thing sucks?"

The woman's eyes twinkled as she smiled, telling Cailey that she thoroughly enjoyed watching the struggle. Sadistic bitch. "You can say whatever you like. But that won't change anything."

"Why'd you do this to me?" Cailey snapped as she tried to sort out her options.

"Because you needed me to."

"Hah. Needed? Not hardly." Cailey paced back and forth. Walk away from her life, her books, her friends, everything? Or leave Lander? God, how could she live with losing either? "What are you? Some kind of avenging angel, or a demon?"

The woman shrugged. "Neither."

"A witch, then. Like Lander said."

"Have you ever met a witch who could magically transport people into imaginary worlds?"

What to do? Life? Or Lander? The real world? Or the one I created? Why couldn't she have both?

"I've never known a witch, period. So how would I know what a witch is capable of? But I watched *Bewitched* on TV when I was a kid. She could do pretty much everything."

"That show was a joke," the nonwitch scoffed.

"Says you. I loved that show. And so did millions of other people." Cailey gave her best Samantha nose-wiggle.

Yes, it was stupid, yammering on about a television show that had been off the air for decades, while she faced one of the most impossible decisions of her life. But she needed to buy some time.

What the hell was she going to do?

"You must decide now."

"I'm trying!" Cailey snapped, desperation making her edgy. "You're mean, doing this to me."

"Says you. I have my reasons for doing what I have."

Cailey glared at the woman. "Which are?"

The cruel nonwitch clucked her tongue. "Uh, uh, uh! You're not going to distract me again. Make your choice. You have exactly thirty seconds."

"That's not enough time."

"What have you learned about yourself in all of this? Think about that. And think about what you value most, and the choice will be easy."

"Again, says the one who doesn't have to make any decisions at all."

"Hey, at least *you* have a choice."

Now, that little rejoinder silenced Cailey pronto. Whoever, whatever, this person was, Cailey sensed she didn't have too many choices when it came down to important things. Not that she'd exactly said any such thing. It had been in her voice when she'd made that last comment, weighted the word "you."

Even more, she wanted to understand why this woman had done this. But it was clear Cailey wasn't going to get a straight answer. If she had a buck to wager, though, she'd put it on something having to do with choices, freedom.

Cailey closed her eyes. Not that the eternal white emptiness was distracting or anything, but she just wanted to focus inward.

What had she learned about herself? How had she grown since coming to this world of cat-people?

It had only been a week. Seven days. But so much had changed. She had changed.

For starters, she'd faced her fear of cats. That was a no-brainer.

But she'd also grown in other ways.

She'd learned she was not nearly as different from the cat-people as she'd originally thought, that she, too, possessed a darker nature, a beast.

She'd also learned it was okay to feel pain. She'd given herself permission to hurt. And become vulnerable. She could still be strong, even when she was baring her weaknesses.

And finally, she'd discovered how fulfilling it was to submit to a powerful master. How free she felt while being restrained.

I want my friends, my world and—

"So be it," the woman said. "Your choice has been made."

"No! Wait! I didn't say anything . . . oh, hell!" There was a poof. No, more of a *wham*, like the earsplitting crack of thunder.

And then the woman was gone.

Cailey did a three-sixty, searching the whiteness. "Where'd you go? And why am I still here? What's going on?"

Now, if this didn't suck.

Was this what happened when a girl couldn't make a choice? Would she be stuck in this blah nothing place forever? Talk about hell!

She sank to the nonground, wrapped her arms around her bent knees, and rested her chin on them. She'd felt jerked around in the past, but this went beyond anything she'd ever experienced. She wanted to scream. Hell, why shouldn't she? It wasn't like there was anyone here to hear her.

She screamed, loud and long and hard, until her throat burned. The echoing sound was quite satisfying, even if that was all she got out of it.

She rocked her head forward, until it was pressed against her knees and her face was shaded by her arms. Eyes closed, she let images of Lander play through her head. Some made her laugh. Some cry.

God, she missed him.

She felt her mood sinking, lower, lower. Her body felt heavy, like when she'd had the flu last winter. A slight pounding started in her temples, then spread across the front of her head until the excruciating pain had her begging nobody for some Tylenol. Tingles spread over her skin. Hot prickles. She slumped over onto her side and assumed the fetal position.

She had to be dying. What else could it be?

She squeezed her eyes closed and rode out the waves of agony. They washed over her, like swells in the ocean. Faster, faster, harder, harder.

"Please, just let it all stop."

A blinding white light burned the back of her eyelids. Squinting, she turned her head. The pain eased slightly, just enough that she risked opening her eyes.

No way.

She was back at home, lying on her kitchen floor. It was dark. No lights. There was a flash of blue light in the window. A distant roll of thunder. A storm.

She remembered now: her critique group meeting, the storm, Lander bashing in her front door.

Her brains still trying to beat their way through her skull, she rose up on hands and knees and crawled toward the living room.

"Lisa? Mia?"

They weren't there. She glanced at the door, the hanging-wide-open door, and wondered if she'd popped back home before or after Lander had hauled her away.

Using the couch, she dragged herself to her feet. Damn, her head was killing her. She fingered the spot where the pain was the worst and found blood, warm and sticky. Ouch. She looked at her fingers.

Had she been conked on the head by something? Had the whole kidnapping thing been some kind of dream? Her imagination run wild while she lay unconscious on her floor for who knew how long?

Her insides dropped to her toes. If it was, then Lander didn't really exist, and . . . ohhhh, her chest hurt. Was it possible to have a broken heart over someone who didn't exist?

She plopped onto the couch and fingered the growing knot on her head. Meanwhile, she glanced around, trying to find a clue as to what might have happened to Lisa and Mia. She found what she was looking for on the coffee table, beneath the bowl of chips.

A page from Mia's Egyptian god story. It looked very familiar.

Jafari cradled her in his arms, feeling the life draining from her body, yet powerless to stop it. Lost in agonizing grief, and blind with rage, he cursed all creation.

Again, that which he'd made had turned on him. But this time it had been much worse. Because now, he wasn't isolated from the world. He was a part of it. He'd willingly stepped into his own creation and allowed it to become a part of him, to change him.

And look what had happened.

He loved this woman. And like everything he'd ever loved, he was destined to lose her.

Where had Lisa and Mia gone?

Would she ever see Lander again, outside of her dreams?

20

"Lisa! Oh thank God! I can't believe how mean you are!" Cailey stomped up to Lisa and gave her the iciest glare she could muster, with a splitting headache, a broken heart, and a huge dose of relief.

For just the briefest of moments, she was convinced Lisa had written her story. And that Lander was real. And she'd actually met him in person. And his hands had touched her, and he'd said those wonderful, magical words to her, "you're my sanctuary.'"

But, unfortunately, Lisa looked totally bewildered as she stumbled through the door. Her hair was a windblown mess and her clothes were tattered. Her face was pale, her eyes wide with shock. "What are you talking about?"

Instantly, Cailey felt like a total idiot. Of course those things hadn't happened. How could they? Mia's page. That had to be some kind of weird coincidence.

Worried her critique partner might blow over with the next gust of wind, she grabbed Lisa's hand and led her to the couch. "What happened? Are you okay?"

"I-I'm not sure." Lisa sat, glanced around the room, then met Cailey's gaze. "What about you? Are you okay?"

"Yeah." Reminded of her cracked skull, she gave it a gentle rub. "I think something fell on my head."

Lisa's already pale face went three shades whiter.

"What?"

Brows dipping low, Lisa shook her head. "It's . . . nothing."

Cailey sensed something was going on. Could it be? Had Lander really come stomping into her apartment? "No, what?" She needed to hear someone besides herself say the words. She couldn't trust herself right now, didn't seem to know the difference between reality and fantasy. But if Lisa said it had really happened, then it had, and Lander was real, and maybe, just maybe, he would come back for her. Cailey looked at her friend's trembling hands. "Why are you shaking?"

"I could swear . . ." Lisa shook her head again. "This is crazy."

"Maybe not."

At Cailey's encouraging words, Lisa continued, "A man came in here and kidnapped you. And then another one took me away."

"Yes!" Cailey shouted, leaping up in the air. Poor Lisa nearly jumped out of her skin. "Sorry. Didn't mean to scare you like that."

"Then it wasn't a dream?"

"No, not unless we're both having the same dream."

"Oh, thank God!" Lisa's face regained some of its color. After a tense moment, where neither of them spoke, Lisa added, "Oh, I get it now. You said I was mean because you didn't like the way I wrote your story."

"No, I did not! What's wrong with writing sex, and more sex?"

"Uh, that gets a little old after a while."

"Not if you get creative."

"Hey, I gave you a scene where you watched two gorgeous

man-lions do it with each other. I'd say that was pretty creative."

"Yeah, that was yummy." Cailey felt herself smiling at the memory. "Yes, very, very yummy. But you still could've saved Lander's brother. Why wouldn't you at least do that?"

"Because look what that trial did for you two."

Cailey thought about it. Would their love be any less wonderful if they had avoided that whole trial and near execution thing? Maybe. Then again, maybe not.

She felt herself frowning. "What about you? I hate to ask what kind of hell Mia put you through."

Lisa grimaced. "Let's just say I was kind to you and leave it at that."

"I was almost executed."

Lisa nodded. "As I said."

"No way."

"Yes way."

Silence.

"What'd she write?" Cailey asked.

"Oh, I was shot and nearly killed, among other things."

"Man, how harsh. Speaking of harsh, did that creepy woman who sent us into our stories talk to you?"

"Yeah."

Cailey leaned forward. "Did she tell you how or why she did this to us? Or whether we'd get to see our heroes again?"

"No."

She slumped back into the couch. "Damn."

More silence.

"Did you get over your fear of guns?" Cailey asked.

"I'm not sure. I think so. What about your fear of cats?"

"Haven't tested it yet, but I did fine while I was in Lander's world."

Lisa glanced at the door. "I wonder where Mia is."

"Yeah. I wonder." Cailey looked at Lisa. Lisa looked at Cailey.

Then Cailey tiptoed to the door again, half-expecting to find Mia staggering in the storm like Lisa had.

The hallway outside looked like a tornado had ripped through it. The wallpaper was flapping off the walls in long strips, whipping in the wind like shredded flags. And the carpet was squishy under her bare feet, soaked through. "What happened out here? Did we have a tornado or flood or something?"

"I'm as confused as you are," Lisa said from her door. "This is too strange for words."

"Yeah." Cailey poked her head outside. No Mia. Just some wicked winds, sheeting rain, and lots of lightning. She motioned to Lisa. "The storm's still kicking pretty bad. We'd better get back inside."

"Okay."

They flopped on the couch, side by side. Cailey stared straight ahead, jolting with every crack of thunder. Each time, she wondered if the sound was from an alpha romance hero barreling through a door somewhere. Each time, she was disappointed when Lander didn't appear in her living room.

Lisa seemed to be reacting the same way.

The storm raged on and on, only making the waiting that much more agonizing. It was bad enough she missed Lander. She hadn't wanted to come back. She'd been about to tell whatever-her-name that she was going to stay in catville with Lander. The witch hadn't given her the chance.

Her insides hurt something fierce, and as time went on, she realized how much Lander meant to her and how hard it was going to be to move on with her life, pretend he didn't exist.

She wondered what would happen if she read the book Lisa had written.

"Hey, you don't happen to have a copy of the manuscript you wrote, do you?"

"No. I came back empty handed. What about you?"

"Same thing." Cailey sighed. "Can you tell me how it ended?"

"Wish I could, but for some reason I remember writing it but don't remember the details."

"That's odd." Cailey remembered what she'd written . . . or did she? There'd been the Egyptian guy. And some water. And some sex . . .

Okay, her memory had been wiped out, too.

Cailey grunted. "That nonwitch doesn't play fair."

"I agree. Nonwitch?" Lisa giggled.

"She claimed she wasn't a witch. Or an angel. Or a demon. So what's that leave?"

"Don't know. A nonwitch, I guess." Lisa pointed at her bag, strewn in a corner. "Maybe my story's in there." She rushed over and scooped it up, stuffed her hand inside, and gave Cailey a wishful glance before looking down.

"Darn! This is the version I wrote."

"Again, I say that nonwitch doesn't play fair."

Just then, there was a noise outside, a thud.

Cailey and Lisa swapped grins.

Could be the super. Or Mia. Or one uber-sexy man-lion from another world.

Cailey sprinted toward the door.

Mia, who looked as beat up as Lisa, stumbled inside on visibly shaking legs. "What the hell?"

Cailey stepped aside to let her friend in, then checked the hallway.

"What're you looking for?" Mia asked.

"Them."

"Who them?"

"The guys."

They weren't out there, dammit.

Mia looked puzzled. "Then it wasn't a dream?"

Cailey made an attempt at closing the door—not easy, since the hinges had pretty much been torn off—and trudged back to the couch. "Nope. It was real and so were they."

"Then I hate you," Mia said.

"Yeah, well, I hate Lisa, so no biggie."

Standing next to the window, Lisa sighed heavily. "Looks like the storm's over. I should go home. Maybe I'll do some writing. Who knows? It might change something."

Mia rubbed at red, watery eyes. "You two fell in love with your heroes, too, didn't you?"

Lisa shrugged. "Doesn't do any good to talk about it now. Who knows, maybe we were dreaming or something."

Cailey shook her head. "You know that's not true."

"Yeah." Lisa dragged her feet as she walked toward the door. "I'm heading home. See ya next week."

Cailey sighed, realizing that soon she'd be alone. "Okay."

"I think I'll go home, too." Mia followed Lisa, rubbing her arms. "I'm really tired."

That left Cailey alone and lonely, wondering if she'd ever see her man-lion again. Exhausted, but too wired to sleep, she sat at her computer, opened her work in progress, and started typing.

Maybe Lisa had the right idea, that they'd write their own story. And the magic would somehow work one last time.

She figured it was the only hope they had.

That was it. The end.

Cailey wiped a tear from her eye and hit SAVE, backing up the story of her heart onto her flash drive.

It had taken her three months to write her version of Lander's story. Three long, lonely months.

With a few exceptions, she'd written it as she'd lived it, with all the terror, ecstasy, and heartache she'd felt firsthand. While she'd worked, she'd relived every moment of those magical days and nights, both the good and the bad.

She was pretty sure this was the most powerful book she'd ever penned.

She glanced at the clock. Lisa and Mia were due any minute

for their critique group. They'd been meeting every week, sharing their stories, swapping critiques. They never once talked about the guys coming back. That topic sort of hung in the air, like a foul odor no one wanted to talk about. It was like they were afraid to, thinking if they did, they'd curse themselves, and the ends of their stories might not come true.

Well, to hell with that (really stupid) logic.

Keeping all the frustration and pain inside wasn't going to do anything for any of them.

She was breaking the silence. Tonight.

Cailey prepared for their critique group the same way she had every time since *that night*. She put out the snacks and beverages, printed off the final pages of her manuscript, gathered a pen and notebook, and headed for the living room.

This time, however, there was a little change of plans. Instead of the usual munchies, she decided to order takeout from the local steak place and fork over the cash to have it delivered. Regardless of the fact that she missed Lander something fierce, and she guessed Lisa and Mia were in similar shape, they all had something to celebrate.

Not only had they all finished their novels, but Cailey confirmed she had conquered her phobia. Cats no longer struck terror in her. In fact, thanks in part to the heartache of missing Lander, she now looked upon them with a certain sad yearning and camaraderie. She was actually considering buying a kitten.

A knock at the door signaled the arrival of at least one of her critique partners. It was too soon for their surprise dinner to arrive.

She rushed to the door and opened it, finding Mia and Lisa debating something hotly. The dialogue didn't stop when they saw her.

"I don't care. It's totally unacceptable for a major character to die in a romance," Mia said, over her shoulder. "I'm starving. I should've eaten before I came."

"Don't worry about it. I told you we'd be having something special tonight, my treat." Cailey shut the door behind them and glanced at the clock on her VCR. "It should be here in a bit."

"Mmmm. You ordered something to be delivered?" Lisa asked.

Mia scowled. "Pizza?"

Excited, Cailey couldn't help grinning. "Nope. Not this time. I decided we deserved something a whole lot better than that."

"Here, here." Lisa lifted a freshly poured glass of diet cola.

Mia mirrored her. "That's nice of you, going to all the trouble and expense."

Cailey plopped onto the couch. "Yeah, well, I was in the mood to celebrate. It isn't every day that all three of us finish writing a book at the same time."

"And cure ourselves of some obnoxious fears in the process," Lisa added.

"I have to admit, Mia, you were right," Cailey confessed. "I won't ever look at a cat again and not think of Lander."

Mia's grin was not smug. It was genuine, although there was a hint of shadow in her eyes. "Yeah, and I have some pretty low power bills now that I'm not burning lights in every room of my apartment all night long. And get this, I'm planning a vacation. A cruise!"

"That's great!" Lisa took a sip of her cola before setting it down on the coffee table. "And I've signed up for gun safety class at the range."

"Good for you."

It was terrific to see how far they'd all come in the last three months. Strangely, not only did the magical trip into their stories change them, but the fallout afterward had done something as well.

They all seemed to live life a little differently now. Rather than cruise through their weeks on autopilot, they each seemed

to be doing more, taking risks, challenging themselves and looking for more opportunities to experience new things.

To live.

It was as if they'd had a near-death experience, she supposed.

"I signed up for classes, beginning in January," Cailey announced.

Both her critique partners let out a whoop.

"I have to take a few refresher courses before they'll let me
start my internship, but at least I don't have to take everything
over again."

"I'm so happy for you!" Mia threw her arms around Cailey
and gave her a hug.

"I owe it to you and your crazy idea." Cailey hugged her
back, hard.

"And one mean nonwitch who doesn't play fair," Lisa
added.

"Yeah, her, too."

There was another heavy silence where the three of them just
sat there, looking at each other. Finally, Cailey set her printed
pages on the coffee table. "Who wants to read the last bit of
Lander's story?"

"Me!" Lisa had those pages in her hands so quickly, Cailey
didn't see her move. She stuffed one hand in her tote bag and
dropped a folder on the coffee table. "Volunteers?"

Mia snatched up Lisa's, then pulled hers from a manila envelope and handed it to Cailey. "Here, how about reading mine?"

They giggled and sighed and cried as they read the endings
of each others' books, then they swapped again. This time, Cailey had Lisa's story and Mia had hers.

Before Cailey had read the last page of Lisa's extremely satisfying ending, the delivery guy from the restaurant knocked
on her door. She sprang to her feet and headed for the door.
"Time to eat. Hope you're really hungry."

"Starved!" Mia rubbed her hands together, eyes a little watery.

"Me, too."

"Great." Cailey went for her purse, dug out a few bills to tip the delivery guy, and then opened the door.

Something huge jammed in her throat, or at least that's how it felt. Standing frozen at the door, she audibly gulped, drinking in the most beautiful sight she'd ever laid eyes upon.

Lander.

She wondered for just the briefest of moments if he knew her, or if his memory had been scrubbed clean. But her worries ended the instant he gave her one of those naughty grins, yanked her into his arms, and crushed her body against his.

In her bliss, she vaguely noticed Lisa and Mia tiptoeing past them.

"You came here? For me?" she said to his chest.

"Yes."

"You left your home, your pride."

"You are my home, my pride. My life." He cupped her cheek in his hand, and she didn't care that they were still standing in the hallway.

Everything was as it should be.

Hot tears streaked down her cheeks, dripping from her jaw. "I've spent the past three months missing you."

"I've missed you, too. I couldn't stay away. You bewitched me." He kissed her. Tenderly at first. Then harder. He curled his fingers around her upper arms, holding her tightly. Tighter still. And then his kiss deepened, growing desperate and possessive. He backstepped her into her apartment and kicked the door shut, and she giggled into their joined mouths. The instant the kiss was broken and their mouths separated, she let a whoop of glee burst from her throat. She literally hopped up and down. A half dozen questions flew from her mouth.

"How did you find me?

"Can you stay here with me forever?

"What'll you do for a job?

"Do you still turn into a lion, even here in my world?

"How will I keep you from being thrown in the zoo?

"What does this mean?"

His eyes glittered with laughter as he looked down at her. "It means you're mine. Right now, that's all I care about." He gave her a look, the kind she'd grown so very fond of. "How about showing me around? I'd love to see where you live, sleep . . ."

Instantly, her face flamed. "It would be my pleasure."

21

The second Cailey stepped into her bedroom, she found herself slammed up against the wall. Funny, she wasn't complaining a bit. Mostly because of who had done the slamming.

Lander. Her Lander. He was here. In her apartment. In the real world. He wasn't a dream. Or a fantasy.

She shuddered as he slanted his mouth over hers and drew her into a kiss. This was no shy kiss either. It was exactly what she craved, the kind that made her head spin and her lungs implode. Meanwhile, he ripped her sweatshirt, right down the middle, and peeled it from her body. Her shorts were next. His desperate grappling, his clawing at her clothes, only made the simmering heat in her body crank up a few dozen degrees or so.

Yes, oh yes, she loved her dominant man-lion. More than she could say.

She tried to return the favor, but he stopped her by pinning her wrists against the wall, over her head.

He angled his hips forward, holding her body against the wall, and gathered both her wrists into one fist. The free hand went wandering, down the side of her neck to her shoulder, her breast.

She felt the rigid lump hidden beneath his clothes grow harder, the heat radiating off his body edge toward lethal levels. She watched his hand kneading her breast through her lace bra. Long tapered fingers. Fingers that had given her hours and hours of pleasure.

They were the most wonderful hands on earth.

"It took me so long to find a way back here. I nearly died, I missed you so much."

Those words touched her so deeply, a little sob tore from her throat and her eyes burned as tears gathered. Lander kissed each eyelid, swiping the tears with his thumb.

"I missed you, too. I didn't want to leave. I wanted to tell you so many things. I tried to—"

"It's okay." He shushed her, tracing her lower lip with his index finger. "We're together now. That's all that matters anymore."

"Thank you for coming for me."

"You're very welcome." He kissed her again, this time softer. He released her wrists, using both hands to work at the front clasp of her bra. As soon as he had her bra off, she tangled her fingers in his silky hair and held tightly, kissing him back with all the love she had.

Evidently it was enough to get to him, because he groaned into their joined mouths, slid his hands around her hips, and cupped her fanny. He lifted, and she wrapped her legs around his waist and kept kissing him. Their tongues caressed each other, stroked, an intimate, erotic dance.

She couldn't get enough of him. He tasted so good. He felt so good. He smelled so good.

It was killing her that he still had clothes on. He hadn't thrust that glorious cock into her wet pussy. She was ready for him. Achingly ready. She tingled from head to toe.

This time would be different from all the others. There was no dungeon. No other lion-people. No fancy bondage equipment. It was her bed. Her room. And just them.

Yet, even though her previous experiences with vanilla sex had been rather unremarkable, forgettable, she had a feeling this time it wouldn't be. Even without all the trappings of his dungeon, Lander was still the same powerful, dominant, slightly dangerous man in her eyes. Her body was his.

He broke the kiss and walked them to the bed, then, bending at the waist, lowered her onto her back. Gazing down at her with glassy eyes, he hooked his fingers in the waistband of her panties and slid them down her legs and off her feet.

His eyes flashed as he gazed at her freshly shaven pussy. His nostrils flared ever so subtly. "I love your scent." His tongue swept along his lower lip. "But even more, I love your flavor." He eased her feet back, forcing her to bend her knees. "Open for me, kitten. Let me taste you."

She could literally feel every beat of her heart in her pussy. It was the most amazing, agonizing sensation. But that was nothing compared to the sensation of Lander's tongue flicking over her clit, his fingers teasing her slit, her anus. He thrust two fingers into her vagina, hooking them to rub against that sensitive spot that only he seemed to be able to find. With the next thrust, he added a finger in her ass, too, and she was ready to come.

Eyes closed tight, hands fisted, body thrumming like a struck gong, she stretched her legs wider and tilted her hips up. His fingers and tongue were performing magic on her body, but there was still only one way she'd come. She needed his cock inside her. And she needed it now.

"Please, Lander. Oh God, don't tease me now. I've waited so long."

"Hmmm," he said, his mouth still devouring her pussy. "But I've waited a long time, too, to taste you." He gave her pussy a slow swipe. "Mmmm."

"Ohhhh." She bucked as white-hot blazes raced along her spine and light exploded behind her eyelids.

He pumped those fingers in and out of her pussy and ass, filling, stretching, possessing. It was enough to make her go crazy, to weep and beg, rip at her coverlet and alternately sigh in bliss.

He was too fucking good at this! It was so unfair. She wanted him—Mr. Control—to lose it for once. To be so crazy with desire that he couldn't wait another second for release.

He inserted a second finger into her anus, stretching her. That was it, her undoing. She gave up trying to fight against the intense heat he'd oh so deftly stirred within her. Her orgasm blazed through her body like a nuclear reaction, a wave of tingly heat following a rolling inferno.

Seconds later, while her pussy continued to spasm, Lander's thick cock drove into her.

"Oh! Yes!" She drew her knees back, held them with her hands.

"Touch your tits," a breathless Lander demanded.

That was a request she was eager to comply with. She pinched her nipples between her thumbs and forefingers, rolling them to produce the pleasure-pain she'd come to enjoy so much. The sensation added yet another layer of ecstasy to what was already the most intense moment of her life. She opened her eyes, meeting Lander's golden-eyed gaze. And while he fucked her, she didn't look away. Not for a single moment.

She didn't want to close herself off into the dark place this time. She wanted to share every microsecond of this experience with Lander, every inhalation, heartbeat, blink of the eye. She could literally see his orgasm building, in the taut muscles of his shoulders, the rigid column of his neck, the reddening of his face.

Her own release was right there, too. They were at the pinnacle together, their breathing synchronized, their bodies working together perfectly, made for each other.

"I love you, Lander."

"I love you, too. Will you take me now the way I've been waiting for? In your ass?"

She quaked at just the thought of his engorged cock filling her there, stretching her anus. But she knew she was ready. It wouldn't hurt, as long as she relaxed.

It was one gift she could give him now. One gift he wanted only from her.

"Yes, Lander. I will. Fuck my ass."

He kissed her, almost sweetly. Then, looking at her as if she'd just agreed to fly to the moon for him, he cupped her cheeks in his palms and whispered, "Thank you." He slowly eased his cock from her thrumming pussy and, after she handed him a tube of lube she kept stashed in her nightstand drawer, shifted their position slightly to allow him to gently enter her ass.

She felt every inch go in. Relished the delectable sensation of him filling her completely. It was heavenly.

"Now, touch yourself." He moved slowly inside her. Innnn. Outttt.

She reached between her legs and touched her clit, stroking it slowly first then faster as the tension coiling inside her body increased.

Hotter. Tighter.

The soles of her feet tensed. Her thighs. Waves of heat swept up her chest. A storm of simmering passion boiled inside her belly. She was right there, and oh God, it felt so good, so right.

"Come, kitten. Come now."

Orgasm felt like a hot wave rolling over her body. Her pussy pulsed as Lander's swelling cock drove into her. Harder, faster he fucked her until he joined her. She watched the tension in his face drop away, leaving pure bliss.

God, she'd never in a million years imagined herself being so happy, so in love.

Could it be like this forever? With her history, she'd never thought it was possible. She was almost afraid to believe it now. This was ten times better than the happily-ever-after she'd written in her story, so obviously she hadn't done this. The story she'd written wasn't tied to reality. At least, not anymore.

"I have something to tell you," he said, his voice taking a serious tone. Instantly, her body went icy and she started listing the many bad things she half-expected him to say next.

"Please. Just let me be content for a few minutes? I beg you."

"Okay. But we need to talk."

"Yes, later." She snuggled closer, pulling the covers over their entwined bodies, and tried to pretend like she wasn't ready to cry.

"Okay, time to talk. I've waited long enough." Lander pulled Cailey away from the sink, piled with dirty dishes.

"How about I clean up first? I mean, this stuff is murder to get off once it's dried." She pointed to a plate with eggs glued to it.

"Later." Obviously, he wasn't going to let her get away with stalling anymore.

As it was, she'd managed to hold him off for almost a full twenty-four hours, while she went shopping for groceries, cooked them a couple of meals, vacuumed, dusted, and ran up to the mall for some new clothes for Lander. She figured if she pretended he was going to be with her forever, maybe something would change. The entire time, Lander marveled at the many things she'd long taken for granted. Cars, electric lights, microwave ovens. Radio.

"Okay. We'll talk later," she said cheerily, hoping her intentional misinterpretation of his words would buy her a little more time. She wriggled out of his grip and returned to the sink.

She simply wasn't ready to face reality yet. This new fantasy, where Lander was living in her world and they were together and happy, was too great to let go.

"No. Clean later." This time Lander moved her completely out of the kitchen. "I've been waiting long enough."

Fuck. The fantasy was over. "Fine. Okay. Sorry." She dropped onto the couch, feeling like her bones had gone soft and her stomach was in her toes. "It's just been so great with you here."

He sat beside her. "Hey, I'm not going anywhere. What made you think I was?"

"What you said, right after we . . ."

"Made love?"

"Yeah." Her cheeks heated. "Made love. I mean, that's what guys do. They screw a girl and then they drop the bomb and make their quick escape."

"Well, this guy's screwing no one. And he's not dropping a bomb either. I won't ask what a bomb is. I assume it's a bad thing."

"It's very bad, yes. But you're not leaving?" Those were the only words she cared about. Although, at the same time, she felt a little guilty for asking him to stay with her.

Lander had been king of his people. A ruler who was well-respected, adored even, by most everyone. Where would that leave the rest of the Werekin?

In her version of the story, the heroine traveled back to his world and they lived as king and queen and birthed a few adorable babies-slash-cubs. Of course, she made it so that the poor queen could take some magical potion to kill the pain of birthing. There was no saying if or when she might find herself in that position, so she'd wanted to cover all the bases. And she'd also written it so that their curse had been lifted with the birth of their first baby, and Lander's people no longer struggled with the beast.

At any rate, the newly cured Werekin had their beloved king.

Unlike now.

He twined his fingers with hers, stared down at their joined hands. "I can stay here with you. For as long as you like."

"Forever?"

"As long as we both live."

She had to ask. She had to know. "What about your home, your people? I know you cared about them. Very much. Isn't it hard to leave them behind? Who's ruling in your place?"

His expression brightened. "I shouldn't be surprised you asked about that, but I am." He kissed her forehead, his eyes sparkling with love. "Kitten, my people have a very fine, honorable, and trustworthy king now. So there's no need to worry."

"Okay. I just wanted to make sure."

"I appreciate that. My brother Kir has stepped up to take my place, and I have the utmost faith in his ability to rule the Werekin—to treat them well, put their needs above his own."

"Kir?"

He nodded. "Thanks to you, Jag has been stopped and the population of smaller animals is returning to normal. All Werekin have plenty to eat. Peace has returned. The curse was lifted. The beast within us no longer battles with our humanity. But more important, because of you, Kir is alive."

"I'm so glad, Lander. I didn't know if it would work." Tears were blurring her vision again. Tears of profound joy and gratitude. More than having Lander back, she had wanted him to have the brother he loved so much alive, healthy, there by his side. That had been the first of the few changes she'd made to their story. "With the curse lifted, you won't change into a lion anymore?"

"No. I still retain some of my feline traits and instincts, the heightened senses and strength, the instinct to hunt. But I no longer change physically into the beast."

On top of being overjoyed, she was relieved. Not because she was worried about Lander turning into a lion around her, but because of the relief she saw in his eyes. "It was painful, the changing?"

"Extremely."

"I'm glad, then."

"You see?" He cupped her face in his hands. "I was right. You did possess magical powers. You changed the events of the past. You lifted the curse. You brought Kir back to me. You changed everything . . . me."

"No, you changed everything for me." She kissed Lander, the man who would always be her man-lion.

"I have something for you." He went to his clothes, rooted in a pocket, and withdrew his fist. He unfurled his fingers, revealing the beautiful collar he'd given her.

Tears blurring her vision even worse than before, she lifted her hair to let her master fasten the collar around her neck.

She was Lander's. For always. And he belonged to her.

The wild, powerful master of her heart.

Turn the page for a look at
Jodi Lynn Copeland's "Captive Heat"

From the sizzling new anthology
DANGEROUS TIES!

On sale in April!

1

"Goddamn you!" It wasn't enough he'd been an asshole when he was alive—Ken had to haunt her from the depths of hell.

This time it wasn't Leia Jenson's mind or body her ex-husband abused, but the priccy pumps she'd flung at the burning, back-woods hovel she'd once called home.

Who the hell paid over half a grand for shoes anyway?

A women trying to outrun her past.

"I don't have to outrun it now, you bastard!" A self-inflicted bullet to Ken's temple took care of that. Not niccly. But messily.

The rotting paneled walls of the one-room shack were splattered with the grisly remains of what had been his suicide scene. Leia hadn't gone inside. She couldn't even stomach the thought of peering through the set of dirt-stained windows for fear old memories would grab hold. The sheriff who called to tell her Ken was dead and that her ex had left her the shack in his will—apparently to give her a final taste of his sick sense of humor—had forewarned her about the shape of the place. The cop had been scanty with the details. Just told her enough that her mind could fill in the gruesome blanks.

Only the blanks weren't so gruesome.

She was glad Ken was dead. Glad the asshole was finally getting his due. If she'd ever questioned the afterlife, then Leia had to accept it now. Had to believe he was dancing to the flames of the devil's caustic beat.

Which meant he would be too busy to fuck with her shoes.

It wasn't the bastard reaching from the gates of hell to destroy the slingback gold-sequined Manolos she'd bought two years ago as a final severance to the pathetic woman of her past. It was the acrid smoke rolling off the shack's dilapidated roof, stinging her eyes and screwing with her mind. Making those old memories surface even though she hadn't gotten any closer than what kicking the barely hinged door in and tossing a gasoline-soaked rag, followed by a pack of lit matches, had required.

Either grey matter was a hell of a fire conducer, or Ken still kept stacks of porn magazines lying around. Her little rag fire had turned to an inferno in minutes.

Flames licked at a small, dirty window on either side of the doorway, blackening the glass. From Leia's cross-armed vantage point fifteen feet away, the heat coming through the open door turned from steamy to sweltering.

Mindful of her bare feet and how stupid it had been to walk even a quarter mile down a decently cleared trail in three-inch heels, she put another ten feet between herself and the hovel.

She wouldn't be escaping this overgrown, secluded stretch of woods and returning to her life in the city until the shack was ashes. Looking skyward, past the towering tops of decades-old elms, she attempted to escape the memories.

Hazy purple-black filled a summer sky that had been blue minutes ago. The color erased any chance of escape, watering her eyes and fucking with her mind even more. Reminding her of all the times she'd worn the ugly shade on her body, of all the shit she'd endured. The way Ken had handled her, called her a fat ass, good to be nothing but his house bitch and sex slave.

Her ass *was* big—she'd come to terms with her size along with a whole lot of other things the last two and a half years. But she was no one's slave.

Then why won't the memories quit?

An explosion erupted from somewhere inside, knocking the question from Leia's mind. She focused back on the doorway as a second blast followed. Then more.

The first of the windows exploded, spewing fragments of glass for yards as if the winds of hell themselves spurred them on. Panic slammed into her belly as the last of those fragments barely missed clipping her side, and she backed further down the trail on rote.

Son of a bitch! This was supposed to be an easy means of destroying Ken's meager possessions while severing any final ties between them. It wasn't supposed to be dangerous.

But just as the ties between them had been dangerous from nearly the moment they'd said, "I do," this situation became dangerous as hell in the blink of her stinging eyes.

Pure TNT seemed to detonate inside the shack, the caterwauling sound near deafening. Reflex had her hands jerking to her ears. Too late, she realized she should have covered her body. The second window exploded in a blaze of orange and black fury. Shards of discolored glass arced toward her. This time they didn't miss, but moved past the lavender silk of her designer shorts and tank combo to slice at bare skin.

Covering her head with her hands, Leia half fell, half dove to the trail. The air whooshed out of her as her breasts and belly collided with the hard earth. The breath dragged back between her lips, even the low air pungent now, and she gagged out a cough. Pain scorched through her thigh. Burning frissions of ache speared upward. She bit her lip against the hurt, tasting blood, savoring that bit of life-confirming metallic warmth as she pinched her eyes shut and waited for the explosions to end.

A deceptive calm descended after nearly a full minute, broken only by the crackle and hiss of the fire. Adrenaline pumping through her system, she gingerly turned on her side. Through bleary eyes, she took stock of her injuries. Dirt and nicks covered her legs and a chunk of concave glass protruded from the inside of her lower thigh, just past the cuff of her shorts.

Brown bottle glass.

"Shit. Shit!" Of *course*, the bastard had alcohol inside. Drunkenness had always been the fuel that fed his rage.

Popping sounded to her right, keeping her attention on the present when it threatened to stray to the past. The popping was far too close. Holding her breath, Leia followed the direction of the sound . . . and panic closed in all over again.

The fire was no longer confined to the shack, but eating away at the rain-deprived woods and quickly making its way toward the trail.

Sickness settled in her gut along with bleak reality. She hadn't set out to be dangerous. But she'd been damned dangerous, damned harmful. And there was nothing she could do but run.

Panting, despite her attempts to not take in more of the toxic air, she shoved to her feet. Razor-edged pain rifled up her leg and had her sucking a hard breath between her lips. She pushed the air back out and pushed her feet down the path, ignoring the sting of fallen twigs and brambles as they cut into the soft pads of her feet. Ignoring everything but the need to find help somewhere in this godforsaken nowhere.

She almost made it to her car when another explosion hit. Once again, the sound was too close. She'd come nearly a quarter mile. But it was right there, right behind her, emitting a force strong enough to topple her to the ground and knock her out cold.